THE SLAVE MAKER

A SOUTHERN GOTHIC NOVEL

FIONA SHANAHAN: BOOK 2

KATHLEEN MORRIS

ALSO BY KATHLEEN MORRIS

The Lily of the West

The Transformation of Chastity James

Risk

Fallen Child

Golddigger

Never Touch Down

Fiona Rising (Book 1: Fiona Shanahan)

The Slave Maker (Book 2: Fiona Shanahan)

Copyright © 2024 by Kathleen Morris

All rights reserved.

This book is a work of fiction. Names, characters, places and incidents are either the product of the author's imagination or if real, used fictitiously.

No part of this book may be reproduced in any form or by any electronic or mechanical means, including information storage and retrieval systems, without written permission from the author, except for the use of brief quotations in a book review.

First Edition, First Printing, December 2024

Ebook Edition ISBN 979-8-9874563-7-8

Paperback Edition ISBN 979-8-9874563-8-5

Hardcover Edition ISBN 979-8-9874563-9-2

1

NEW ORLEANS, 1883

Raphael Benoit loved his job. He loved everything about it: the elegantly decorated offices, the access to the adjoining art gallery through the secret door, the most fashionable location in New Orleans at 416 Royal Street, so close to his favorite boulangerie whose still-warm croissants were now tucked safely in the paper bag he carried. Yes, all those things were true, but most of all, Raphael loved two even more important things: the sense of mystery and excitement that permeated the very fiber of the place but even more, the enchanting Fiona Shanahan, his employer, the "S" of S&H Investigations. He didn't have the same feeling for the "H" half, Mr. Henley, but just being around Fiona every day was worth every second of Henley's somewhat terrifying presence, even though the most intimidating thing Henley had ever directed towards Raphael was a slight frown. Still, Raphael had heard things. He was no naïve ingenue at the game of life.

He unlocked the black door with its brass sign and stepped inside, immediately stumbling into something soft but unyielding that groaned piteously.

"*Bon Dieu,*" Raphael said, nearly dropping the croissants.

"She's done it again." If there was one thing he shared with Henley, it was a distaste for Fiona's habit of taking in street orphans, and this one in particular. She'd even given him a key. If Raphael hadn't come in early this morning, he'd have never known and, he suspected, neither would've Henley since Fiona was the early riser of the group.

"Get out," Raphael hissed at the rather pungent lump of clothing lying on the Persian rug, one blue eye visible under the mop of black hair.

"Piss off," the lump said. "I'm on the job 'ere, mate. *She* said."

Raphael raised his foot for a hefty kick but before it could land, the little wretch jumped up and snatched the bag of croissants from Raphael's hand, laughing as he ran down the street.

"*Cochon batarde,*" Raphael said, shaking his head. He'd never deign to chase him down. Instead, he strode to his desk and the petty cash drawer. S&H wanted croissants today, they'd have to pay double. He locked the door and headed back down the street to the boulangerie. His temper improved the second he scented the baking pastries. He smiled in spite of himself. Hopefully, the little bastard was enjoying his breakfast.

"It sounds like Raphael was early this morning," Fiona said, turning close to Henley's ear on the pillow beside her. "But then he left. Hmm."

Henley grunted, as he often did before coffee. "You have the hearing of a bat, my darling, or some other creature of the night. I do wonder, sometimes."

"It is peculiar," she mused, looking innocently at the ceiling. "I seem to see in the dark better than most as well."

Henley snorted. "Let's not stray into mythical territory, Irish. The reality of life is mystery enough." He threw off the sheets and pulled on yesterday's breeches for a quick trip to the kitchen downstairs. "Hopefully our dashing little Frenchman returns soon with croissants and makes some coffee. Truly, we pay him for his beautiful face and charming manners, which are important to you, but to me his most valued asset is concocting café au lait, a task at which he's proven quite adept."

She watched him as he strode to the door. Henley was truly something special to watch, especially without a shirt, muscles rippling and long legs striding with such purpose. He stopped and looked back at her over his shoulder with a wolfish grin. He thought it made him look dangerously sexy but to her, the grin was that of the charming boy he'd likely been. She fell back into the pillows with a smile. Henley. Easy on the eyes and even easier to love.

She stared at the plastered cherubs and flowers on the ceiling, early morning sunlight filtering into the bedroom, the leaves of the plane trees dancing patterns through the latticed shutters. In the three years they'd been in New Orleans, she'd come to feel at home in this place like no other, an unusual haven for an Irish orphan who'd never before had a safe and beloved sanctuary. That it was shared with a man she loved beyond imagining and who ensured she was safe and beloved was a reality Fiona had only dreamed she'd ever have. Even better, she and Henley had the opportunity to help people find justice and be a part of changing things for the better, thanks to their sponsor, Julius DeMonte.

S&H Investigations was the New Orleans security arm of Julius's business interests, not all of which were legal, as Fiona knew only too well, but all were dedicated to helping others and making the world more equitable. Right now, Julius was once again on his way down the Mississippi on his showboat, the Queen of Dreams, where Fiona had once been the featured actress in Julius's productions on its maiden voyage. Julius had offered Fiona a refuge from law enforcement that sought to detain her for questioning in an incident in New York. While on the river, together they had weathered a conspiracy and attempts on both their lives which convinced Julius that S&H Investigations was a much-needed part of his business.

That the Queen and a few other riverboats carried valuable contraband of one sort or another was a well-kept secret. While Julius was from an aristocratic English family, his ambitions and support of causes required more money than a theater producer or even a well-provided-for black sheep younger son could possibly provide, so many years ago Julius had established a smuggling network that could, centered from his headquarters in Chicago. Fiona had first-hand evidence of some of the good he'd done and was gratified to be trusted enough to be part of his network, partnering with Henley, who'd been Julius's right hand for years. Now Henley was her partner in life as well as business.

A rustling on the balcony was followed by a whispered "Miss!" and Fiona sat up, peering through the filmy white curtains swaying gently in the early morning breeze, the French doors open. It had to be Nico Cooper, her young protege, always eager to bring her information and gossip from around the Quarter. Sure enough, bright blue eyes and a mop of black hair were just visible through the thick bougainvillea vines.

"What is it, Nico?"

"Just wanted you to know that Raphael nabbed me this morning and the bugger'll waste no time in telling Henley. Sorry, miss."

Fiona sighed. Well, she'd deal with that. "Be more careful, Nico."

"Yes, ma'am. Also, Marie Laveau needs to see you."

"Oh really?" The voodoo queen was a client, off and on, and had come to trust S&H with some issues she couldn't deal with herself, not that there were many. Fiona found herself reluctant to return the same, fascinating as Marie was. That she was a valuable source and sometimes an asset was in no doubt. "Did you see her this morning?"

"No, last night. Someone broke into the store, late-like. Rene had saved me some crawfish boil back in the kitchen of the Absinthe House, and we heard the commotion."

Fiona's sigh this time was more like a groan. Who would be foolish enough to rob Marie Laveau? Someone either desperate or insane, most likely, and Fiona wasn't eager to track down a villain of either stripe. Julius would be arriving soon and she and Henley would be very busy.

Henley returned, whistling a tune from the operetta they'd seen the night before, The Pirates of Penzance. He deposited the heavy silver tray on the bed. A silver coffeepot, cups and a plate of croissants with a pot of strawberry jam drew Fiona's immediate attention while Nico took the opportunity to vanish without a sound, as she knew he would. Likely Henley did too, but never would he mention it.

2

Autumn in New Orleans was the beginning of weather people could enjoy living in, unlike the humidity of the summers, a dictum which even Fiona, who loved the place, could agree. Fans, the occasional thunderstorms, evening breezes, the intoxicating scent of jasmine and the chilled wine helped, but not enough. Conversely, not even the winter rains could dull the spirits of the denizens of this unique city, but simply send them to shelter, to the fireside comfort of fine food, drink, music, entertainment of various and esoteric diversions and delights, and the planning ahead for the costumes and revelry of Mardi Gras. But autumn, and blessed spring...now that was as close to heaven on earth as Fiona had ever experienced.

Fiona stepped out the door of S&H, adjusted her hat over her occasionally wayward black curls, a quite beguiling green velvet confection from Colette at Madame de Chantilly's, that matched her eyes. She breathed deeply of the cool, rain-washed sparkling air. She had loved the Crescent City since the first day she'd walked its streets and that hadn't faded a whit.

The rain hadn't been enough to turn the dirt streets into a

muddy morass, but just enough to clean the air and the sidewalks. It was only a short three blocks to Marie Laveau's compound on Bourbon Street, and Fiona loved walking through the Quarter, the lace filigree iron balconies and columns bedecked with flowers and vines. She smiled and greeted everyone she met, as was her way, secure in her ability to be safe, from the general neighborhood to the knowledge that she had a straight razor as well as a pearl-handled derringer in her beaded reticule. In their time in New Orleans, Fiona had never needed to utilize either of them on the streets of New Orleans, but a life of some turbulence in the past had taught her to be prepared and that forethought had served her well.

When she reached 628 Bourbon Street, it was clear something drastic had occurred. The glass windows of Marie's shop, which fronted the entire square she owned, were being hastily covered with wood and cardboard, the shards of their previous existence being swept up by a crew of workers, supervised by a tall man in impeccable white linen, whom Fiona had met before.

"Mornin', Miss Fiona," said Jim Washington, Marie's right hand man of business and, Fiona suspected, much more. He shook his head in disgust. "Be careful where you step. It seems some people have no damn sense at all."

Fiona nodded in agreement. "This indeed quite awful, Jim. Do you know anything more?"

"Not so far. But news travels fast in the Quarter, Miss Fiona. Don't think it'll take long for some inklins' to surface. Then the Queen can decide the best course."

"As always," Fiona said. "She wants to see me?"

"Yes." He escorted her through the destruction and up to a side door. "She's up in the parlor on the second floor, you know the way."

"*Merci.*" Fiona ascended the stairs and entered Marie

Laveau's study. She'd been there twice before. It was a delightful room, ringed with floor-to-ceiling bookshelves on three sides, complemented with a wall of glass-fronted shelves that housed a quite extraordinary collection of artifacts, some of which made Fiona's skin crawl if she looked at them for more than thirty seconds. She'd learned that perhaps any skulls – human or otherwise, unusual preserved animal and amphibian specimens and quite a few other items in this place were not something she wanted to see or dwell upon again. Henley, after one visit, refused to return, leaving Fiona as their spokesperson. She couldn't blame him. Besides, she and Marie Laveau got along famously. At least Fiona thought so, given the fact the Voodoo Queen of New Orleans was someone very difficult to read. Marie did seem to find her Irish accent amusing, so there was that. Maybe today Fiona would have to forgo her stage training and turn it up a bit.

Marie herself sat at her desk, an ornate Louis XVI antique that she revered, similar to Fiona's own, its beautifully curved and crafted legs and gilded walnut top as much of a work of art as the woman who sat behind it. This Marie Laveau, Marie Laveau II, who, after the death of her mother the year before, the original Voodoo Queen, had taken up the mantle quite seamlessly after her mother's passing. She was a beautiful and regal woman, her café-au-lait skin smooth and flawless, today's headdress not the often-seem white cotton tignon but a silken gold and red confection atop her head, some braided strands of hair flowing easily across her shoulders. She looked remarkably like her mother, stoking rumors that she had concocted some magical elixir that allowed her to live forever, but Fiona knew better. She and Henley had attended the first Marie's funeral the year before, earning the daughter's respect. Now, Marie's dark eyes were fixed on Fiona as she came through the door.

"Good morning, Miss Shanahan. I appreciate your visit."

"Of course. How can S&H help you?"

"Please," Marie gestured to the chair in front of her desk, and poured a cup of the chicory coffee she favored into a delicately painted Meissen cup. "You've seen the mess out there. I was hoping you and your colleague could assist me in finding and dealing with the culprits, as you have before."

Fiona nodded, accepting the cup and saucer and settling into the chair. "Anyone in particular come to mind? Just to save us some time, of course."

Marie laughed, a rich hearty basso that was unexpected from her delicate frame. "Oh, *mon cher*, I have so many enemies it is hard to distinguish one from another. Those enemies, however, seem to forget that I have so very many friends as well. It is always the way, *n'est pas?*"

Fiona sipped her coffee, which was excellent. "Sure and true, 'tis. And they cannot hide forever even though they might think so. Still, any new threats in the air besides our usual?"

Postwar New Orleans had been a turbulent place, then calmed, but was now picking up its racist past and contemplating new laws to quell people of color from positions of power and political and financial equality, a large step away from a city that had welcomed equality in the early years after the war, and one that always had a goodly portion of free people of color making up its business and cultural sector. Southern racism was resurfacing, with the emergence of white supremacist groups like the White League and the Ku Klux Klan throughout the South, and certainly in New Orleans itself. Fiona, Henley, Julius and Julius's vast network were actively working against the formation of any of that. Their work might be a weak levee against a rising tide of hate, but every inch and every brick counted.

"Only one I might consider," Marie said, taking a sip from her own coffee cup. "Dwight Furley, because he threatened me a few days ago. He should know better, but he's a stupid man."

"Ah," Fiona said. Dwight Furley was a city councilman, a porcine and vulgar little man, who frequented Marie's balls, as did most of the gentlemen of consequence in New Orleans, drawn like helpless moths to the flame of the beautiful young women and men who worked for Marie. She and Henley had met him at a few civic receptions, and they had both found the man quite distasteful, as was the case with quite a few of the new politicians that had begun to populate city and state governments in the South, driving out the moderate and truly democratic people who had been beneficial in rebuilding after the war. Most were racists, and nearly all were greedy and corruptible, a dangerous combination.

While the balls, the bars and restaurant that did business behind the doors of 628 Bourbon Street, known as Maison Blanche, were profitable and long-established businesses, they were separate from Marie's retail and client-based voodoo enterprises. Her mother had established them long ago and Marie II had kept the tradition alive, not out of nostalgia, but because they were the cornerstones of her power. Secrets were whispered, plots were hatched, nefarious deeds were spoken of by those whose tongues had been loosened with alcohol and passion, and Marie and her people gathered and tracked them all.

Few were aware, unless they had run afoul of her, and remarkably even when they did, the dark and beautiful enticements she offered were too much for most of them. Ignoring the rumors and common sense, they told themselves they would be more discreet, or drink less than their unfortunate friends. Of course, they did not.

"What do we know about Mr. Furley besides the fact that he's a dishonest grasping politician of the worst sort? I've seen him at gatherings here and there but never took much notice."

"He has peculiar tastes," Marie said, "and he likes to hurt pretty things. I have a girl that's damaged and that I cannot countenance. I asked him for payment, but we couldn't come to an agreement, even though I reminded him that there could be consequences if not. Of course, I also banned him and word is already swirling around town, but not, so far, to his wife or the governor, a situation I can remedy quickly."

"I think I understand." Fiona put her cup and saucer down on the silver tray on Marie's desk. Fiona disliked a great many things about a great many people, but men who liked to hurt women outpaced them all. "Our usual arrangement?"

Marie nodded. "Of course."

3

Fiona dipped her finger in the remoulade sauce, touched it to her tongue and rolled her eyes in appreciation as Henley watched her with an inappropriately lascivious smile. He looked very handsome today, especially dashing in the new embroidered waistcoat she'd surprised him with from his favorite tailor, Fontaine's on St. Anne's street.

"You do rather like your shrimp, Irish," he said, "and I like nothing more than watching your enjoyment." He uncharacteristically waggled his eyebrows, a movement exceedingly unfamiliar on the handsome patrician face of Michael Henley. At that, Fiona nearly laughed out loud, but the elegant lunch clientele at the Ponchartrain House would have likely disapproved, not that she cared much.

"It's only one o'clock, darling. You'll have to wait for more of it. Besides, we have to discuss our new case. Any ideas on bringing Mr. Furley to some sort of justice? Marie is somewhat anxious because the repairs will be extensive and recompense would be helpful. Not to mention the girl. I'd like to see her go to New York or Paris to see competent surgeons repair the damage to her lovely face."

"Yes, we do have some loose ends to finish up before Julius gets here with the Queen. Things will get busy then, as you know."

"Then there's the issue with Tim O'Leary and his whiskey business, and Mrs. Brown's son-in-law," Fiona said, sneaking a plump shrimp from Henley's plate.

"Tiresome, but necessary." Henley held up a discreet finger and their waiter, always attentive, nodded, and returned with another platter of shrimp remoulade. He knew them well, refilling their wineglasses with more of the chilled Pouilly Fuisse they'd come to favor.

"Yes, yes," Henley said. "I think from a politic standpoint, we deal with Marie's problems first. Who do you think we should approach on the city council? They're mostly a collection of corrupt vulgarians like Furley but some more amenable than others."

Fiona smiled. "The likeliest candidate, sitting two tables over," she gestured with her wineglass. "The most Catholic Monsieur Montell. His mouth puckers at the very suggestion of sexual impropriety. I do pity his wife."

The gentleman in question was gorging himself on a large dish of coquilles St. Jacque, making Fiona feel sorry for the scallops and shrimp that gave their life for someone who didn't appreciate their culinary sacrifice.

"Excellent choice," Henley said. "This afternoon, in about an hour or two, after he's had a nap?"

Fiona smiled and held up her glass in agreement, and they gently clinked the crystal together, with promises to come.

The shrimp remoulade was truly delicious, as always.

∼

HOUSED in its imposing white marble building, many of the denizens of City Hall were familiar to S&H Investigations, because Julius had arranged introductory dinners and events to insure that everyone in New Orleans who mattered when it came to business, legal and financial dealings were well acquainted with DeMonte Enterprises and all their subsidiaries. Favors were granted, deals were reached and relationships established, to everyone's advantage, none more so than those that concerned DeMonte Enterprises, whether their new friends were aware of just how much or how different DeMonte's goals might be from those who profited from their official positions at city and state level. Julius had a loathing for politicians and their machinations that was thoroughly shared by Fiona and Henley.

"So good of you to receive us this afternoon, Mr. Montell," Henley said as he and Fiona were seated across from the man's ostentatiously wide desk, empty of papers. "We have a concern that we felt you especially might find as disturbing as we do."

Interest sparked in Montell's eyes. He liked nothing more than to ferret out what he considered bad behavior anywhere, but especially among his rivals on the council.

"I am happy to help you and of course, Mr. DeMonte, in any way I can," Montell said, leaning his ample stomach against the desk. "Please tell me what troubles you."

"It is a delicate matter," Fiona said. "I will attempt to relay as much as I can, with Mr. Henley's assistance if it becomes too much for me." She touched her forehead lightly with a lace-edged handkerchief and took a deep breath.

"Yesterday, in my usual visit to St. Mary's Hospital, I met with a young woman who was severely injured, among other wounds, with a disfiguring knife slash to her beautiful face. It was horrifying, but the story she told me of how it occurred was even worse." A tear dropped which Fiona quickly dabbed at with her handkerchief, and Henley touched her hand.

"I'm fine," she assured him. *Don't overplay this*, Fiona

thought to herself, *it's not Lady MacBeth and this is no stage you're treading here, tempting as it was.*

"Oh dear," Montell said. "Do you need some water, Mrs. Shanahan?"

"No, no, thank you," Fiona said. "Just let me finish and I'll be fine." She straightened her spine and stared at Montell. "This poor girl was raped and beaten, a victim of Mr. Dwight Furley, your colleague on the council. He is a beast who must be brought to justice, and should hold no place in the esteemed office he shares with respectable and moral gentlemen like yourself."

Montell's eyes gleamed with zealous attention and he struggled to keep the glee from his voice while he put on a shocked face. "This is terrible. Are you certain of your facts?"

"We are positive, sir," Henley said. "As you know, S&H and Mr. DeMonte are meticulous and conscientious in their dealings. There is no question whatsoever. Mr. DeMonte himself will return shortly and we all would wish this matter be dealt with before he returns. He asks for your assistance, Mr. Montell."

Montell didn't skip a beat. "You shall have it. Transgressions like this are an insult to God and man both. I will make it my personal mission to insure Hurley meets his obligations, and takes responsibility for his actions, praying for his redemption. What recompense does the young lady require for her medical needs?"

Henley looked at Fiona. "My colleague has had more direct contact with the physicians. Could you estimate, my dear?"

"Of course," Fiona said. "She needs specialists, only available in New York and other European capitals. We have discussed it with Mr. DeMonte via messenger and believe $30,000 should be adequate for those needs as we must consider travel and lodging costs. Mr. DeMonte wanted me to remind you of his gratitude in resolving matters like this."

She could almost see Montell's brain, flawed as it was, working like a squirrel hunting acorns. Not only would they now have Montell on their list, along with Hurley, all of whom would be under control should the need arrive. She and Henley had learned well from Julius.

Montell stood up and held out his hand to Henley. Rarely did men of Montell's stripe shake hands with a woman, Fiona had learned. She sorely desired retribution for that but she was no fool. Deserved respect might take quite some time.

"Have no fear," Montell intoned in what he mistakenly thought was a senatorial-like tone. "I will see that Mr. Furley meets his obligations, you can count on me. I'm gratified you've brought his actions to me to achieve justice. You can expect financial restitution for your client very soon. Give my regards to Mr. DeMonte. I'm looking forward to seeing him."

Fiona and Henley stood outside the door of city hall, looked at each other, and grinned. "That was a masterful performance, my love," Henley said. "I think we deserve an absinthe, what do you say?"

"Beyond a doubt," Fiona said. "Next on my list, though, is that nasty prig Montell. I'm sure he's got a flaw or two. I bet his housemaids have a tale to tell."

Henley sighed. "You're relentless. I love that about you."

"No more relentless than you, my heart." Fiona took his arm as they strolled down the street towards Marie Laveau's. She had the best absinthe in town, as everyone knew.

4

"Exquisite, is it not?"

Jean-Claude St. Clair stood in front of his latest acquisition, a fifteenth century Italian painting Raphael had just unpacked, excelsior and wooden shipping frames scattering the floor. He was dressed to the peak of fashion, as always, a dashing figure, his pale blonde hair clipped nearly as short as his artfully shaped beard. Ladies always sighed when he entered a room, with good reason and he delighted in that, rake that he was, although a discreet one. Jean-Claude said no husband ever wrote a large check to a man who had cuckolded him.

"Absolutely," Raphael said and Fiona stifled a snort. Raphael was trying diligently to become sophisticated and knowledgeable about art among many other things, but she knew full well he wouldn't know Michelangelo from the Cajun painter who dazzled the tourists in Jackson Square.

"Truthfully, Jean-Claude," she said, "I find it quite gruesome, and cliched religious art is not to my taste. However, it is very valuable and a fine acquisition to your gallery or your collection if you can't bear to part with it."

Jean-Claude eyed the bloody depiction of an agonized Jesus on a cross, God's anger expressed through the turbulent dark clouds massing over Golgotha. He gave her a mock frown. "Fiona, my darling, how deflating your plebian tastes can be." Then he laughed and kissed her cheek. "You're right. Even though I have assurance it is a Canaletto, I hate it too, but I will make a bloody fortune on the thing."

"I've got just the customer for you," Fiona said. "Councilman Montell is a most devout Catholic gentleman who would find this painting just to his taste. I believe he has just come into an unexpected financial windfall. I'd be delighted to send him a note about this rare opportunity."

"Ah, Fiona," Jean-Claude smiled. "I can always count on you. I sense a dinner at Antoine's coming soon."

Henley strode through the connecting gallery door and stopped short at the sight of the large gory canvas.

"Holy Christ, that's awful, St. Clair." Henley was never one to dissemble. "Sell it fast so I can sleep at night with that horror lurking down here."

They all laughed, even Raphael. "I've just suggested Montell as the lucky buyer. I'm sure you'll agree," Fiona said. "It seems to be quite his sort of thing."

"Hell yes. Perfect." They both knew the money Montell received from Furley for Marie and the girl came with a hefty commission, straight into Montell's pocket.

They left Jean-Claude to his work and closed the connecting door.

"Anything new today, Raphael?" Henley leaned against Raphael's writing desk. "Give us something juicy, something devious, and please God, something non-political."

Raphael shrugged in typical Gallic fashion and threw up his hands. "Just the whiskey thing and Justin Glover. If you don't want anything political, given the state of things around here, business is slow."

Henley grinned. "Just as it should be, with Julius set to arrive soon. We'll have a lot to manage with the cargo and all and Julius always comes up with other issues." He glanced over at Fiona. "He'll likely want you to star in some production he'll arrange at the Opera House, like he's done before. Are you up for that?"

Fiona rolled her eyes, but in truth she was rather looking forward to being back on stage, her first love. "I'll manage, darling."

Henley gave her a look and she knew she wasn't fooling him for a minute. He grinned. "I am quite sure you will, Juliet."

The front door was flung open and Nico stood there in the late afternoon sun, hair wild and his chest heaving from exertion. "Imogene Carondolet just shot her husband. You've got to help her."

Raphael rolled his eyes. "The whole town saw this one coming. You must go. Whiskey can wait."

∽

THE CARONDOLET HOUSE was in the Lower Quarter on Ursulines Street, so rather than take the time to harness their own mare and rig in the carriage house in the back of the square, Henley grabbed a passing cab for hire, and he, Fiona and Nico quickly crammed inside, to make their way through the muddy and reeking streets.

"Who else knows?"

Nico shrugged. "I can't say at this time. My friend Ellie works in their laundry and she came to get me at the Market. The bastard deserved all he got, Mr. Henley --"

Henley cut him off. "I'm sure he did, Nico, but what I need to know right now is, are the police involved yet?"

"They weren't there when I left, and I told Ellie to try and keep a lid on it so's I could get y'all to help."

Henley looked over at Fiona and she shrugged. There was nothing they could do until they got there and took a measure of the entire scene. If the New Orleans Police had been called, it would be much more difficult to deal with. The notoriously corrupt current chief Boylan was about to be replaced by a new man, one Richard Rowley. Fiona held little hope he would be much better than his predecessor. S&H Investigations owed its authority and autonomy to Julius's assiduous courting of the mostly corrupt and racist municipal government, much as he detested them, and that included the Police Department.

Imogene Carondolet was the daughter of French aristocrats who had been in New Orleans for decades. Her family had been an ally of Julius and his many friends in the colored community, free and slave both, before and after the war. After the war, young Imogene had made an unfortunate choice of a husband in Philippe Carondolet, a weak-willed hedonist whose younger beauty had been ravaged by a lifestyle now long fueled by alcohol and dissolution. His tastes ran particularly to the pupils in Imogene's boarding school that she had established for young women of color to prepare themselves for a better life.

Trouble had been brewing for some time at 750 Ursulines St. and it was no surprise nor a tragedy to Fiona that Philippe had met his demise, a fate easily foretold. Their task today was to make certain Imogene was not held legally responsible for a justifiable crime, especially when it likely involved protecting a young woman who could not protect herself.

Serenity reigned on Ursulines Street when they stepped down from the carriage. Henley spoke to the driver, money changed hands and he pulled over to wait for their return. They stepped up onto the porch and the door opened by Imogene herself, who had clearly been awaiting their arrival. She hugged Fiona and pulled her and Henley inside the foyer and shut the door.

"Thank god for you. I don't know what to do."

Fiona clasped Imogene's hand while Henley took charge, his forte.

"Show us, Imogene."

The pretty and very distraught woman led them down the hallway to the kitchen. There Philippe Carondolet lay in a pool of blood on the black and white floor tiles in front of the stove, his arms outflung, his handsome face now disfigured by the bullet hole in his once perfect forehead. His trousers were open and disarranged. Aside from that minor flaw, Fiona thought it was an infinitely better death scene artistically than Jean Claude's pallid Jesus.

"He was raping Maisie and I'd just…had enough of it. Not one more girl, not one more time." She looked at Fiona. "I know you understand. I'm only sorry it took me this long. I failed too many before."

Christ Jesus. Fiona looked at Henley and back at Imogene. "Has anyone sent for the police?"

"Not that I know of," Imogene said, her face pale. She looked over at the kitchen counter and picked up the small derringer she handed to Fiona. "My neighbors are friends and quite discreet."

Fiona couldn't argue with that. If anyone had sent for the police they would have been here by now. Imogene sank down on a bench beside the sink. "The girls are in their rooms and I know they will say nothing. No matter what, I'm willing to pay whatever price it takes to ensure Maisie's safety and the rest of theirs as well, even it means prison or worse for me."

Fiona looked at Henley and he jerked his head towards the hallway a few feet away. She followed him through the doorway. He leaned down, his voice low and his breath warm near her ear.

"We can take care of this our way, Irish, and I highly recommend we do. The alternative is Imogene stands trial for murder because no one cares about the violation of a young girl of color, not right now in this town. I'm not willing to take that chance, are you?"

Fiona stared at him. "Are you seriously asking me this? From the second we walked in here I knew Mr. Philippe Carondolet was going to be the main entree for the gators of Bayou St. John this evening. For faith, I was only thinking about whether the sauce should have garlic or basil."

Henley grinned. "Basil, certainly."

"You have such good taste, my love," Fiona said. "Basil it is. Imogene will have to sacrifice a rug for a shroud but I'm sure she won't have the slightest regret."

5

"Halloween, Henley. We should at least have a reception. I think Jean-Claude would agree. We can open the doors to the gallery and it will be a joint gala. Jean-Claude could even entice a new client or two."

Fiona sipped her wine and leaned her head back on the comfortably upholstered arm of the sofa, her bare feet on Henley's lap. "We always attend other people's parties, but we rarely allow anyone into our inner sanctum, as it were." She arched her foot that rested in Henley's capable hand. "After a time, it does look a bit suspicious. Or, at least displaying a disdain for society, which of course we have as most of them are idiots, but since 'fitting in' is a part of our façade, it would do to maintain it, nonetheless."

Henley shrugged and she knew he didn't disagree. He'd been playing the game long before she had, and even without the theater training, he was a master of the art. "Perhaps. But we can't have the caterers breaking their wrists carving faces on turnips, which you Irish seem to prefer. In New York, they've gone to pumpkins so if we can find them, that would be an improvement. Otherwise, too much trouble." He pushed down on a particularly sore area on the ball of her foot with his thumb and Fiona couldn't help but yelp a little, even though his skilled fingers eased the pain with comfort.

"Ahh, ahh. Yes, pumpkins," she managed. "Good idea." If he kept this up and moved those talented fingers any further up her leg, coherent conversation was going to dissolve for the evening. She knew that was Henley's favorite way to end discussions he didn't want to have and too many times she'd fallen prey to that tactic. She swung her legs to the floor.

"I'm serious. This is a good idea. Just so you're thinkin' proper, I've never carved a turnip in my life, the nuns at the orphanage wouldn't allow such scandalous pagan practices, by the way." She dropped one shoulder and the silk strap of her chemise slipped down her arm. "They sounded a great deal more interesting than plain old All Saints Day, though.

"I think Marie Laveau would love to join us in this celebration and add an excitement that no one else is capable of doing as well. Voodoo and Celtic folk tales merged into one, that would be a grand mix. Something America would thank us for in the years to come."

She could see the alarm in Henley's eyes at that last couple of statements. His frown deepened and he cleared his throat in anticipation for delivering an admonishing speech. Clearly, there was no time to lose and she needed to employ *her* favorite method to end a discussion she needed to win. She gently unbuttoned his shirt, baring his chest, and then proceeded nimbly onto the buttons on his doeskin trousers. Henley became quite helpful in this endeavor, shifting his backside to accommodate her efforts.

Fiona hid her smile and ran her tongue down his muscled torso. Convincing Henley had become her favorite occupation and there was no question it provided significant rewards.

∾

"No, no, no, *mon cher*, all the way to the front wall," Jean Claude said, waving his arms as though that would demonstrate his wishes to the comely young man on the ladder who was putting up an eerie garland of small plaster skulls and bones. "And the same on the opposite wall. Do be careful of the Caravaggio, of course."

Jean Claude had enthusiastically embraced the Halloween gala concept and gone beyond even Fiona's imagination when it came to decorations. Henley always averted his eyes and then sighed heavily into his bourbon each evening when he glimpsed the décor on his way to the second floor.

"Good Christ, Fiona, you're creating a house of horrors down there between the two of you, not to mention what Marie Laveau will contribute."

Fiona grinned. "Delightful, isn't it? Darling, you have to calm down. Décor never hurt anyone." Henley could be so prickly.

"Ha." Henley poured himself another glass. "Tell that to Marie Antoinette."

Fiona sensed a change of subject could be beneficial. "This morning I received a message from a flatboat captain that Julius's arrival is imminent, sooner than we expected." Fiona had sent their housekeeper Mara and the maids to open and refresh the wing of Julius's rooms on the back side of their square that bordered Bourbon street, complete with new candles, linens and fresh flowers. "The Queen could be here by tomorrow even. Wouldn't it be grand if he was here for the Halloween Ball?"

Henley rolled his eyes. "Grand."

Fiona wasn't worried. Julius was a showman, among many other things. He would embrace this endeavor.

"Have no doubts, Henley. I have this well in hand."

She and Jean Claude had decided to have as the main venue the beautiful courtyard behind their establishments.

Julius DeMonte owned the entire block, surrounded on four sides by Royal Street which they faced, bordered by Conti, St. Louis and Bourbon streets, a typical New Orleans squared block. In the hollow center was the usual courtyard the French Quarter was renowned for, a private and refreshingly beautiful retreat from the noise and aromas of the city itself, replete with fountains and paved walkways through the lush and flowering greenery, and benches and tables in which the residents took their leisure and enjoyment. This is where the Halloween Ball would truly come to life after guests passed through the macabre and eerie passageway that Jean Claude was creating in his gallery, his creative décor a sure guarantee of returning patrons and his future art sales. Already word was spreading, invitations were hotly sought-after and anticipation was bubbling for the most unique Halloween festivity ever conceived, which was also, of course, a masquerade ball. Fiona had heard that the Mardi Gras warehouses and costume designers were besieged.

Marie had sent over a wagon full of decorations for the courtyard and Fiona thought they were a bit macabre but the skulls, skeletons and their black lace-covered hangings and robes were effectively eerie. Robert, their gardener, and two boys he'd taken on to help, were placing them throughout the gardens. A spot was cleared for a bonfire, according to Marie's specifications, always a necessity for any voodoo ceremony and most definitely for this one, known as Fete Gede, a tribute to those who had gone before, and hosted by Gran Brigitte, the goddess of life and death, and her consort Baron Samedi, the guardian of the underworld. No doubt they would be personified by Marie herself and Jim Washington.

Fiona had chosen for Henley to become Francois Vidocq, the famous Parisian detective who had pioneered criminology, an inspiration, working with Henley's tailor to fashion a close copy of the dashing black cloak and top hat Vidocq had always worn in pursuit of his prey. For herself, she designed a costume from mystical legend: the Celtic goddess of death, the Morrigan herself, replete with a taxidermic raven that would perch on the shoulder of her black velvet gown.

At last, dark was falling and the evening had arrived. Antoine's was catering the food and the mouth-watering aromas of etouffee and carmelized roasted pork were wafting through the gardens. Antoine's had set up a bartender in the gardens along with a champagne fountain to supply any drinks the guests could possibly require, from absinthe to whiskey. Now, the stage was set, the bonfire lit, the costumes ready, and the guests soon to arrive. Fiona took one last look at the enchanted and somewhat sinister world they had created. Lit with hundreds of lanterns and candelabras, some even floating on the surface of the small lagoon in the center, tendrils of fragrant smoke snaking through the trees, the scene was perfectly eerie. Mingling with the scent of jasmine and honeysuckle, with a frisson of excitement running down her spine, Fiona took the stairs to the second floor to dress.

6

Henley was lounging on the sofa in their small parlor, a book in his hand, seemingly without a care in the world.

"All in place in the dark world of the dead down there, my dear?"

"Yes, no thanks to you."

He laughed. "Not a soul has asked for my input, which has been fortunate, since I have none to give. You little pack of ghouls have done an admirable job, I'm sure. I have been at the helm of the ship so to speak, while the ghastly goings-on have taken all your time. Fortunately, there has not been a crime wave in New Orleans this week."

"Have you ever looked at your costume?"

Henley patted the sofa beside him. "No, I have not. I've been waiting for that delicious sense of anticipation and curiosity to overtake me."

Fiona snorted but plopped down beside him anyway. "That could take until hell freezes over if your past sense of anticipation is any indicator." Her hand roamed over his tight breeches and she snuggled closer. "Unless given some impetus."

Henley sighed and leaned his head back on the sofa's plump cushions. "True words, Irish." He reached for her.

Fiona deftly evaded his arm and stood up. "So are these: follow me to the closet. You're about to be transformed, Michael Henley, like it or not. Hell is awaiting our entrance and fate is never a patient mistress, rather like me."

They stood before the mirror and she knew by the grin on Henley's face that he was more than pleased. He was the very incarnation of Francois Vidocq, black silk top hat, and the cloak, which she'd had Fontaine's make using delicate black silk rather than a heavier material, given New Orleans's October weather. It hung beautifully from Henley's broad shoulders, a perfect frame for the black waistcoat, trousers and tall boots that all fit him perfectly, the cloak fluttering with every move he made.

"I do like it, Irish. But it pales beside your magnificence."

"Not necessarily so, but we certainly make a lovely couple." Fiona twirled around and stopped to gaze into the floor-length mirror again. Her dress was a work of art -- the clinging black velvet pooled on the floor while a low-cut neckline barely seemed to cling to her shoulders. Upon her head of upswept black curls rested a narrow diadem of tiny sequined black bats, and more bats dotted the smoky black and grey silk veils that fell from the crown. With every step she took, the veils shimmered.

"And, the *piece de resistance*..." Fiona fastened the raven onto the shoulder strap of the gown.

"Of course." Henley grinned, giving the lie to the menacing portrait before them. "If we aren't very careful, my dear, people might discern our true nature underneath our sympathetic facades and that would never do."

"Doubtful, my heart, because we do care. Remember our motto: 'to do a great right, do a little wrong.'"

Henley raised an eyebrow but held out his hand. "Shall we?"

They bypassed Jean-Claude's elaborate entryway through the art gallery and entered the courtyard through their own kitchen back door, seeming to appear out of nowhere. They took up a post on the main pathway into the lush courtyard, and personally welcomed each guest as they passed by, some well-known while others were strangers, but strangers that had been invited for a purpose. The crème de la crème of New Orleans society had been invited, and the crème de la crème had come, some from social or political obligation of one form or another, others because they knew Julius, and many because their curiosity was too great to keep them away, as Fiona had planned on.

The small orchestra Fiona had contracted with was half-hidden by a trellis of bougainvillea and were playing Saint-Saens's Danse Macabre, the eerie violins wafting through the garden just like the wispy smoke from the candelabras, setting the scene for mysterious anticipation. The zydeco band Marie Laveau had recommended would play later, after the majority of the guests had arrived and been well-sated with food and drink, ready to dance and more.

"*Bonne soiree, madam et monsieur,* welcome to the Underworld," had passed Fiona's lips so many times she felt like a marionette, Henley's hand on her elbow her anchor to reality. She and Henley complimented each costume and Fiona had to admit there was a variety of clever and wonderfully crafted ones, women everything from Cleopatra to Mary, Queen of Scots and even medieval milkmaids replete with wooden pails. Men were dressed in everything from cowboys to Shakespeare characters to Roman centurions, feathered helmets and all. Fiona was not a social creature, as a rule, although acting had schooled her. This was the first time she herself was the doyenne of her own entertainment.

'*Magnifique,* unbelievable, how enchanting, *fantastique, tres chic,* oh my god this is amazing', and so many other exclamations had flown at her she needed Henley's strength. Organizing this was her forte, enduring it was quite another. She found herself not as steady as she could be and her mood was becoming as black as the bats on her veil. So many silly people, such a long evening ahead. Henley was quite aware, tightening his hold. He knew her and her lack of patience well.

The tide of arrivals slowed to trickle, the courtyard full of costumed guests indulging in Antoine's delectable food and imbibing champagne and absinthe as though there would be no tomorrow, for after all, had they not entered the world of the dead?

"Breathe, Irish. Besides, here come reinforcements."

Fiona scarcely recognized Marie Laveau and Jim Washington, because tonight they were different entities altogether. Gran Brigette and Baron Samedi had arrived and with their royal presence, now the voodoo Fete Gede joined with Samhain, the Day of the Dead and the magic was complete. Marie took Fiona's hand in hers and bent to her ear.

"Tonight is ours, *cher.*" She swept her gaze over Fiona's costume and kissed her on the cheek. She gestured to the mass of partygoers. "They are ours as well, even if they do not yet know it." Marie was frighteningly resplendent as Gran Brigitte, her purple silk dress matched by a parasol trimmed with purple roses and black rooster feathers. A white clay paste had turned Jim's face into a grinning skull, his black frock coat and bowler hat a perfect match for every sketch or painting Fiona had ever seen of the Baron. Round spectacles with only one lens as was tradition, and a silver-topped cane completed the ensemble. As the four of them made their way through the paths and guests, conversation stilled in awe, and whenever they stopped to chat, people behaved as though royalty had deigned to notice them. Now Fiona was enjoying herself, especially after two glasses of absinthe.

That the evening was a resounding success became evident, and the low-key string orchestra retired to be replaced by the zydeco band, drums pounding. People crowded into the dance area with some enthusiasm while others tapped their feet in place, faces flushed with alcohol and abandon. Just before midnight, the bonfire was lit, and Marie stood before it, arms raised, and called for silence. Her wish was quickly obeyed, a quiet spreading quickly through the crowd. At her signal, the zydeco music stopped, replaced by the large conga drums pounding a rhythmic beat. Marie opened the big wicker basket at her feet and took out a large yellow snake, placing it around her shoulders to the gasps of some of the onlookers. She began to dance, hips swaying widely as she turned in circles around the fire. Two other women in brightly colored dresses of purple, green and yellow ruffled layers and matching tignons joined her in her dance and all three of them began to chant. Fiona didn't speak the language but she knew it was Haitian, where Louisiana voodoo had begun. The vibrant colors, the drums, the smoke and the chanting were hypnotic and people began to sway as though enchanted by it all. Fiona had seen some of this performance before but this time it was especially compelling and she was grateful that Henley's arm was around her, keeping her steady.

Finally, Marie lifted the snake over her head for one last twirl, and deposited it back into its basket with a caress. The drums reached a pounding climax and all three women whirled like dervishes and then sank onto the ground, faces and arms outstretched as the drums stopped. The silence fell as though God had silenced the world for a brief minute. Then people began to clap their hands, yelling bravo, amen, accolades of all sorts. Baron Samedi stepped to Gran Brigitte and took her arm, lifting her from the ground. This new year had officially begun.

The spell broken, the band played again, champagne flowed and the guests resumed their dancing, drinking and eating, but perhaps with a little more awareness and a bit more passion for life, even if they weren't quite sure why.

"'If music be the food of life, play on. Give me excess of it,'" whispered a voice in Fiona's ear. "You have outdone yourself, little one."

Julius DeMonte stood beside her, his kiss a fleeting butterfly's wing on her cheek. His eyes glowed in the candlelight, much like the first time she'd ever seen him. Fiona flung her arms around him, this man the father she'd never had. His aristocratic bearing and perfect handsome features hadn't changed a whit.

"Welcome," she managed, as Julius drew a grinning Henley into their joint embrace. "I was so hoping you would be here." In the three years they'd established the New Orleans office that served Julius's enterprises, there was never a definite date when the Queen would arrive from her showboat cruise down the Mississippi, what with prolonged dates, weather and many other variables. It was always a delight when it did.

A moment passed before Julius stepped back and flung his black velvet cloak over his shoulder reaching out towards the tall man standing beside him. "I was in hopes as well, for the Queen is still docking, left in Abel's competent hands. I have brought an old friend whom I hope you will come to trust as you do me."

Fiona looked up at the gentleman beside Julius. Impeccably dressed, his dark hair fell in waves to his shoulders, and his delicately featured face was marked with dark, mesmerizing eyes. He took her hand. He gently pushed aside the black silk veil from her face where it had fallen and smiled. Where his face had been attractive before, the smile gave him a mischievous charisma that was well-nigh irresistible.

Before Julius could make introductions, the man said, "Claude-Louis, the Comte Saint Germain, dear madam," he said, his voice soft but resonant with a slight French accent. "I am delighted to make your acquaintance, Fiona, and that of your esteemed companion, Mr. Michael Henley," he gazed at Henley. "Julius has told me of you both and it is a great pleasure, as is this enchanted tableau you have given us on this special evening. I am sure I shall enjoy my initial visit to New Orleans a great deal."

Marie drifted by and stopped to greet Julius. "I am happy to see you again, Julius, and just in time for our little festivity. And your friend?"

"Ah, yes, madame. Let me introduce you to the Comte Saint Germain," Julius said. "Claude-Louis, may I present Gran Brigitte, the queen of New Orleans, Marie Laveau."

"*Je suis enchante*," that gentleman took her hand, bending to bestow a kiss. Before he could do so, Fiona saw a look of distaste cross Marie's face and she snatched her hand away as though she had touched something undesirable.

The Comte gave a slight nod, his face inscrutable but the smile returned, although it was not reflected in his eyes anymore.

"Come, my queen," Jim Washington said, his hand on Marie's elbow. He doffed his hat to the group. "A lovely evening, but *desole,* the Baron and Brigitte have more appearances to make on this night. *Bon soir.*"

The silence that fell on the little group as the two walked away was broken by Julius. "Absinthe, my friend?" Julius said, leading the Comte towards the refreshments. "We shall catch up tomorrow, my darlings. It is good to be back."

As they watched Julius and the Comte depart, Fiona looked at Henley. "What was that about?"

Henley shook his head. "I don't know, yet. Definitely something we shall have to investigate. How fortunate that is exactly what we do, Irish."

7

Fiona groaned, flinging out an arm towards Henley. Instead of warm flesh, she was met with cold sheets on his side of the bed.

"He's been gone for an hour or more, love. Off with the silver-haired devil from across the way, don't you know." Nico sat at the small breakfast table by the French doors, munching on a beignet, powdered sugar a sprinkling of snow on his shirt. "Fortune waits for no woman. Or whatever they're up to. I don't like to ask questions, being the canny lad that I am."

"Quiet, my canny lad. Is there anything in that pot or plate you haven't consumed? If so, bring it here now."

The brat could move quickly, she'd give him that. Within seconds, a cup of café au lait and a beignet appeared on her bedside table. Fiona sat up, grateful that in the miasma of absinthe the evening before, she'd thought to don a cotton nightgown. Her head began to clear, and she held out her cup, which Nico nimbly refilled from the silver pot on the table.

"What time is it?" She had a feeling the answer was one she didn't want to hear.

"The last bell from the Cathedral said eleven, milady."

"Christ Jesus." Julius's favorite epithet came out of her lips like she'd heard it last night, which likely she had, but memory failed.

She finished her second cup and sat up, the room steady. She fixed her gaze at Nico, who looked to be settling in and waiting for lunch. She pointed at the balcony, his favorite entry and exit.

"Out."

Feigning disappointment, the imp grinned and headed to the balcony. "Of course. I'll be around, if you need me."

"This is a world fraught with uncertainty but that is one fact I'm quite sure of," Fiona said, flinging back the bedcovers.

An hour later, after a bath and piling her unruly black curls in a type of pompadour, dressed in what New Orleans considered fashionable, although the silken layers were too much for Fiona's taste in the humid climate, having grown up wearing rough cotton shifts in a Ballyowen orphanage. Still, she felt ready to take on what was left of the day. Needs must, she'd learned long ago. She descended the staircase and was greeted by Raphael, clearly eager to impart the latest news.

Fiona held up her hand before he could say a word. "The warehouse, I presume?"

Deflated, Raphael nodded. "Should I call a carriage? They took ours."

Fiona sighed. "Of course they did. Yes, please, Raphael." She hated public vehicles, they were usually dirty and the drivers were a mixed lot.

"There's a lot of cards and messages, Miss." The silver tray on his desk was full of envelopes.

She rifled through them while he went to the street to flag down a carriage. The usual fawning thank-yous and platitudes, a few requests for assistance with one trouble or another, and a couple she'd need to devote more attention to later.

Raphael helped her into the carriage and within only a few

minutes, they stopped before a two-story wooden building with a large peaked roof. She impatiently kicked down the steps before the driver could manage it, leaving the fare and a generous tip on the seat. She stood before the immaculately painted warehouse at Number 27. No company name adorned this well-kept building, its sleek façade as discreet as its owner. The Queen of Dreams sat quayside nearby, the ramps still down, although all activity had ceased. Fiona knew that the cargo had been unloaded during the wee hours this morning. She gazed at the showboat she'd traveled on during its maiden voyage down the Mississippi and smiled fondly at both the memories and the beautiful boat before her, its white paint gleaming on all decks like a wedding cake confection, the momentum of its great paddlewheel stalled for a time. She knew Captain Abel would pilot it upriver in a couple of months for the winter maintenance before he guided the Queen on her journey south again in the late spring when all the ice had melted.

Fiona took the key to the small door on the street side of the warehouse from her reticule and inserted it into the lock, swinging the door open. Julius, Henley, Sean McKean, Abel Hamilton and two other men she didn't know looked up as she slammed the door shut.

"Shame, gentlemen. Could you not wait for the lady in this play on such a fine day?"

After a second or two passed before Julius bowed. "Apologies, fierce one. We only were concerned for your welfare."

Fiona rolled her eyes at that before Captain Abel Hamilton took three big steps and swept her up in his arms, his grin dazzling in his dark face. "You never change, Fiona. Amaro sends her love."

She kissed his cheek before he deposited her back on the floor, quite a distance given Abel's height. "And give her mine and tell her I miss her. And Heart's Ease, that piece of heaven." The Hamiltons had restored the plantation near Greenville, one they'd formerly been slaves on, renaming it Heart's Ease. Sean McKean, Julius's gruff Irish bodyguard, was next to bestow a hug. "Tis good to set eyes on you, missy."

They settled around the table, perched on packing crates, sharing a delightful wine from Argentina, crates of which were about to be loaded onto the Queen for her northbound voyage, along with many other things from all parts of the globe, some illegal and all without an import tax or any other regulations, customs or otherwise. Julius had been at this game for a long time, financing his other interests and passions with his carefully orchestrated choices from without and within. Fiona counted herself lucky to be a small part of this endeavor and was well aware of the dangers involved. Because, many of Julius's interests, particularly equality among races, women's rights (of which there had ever been few) and needs (of which there were many), along with widespread educational and cultural opportunities, dovetailed with her own and those of everyone in this room. The two gentlemen she didn't know likely felt the same or they wouldn't be here, at least not for long.

"Let me introduce you to our new colleagues," Julius said. "Alexander Cameron, our new accountant, who better than a canny Scotsman to tally numbers, eh?" A stocky sandy-haired man stood up and gave her a bow, along with an admiring grin. "Delighted, ma'am."

Fiona nodded and Julius turned to the other newcomer, who had remained standing the entire time she'd been there. "This is Daniel Fox. He has a plethora of talents, as you will discover in the days to come."

He was quite tall, maybe an inch or two past Henley, his black hair pulled into a tail that left his face distinctive with its high cheekbones and intense dark eyes. He held out his hand to her, not a common practice, and Fiona put hers into his gentle one. "I have heard much of you," he said, a faint smile in the corners of his mouth.

She glanced at Julius. "Don't believe anything these rogues have to say, especially King Lear there."

Julius feigned innocent outrage but everyone else laughed. "I'm hurt, my darling. You could have at least compared me to MacBeth or Orsino."

Fiona shrugged. "Perhaps. But I did not. That will teach you to leave me behind." She looked pointedly at Henley as well.

"Truce, truce."

"Agreed, Lord DeMonte." Fiona smiled. She knew well how Julius hated to be reminded of his title or his father, the Duke of Sandbrooke, all part of the life he'd been happy to leave long ago.

"Now, to the business at hand," Julius said. "Cameron, break out the inventory sheets."

Alexander Cameron was very good at his job. Sean McKean and Daniel Fox took up sentry duty, inside and out, and the rest of them pored over the cargo sheets and the disposition of the goods ready to go north and the assignment of what remained of the cargo that had floated southward on the Queen. Usually what came south were armaments, guns, cannons, ammunition and other instruments of war, in high demand throughout the world, and some of them found homes long before New Orleans. Julius was judicious in who received them but disliked dealing in death even for causes he championed but that was the sad way of the world. Medicines, books, tobacco, cotton and sugar, among other goods, rounded it out. Within days these would be sent out on the tide in various ships to various locations.

What had entered New Orleans from other lands and was stored in the warehouse to be loaded onto the Queen for its voyage north was quite different. Rare spices, silks, velvets and Italian laces, French and South American wines, brandies and liqueurs and other luxury goods made up the bulk of the cargo. The most valuable and that which took up only a small space, were tiny in size but the largest in value: opals from Australia, jade and pearls from China, diamonds from Africa, the best rubies from Burma and Julius's current favorite, Colombian emeralds.

Secrecy was essential. Very few people knew anything of the shipments that sustained Julius's empire, just as most assumed that empire was about entertainment -- his theaters, the traveling troupes, and the showboat. That was the frosting, but the cake itself was an intricate network that supported those unspoken causes and people who needed help, those who could make a difference in an increasingly divided world, and those who fought against inequality, whether it was because of race, gender, grievances and greed, and the grasping corruption of politicians and their financial bankrollers. It was a battle that was always fought even behind the scenes and needed its champions. Julius was one, and she loved him for it.

Inventory tallied, books perused, allocations made, by late afternoon, everyone seemed satisfied. Julius held up an especially large emerald from a pouch in his hand and turned to Fiona.

"Open your eyes wide, little one," he said, holding the stone near her face. "I do believe it matches.

Fiona took his hand and the emerald in hers. "Of course it does." She dropped the stone back into the bag. "I figure it could better finance a new orphanage in Cairo, Illinois rather than be compared to me. But, thank you."

"And it will, of course," Julius said. "But it does no harm to give beauty its due, Fiona, never forget that." He stood up. She felt chided, but she deserved it, really.

"Good work. Let's call it a day, shall we?" He turned to

Henley. "The night crews are ready? As we've found before, this is the most crucial time for security."

"They're waiting outside. Sean and Daniel will be here until six and then the others will take over until morning."

"Excellent. Dupree's at nine, then?"

8

In an intimate private dining room within Dupree's, a welcome dinner for DeMonte Enterprises was well underway. Fiona was disappointed that Mama Rosa, the turbaned Romany woman whose dark knowing eyes registered everything, both on this side of the veil and the other, Julius's long-time advisor, had stayed at home in Chicago on this tour of the showboat. She greatly admired the wise woman. Her son Ramon, Julius's favorite leading man, was in attendance, seductively handsome. Beside him were the St. John sisters, Ellen and Merry, Julius's dear friends, beautiful actresses and dancers who had become close friends of Fiona's ever since their initial voyage down the Mississippi. Sean McKean, Daniel Fox, and Alexander Cameron rounded out one side of the table, while Henley, Fiona, and the enigmatic and mostly silent Comte Saint German sat at the other. Julius anchored the seat at the other end or, as Fiona knew he preferred, the head.

They'd swiftly consumed the crab soup and shrimp remoulade, when the waiters opened the champagne, poured it and discreetly disappeared. Julius smiled benignly, and stood up, holding his glass.

"My dear friends. Another successful season has passed, and we all look forward to the next. Each and every one of you is important to me and I want to commend all of you on the excellent work you continue to do. We do make a difference in this world in our own small way, and will continue to do so, I have no doubt. Thank you for sharing my sentiments and vision." He drank, as did they all.

Julius turned to the Comte, sitting to his left. "I want to introduce you to an old friend of mine, who will be in residence here this winter. I have known Claude-Louis for many years and I owe him my gratitude for his friendship and knowledge. Treat him as you would me." Everyone at the table knew what that meant. He held up his champagne glass again, as did they all, and drank to the Comte. That gentleman rose, bowed and Fiona saw him smile, a small upward quirk of his lips.

"*Merci beaucoup, mon ami.* You do me honor."

Working their way through asparagus, shrimp Creole and filet with Marchand sauce, conversation sparkled, stories were told, memories shared and Fiona's impatience abated as each delicious bite filled her stomach rather than her curiosity. Finally pushing aside the remains of crème brulee and raspberries, she felt content, or at least as content as her suspicious nature allowed her to be. Truly she delighted in Julius's arrival each year, but there hadn't been time to have any time alone so far on this visit and she half resented Saint Germain for that whether it was justified or not.

Ah well. There would be time. It was New Orleans, the best time of the year was here and she must remember the rule: in the South, all things are taken in proper order with no strain or disquiet. In that way, all things are dealt with as they should be.

As they left the restaurant, Julius whispered in her ear. "You are doing a commendable job of hiding your curiosity, Fiona. I will see you in the courtyard early in the morning. Sleep well."

Henley remained snoring softly as Fiona slipped into a simple cotton morning dress and tiptoed downstairs into the garden, her feet bare and hair tumbled. It was barely light, but even so, her favorite time of day. Dew glistened on the leaves of the twining vines and trees, flowers were opening to the light, and small unseen birds gave a tentative welcome to the dawn. It smelled of life, hope, and green growing things.

As promised, Julius sat at a table in a secluded corner, a silver tray with coffee and beignets beside him. He smiled as she appeared and sat soundlessly on the other chair.

"Lovely morning." He poured her coffee and handed her the cup and saucer, a smile playing on his lips. "I know you are eager, my dear, but give me a chance to tell you how happy I am to see you, just between us. You are special to me, Fiona."

She blushed, unable to control her pleasure at his words. "As you are to me, Julius. Tell me truly, how are you? You look wonderful, but then you always do."

He shrugged and for the first time, she sensed a tingle of apprehension. "I am doing well, Fiona. For now. There is much to tell you. I thought it might be simpler to acquaint you first with this problem, Irish and myth-laden as your lot is," he grinned. "Having you with me in agreement is an easier premise for our dear hard-headed Henley. I need both of you and your skills."

"Myth-laden, is it now? Coming from someone who chats with Shakespeare over his brandy, I pale in comparison," Fiona sipped her coffee and put it down with a clink, curiosity overwhelming.

"Point taken. But now, listen to me." Julius sat back and Fiona did the same.

"Many years ago, when I was but a rakehell lad in London, successfully disgracing my family name, as my father put it, I met Claude-Louis Saint German at Bolbrooke's, the exclusive London gaming club. I was young, heedless, full of anger, exactly what my father suspected and feared. Claude-Louis and I became fast friends, much alike in our practices and personalities, so much so that we became as brothers.

"We also indulged in every vice imaginable, from procuring the most beautiful and accomplished whores and actresses who would entertain us with songs, dance and other delights before ending their evenings in our beds, to opium pipes that we indulged in for days at a time, enjoying the most expensive and elaborate food and drink available, not to mention the gambling that sometimes went on for days as well, resulting in fortunes and estates sometimes changing hands in the most suspect manner.

"I thought we were much the same, Saint Germain and I, but one evening I learned quite differently, and from that moment on, my life changed forever. Shortly thereafter, we parted company, he went on to his scientific pursuits in the wider world, while I agreed to make my father happy and remove myself to the wilds of America, where I remain today. We had not seen each other for many years until he arrived in Chicago just before I was to embark on the Queen this spring. We had a grand reunion and spent the voyage downriver enlightening each other on our lives since we had last met."

Julius poured them both more coffee. "While we have enjoyed renewing our friendship, there is another reason Claude-Louis has come to New Orleans. While seeking transportation south, he quite by chance discovered my showboat and troupe and not only availed himself of my services but confided in his need for my help with a much larger problem, one I have some knowledge of and a great desire to assist. I am positive that you and Henley, with all the contacts you've made here, and your innate abilities to solve mysteries, are the very people Claude-Louis and I need."

Fiona was intrigued. A torrent of questions was ready to spill from her mouth, but she knew Julius wasn't ready to answer them. Instead, she nodded. "Of course, we'll do what we can, Julius but you're being pretty mysterious yourself. What's next?"

"I need you to talk with Henley about what I've said. For the next day or two, I will be helping Saint German set up his laboratory in the west wing. The man is a dedicated scientist, botanist and alchemist, and needs a secure private workspace which of course, I can provide here. Crates of equipment will be arriving this morning. I suggest the four of us meet there tomorrow evening and discuss the situation further, if that meets with your approval?"

"Of course," Fiona said, more curious than ever. Julius was ever a tricky one but this time he had outdone himself, to her mind. "We'll wrap up some cases we're working on and be available then."

She stood up and so did Julius, who gently pulled her into a hug. "I've missed you, little one, and I thank you for your patience. A delicate matter, this, as you will see."

Fiona gave a sly grin. "Likely myth-laden then, like myself?"

Julius laughed. "Decidedly so."

She could hardly wait to talk to Henley and practically ran up the stairs. He was on the balcony, watching Royal Street come to life, eating a croissant.

"I was wondering where you went so early, Irish."

"We need to talk." Fiona pulled him inside. "Julius and his old friend are in some sort of trouble and they need our help. Sounds very intriguing."

Henley was as perplexed as she was after she told him everything Julius had said. "I don't understand the secrecy quotient myself. It makes me a bit uneasy. He's always had things in his past he's never divulged and I haven't asked. That said, I trust Julius with my life and always have."

"As do I," Fiona said. "It can't be anything stranger than some of the things we've seen at Bayou St. John, or even the tarot card reader at the park."

She would have cause to remember those words very soon and replace them with others, beginning with "There are more things on heaven and earth, Horatio, than are dreamt of in your philosophy,", words Julius DeMonte already knew to be true.

9

That day and the next passed in a blur, Fiona and Henley busily finishing up cases, sometimes solved as easily as sending an invoice or collecting one, while a few required a little more hands-on approach, but by the next evening, they were ready to devote their time solely to Julius and his friend's issue, whatever it might be.

Fiona was skeptical. "I'm irritated."

Henley laughed. "That has been quite evident, my dear. You nearly took Raphael's head off this morning over the Fouquet invoice, and verbally eviscerated Jean-Claude over his complaints about moving his stuff out of the storage space."

Crossing the garden, they were on their way to the west wing to meet in what Julius referred to as Saint Germain's laboratory. Henley stopped and turned Fiona to face him. His hands on her shoulders, he bent down and kissed the top of her head. "Whatever all this is about, we will soon find out, and there is nothing we can't handle, especially together."

Fiona rested her cheek on the soft linen of his waistcoat. "I know. I'll be fine."

"Hell, I know that. It's everyone else that comes within two feet of you I'm worried about. Got your razor with you?"

"Very funny, darling." He knew quite well she did, snug in its pocket in her corset. She pirouetted away and stepped quickly to the door leading to the second floor wing that faced Conti street. "Let's not be late."

Julius flung open the door on the landing just as Henley was about to knock. "Welcome." He flung out his hand and stepped back.

"Christ Jesus," Fiona breathed, stopping four steps into the large room. "Tis the devil's own workshop in here."

She'd never seen a laboratory of any kind before, but she had seen drawings of medieval sorcerers' workshops in old books and this place reminded her strongly of that, and a fanciful stage set from the opera Faust. A long table across one wall held an assortment of glass tubes, vials and retorts, one bubbling away atop a charcoal burner, a bilious green liquid running through its glass coils and into a strange contraption that fed into a large glass jar. She stepped closer and Saint Germain, wearing a black rubber apron over his clothing, turned to her.

"It's an alembic, Fiona. They've been around for hundreds of years and still work just as effectively as they ever did for distilling. Fascinating, isn't it?

"Yes, yes it is." She meant it, too. "This entire place is wondrous. Does smell a bit peculiar, though."

"Sulfur does have an unusual odor, as well as quite a few other elements, compounds and ingredients in here."

A stone sink, fed by tubes from the cistern, sat in the middle of the worktable, which seemed a good idea, especially from a safety standpoint, and also large pails full of sand for quenching fires, she assumed. On the other side of the room, mortars, pestles, wooden holders full of vials, an assortment of instruments and glittering knives cluttered the table. A rack suspended from the ceiling held easily accessible copper pots in all sizes. In the center of the room, a large cupboard full of many small compartments labeled with a drawing and words in French, Latin and English. Leather bound books, some open and others closed, were stacked on the tabletop. Above, another cupboard held drawers of herbs, powders, plants, seeds, roots, leaves, fruit and flowers were all there, some she recognized, like a rose and a sprig of cilantro, and most of the others she did not.

"What do you plan to make here?"

He chuckled with delight at her curiosity. "Anything and everything. Cures, medicines, even poisons, for all are needed sometimes, for one thing or another, *non*? But the true beauty of science is discovery itself, Miss Shanahan. That is the thrill of it, of course. I believe I sense a kindred spirit."

She gazed at him. "You may indeed, Comte. I must admit I am fascinated. Nothing I have seen so far in my life is quite like this."

Julius and Henley were murmuring in the corner while Fiona was flitting from one area to another like a butterfly entranced by perhaps some of the very flowers in those drawers, Saint Germain following like a solicitous governess with an overeager child, so much so she lost all track of time. So many wonderful things that she'd never imagined, and the possibilities of what you could discover by using the equipment here. Plus, the books, her greatest weakness and greatest joy. Saint Germain was a kind teacher, answering every question she put to him. Finally, he glanced over his shoulder to where Julius and Henley sat on a couple of stools. Only then did Fiona feel slightly conspicuous in her enthusiasm, and taking Saint Germain's arm, smiled at him as they stepped over to join the other two.

Fiona smiled and held up her hands. "Apologies. This is so wonderful I forgot my manners, gentlemen. However, I am somewhat puzzled as to how S&H Investigations can possibly help with anything you may need when it comes to your pursuits here."

Henley nodded. "True. Our talents lie in a somewhat different arena."

Saint Germain and Julius exchanged glances and both smiled. "Let's go into the study and we shall enlighten you."

Filled with mellow light from the gas sconces on the walls, the book-lined smaller room was cozy, just large enough for a desk, a small sofa, a bar cart and a table and chairs, which they settled into, Julius handing out crystal glasses filled with brandy.

"I am searching for someone," the Frenchman said, "and I think with your contacts and knowledge of the area, you two can find her if she is here."

Henley sipped his brandy. "Possibly. What information have we to go on?"

Saint Germain winced. "That, you see, is the problem. Very little. I have been looking for her literally the world over, for a very long time, as she was very dear to me. It has been many years since I have last seen her, and then she was in her twenties, blonde hair, blue eyes, very pretty, of medium height and slim of figure, the elegant daughter of a Marquis, and her name is Annette du Chambord. She too is a scientist, specializing in botanical recipes." Here he paused and looked at Fiona. "So, you see, my dear, women are very capable in this field."

"We must assume, then," Henley said, "that she looks nothing like she did many years ago, and if she is aware you are eager to find her, perhaps not eager to be found?"

"Most people would think those are wise assumptions. I doubt the name is the same, however the du Chambord family is notoriously long-lived and shall we say... well preserved."

Fiona doubted that last, but saw little point in arguing. "What makes you believe she may be in New Orleans?"

"An odd thing, but the first real clue I have had in a long time. I met a gentleman in New York last year with a rare medical condition. He has been searching for a medicine that he has learned about that could help him. As we talked, he mentioned one of the ingredients that makes up this medicine, if indeed it exists, a plant that has only ever grown in two places on earth, one in a Nile valley in Egypt, and the other, my own old estate in Chambord, France. My friend unfortunately died last winter, but he did reveal to me that the plant he was searching for, according to a chemist in New York at the University supposedly came from a botanist in New Orleans who specialized in exotic plants."

Saint Germain rose and paced slowly around his chair. "The only possible person in the world who might have that plant aside from me, grown long ago in my garden in France, is Annette du Chambord or whatever she calls herself now. So, this is where the search must begin again."

Fiona glanced over at Henley, who raised his eyebrows but stayed silent, finishing his brandy.

Julius refilled everyone's glass. "If anyone can find her, it is you two. I have complete faith in you."

"As do I, from what Julius has told me, and especially now that we have become acquainted." Saint Germain held up his glass. "To success."

Crystal clinked and brandy swallowed, Fiona thought it best to keep her misgivings to herself. Only a few minutes later, she and Henley sat on their balcony, the breeze from the west sweet with the grassy scent of the sugar cane harvest. She'd never really cared for brandy, and made up two tall glasses of her own recipe, gin and lemonade. She 'd handed one to Henley and had taken one for herself, the ice tinkling softly as she drank.

"Ah, that's better."

Henley nodded. "Agreed."

They sat in companionable silence for a few minutes. Henley finally said, "Spit it out, Irish."

"Well, there's a few things. First, not much to go on, rather like Cervantes' 'needle in a haystack'. Second, I'd like to know more about why he wants to find her, because I think it's more than a plant. Third, I don't –"

"Trust him," Henley finished in chorus. They both laughed softly. They had a habit of finishing each other's sentences. This time was no different. "For the record, neither do I."

"He's lying about something, maybe a lot of somethings, and so is Julius," Fiona said. "It's the Julius part that's bothering me."

"Yes, although I don't believe Julius would put either of us in harm's way, Fiona."

"I agree with that." She sighed. "Ah well. We will see what we can find. The whole thing may be just a puzzle with too many lost pieces, with the lack of information we have. At least it's not so filthy hot, since we'll be scouring the streets, so to speak."

"It's not late," Henley said. "If you're eager, we could start scrubbing tonight."

"I have other plans for tonight and they don't involve scrubbing anything except for your back, if you're interested."

"Ah. Bubbles then?"

"Of course."

"I could be enticed."

"You always are."

"Well, it's not just the bubbles, Hen."

10

An envelope of heavy cream-colored paper was on the silver tray at the desk when Fiona came down the next morning, with her name in elegant black ink script. Inside was a key and a card:

"I would be delighted to be your guide in discovering more of the world of science, botany and alchemy when your time permits. Thank you again for undertaking the difficult task I have set for you. *Bonne chance. SG*"

She stuffed the card back into the envelope and buried both in her pocket. *The man was an odd duck,* she thought, *but a rather fascinating one. When time permits, indeed.*

"Good morning, Miss Fiona." Raphael had done his job well this morning, fresh croissants and strawberries sprinkled with sugar crystals sat on a silver tray on the reception table, with a pot of coffee. Fiona wasted no time in indulging in all of it before Henley came tripping down the stairs as though he was on a mission. He stopped abruptly when he saw her sitting in one of the wing-backed chairs.

"Ah, there you are." He nodded at Raphael and poured

coffee for himself. "I thought you might be off scouring the streets or some such." He grinned. "You're quite skilled at it."

"Shush. We are professionals."

"Of course we are," Henley said through a mouthful of croissant. "So well practiced too." He leered at her over his cup and she laughed, putting down the strawberry she'd just picked up. "Where did you plan to start this morning?"

"Apothecaries, pharmacists, herb stores, that sort of thing," Fiona said. "If we come up with nothing on that front, we are going over to Tulane University to their School of Medicine. If anyone knows about folk remedies or botanicals, it may be them."

"Excellent thinking, Irish." He started in on the strawberries. "This is why I love you, you're so thorough."

She wanted to kick him in the shins but then there was always the possibility he'd choke on his strawberries so instead she finally ate another one herself. It was excellent.

By three o'clock, they sank down on a shaded bench in Jackson Square, drinking iced sweet tea from a street vendor, watching a clever artist draw caricatures for passersby.

"Not a shred to go on," Henley said. "Frankly, I'm not surprised. I knew this was going to be close to impossible when we started."

Fiona leaned back far enough on the iron bench that she felt her spine crackle and sighed with pleasure. Henley chewed on a piece of ice and shook his head. "I keep telling you you're going to cripple yourself doing that. Probably look like you could play one of MacBeth's witches by the time you're thirty."

Fiona rolled her eyes. "You get especially testy when you're frustrated, Hen. Therefore I'm going to be understanding and not retort in kind."

"So let's go over this again. We are looking for a woman, a Frenchwoman, who deems herself a botanist of some kind. If she is that and is here, one would assume she supports herself in some manner by selling remedies or plants or concoctions of some sort to others in that sort of business, and/or buying such plants or concoctions and equipment from the same people, correct?"

"Yes," Fiona said. "However, it is possible she does none of those things but keeps to herself."

"Unlikely. At some point, she would interact with someone in that community or a similar one."

"True. Ergo, we just haven't found that someone yet. Or, at least one of the people we've met is lying. Maybe we don't look threatening enough."

"That could be true. Didn't know I was supposed to be threatening today," Henley said, "but I could if that's your desire, pet. You, on the other hand, look as threatening as a kitten. 'How foolish these mortals be.'".

Fiona rolled her eyes and pulled out the small leather-bound notebook she always carried with her, along with its pencil, attached with a red ribbon. "There are four more we haven't been to, besides Tulane which is over on St. Charles, and two of the last four are in the Garden District. Perhaps we set out again tomorrow in that direction?"

"Likely chasing a rat in a cornfield, but yes." Henley sighed. "However, there is someone we haven't had on our list that we certainly should have and she's much closer. If anyone knows about botany, herbs and mysterious anything, she's on Bourbon Street."

Fiona groaned. He was absolutely right. Ever since meeting Saint Germain, her head had been half in old France and half in some chemist's lab. Marie Laveau likely knew more than anyone about plants and herbs, especially those grown in Louisiana. She downed her tea and stood up.

"Lead on, MacDuff."

Six-twenty-eight Bourbon Street was back to normal, the street in front of the voodoo shop quiet with just a normal amount of traffic. It was as though the events of a few weeks ago had never occurred at all. Fiona and Henley entered the shop, the bell by the door jingling as they came inside. Evangeline, Marie's shop manager, smiled warmly. She wore a simple layered white muslin gown with a neckline that could be off the shoulder, and a red headscarf, defiantly harking back to the old Tignon laws in 1700s Louisiana that required women of color to wear just that costume. Evangeline, Marie and many of their acquaintances adhered to this style often as a symbol to demonstrate how much had changed, and a warning that it could happen again.

"It is lovely to see you both again," she said. "Unfortunately, if you are wishing to have an audience with Marie, I must disappoint you. She is upcountry for a few days or more."

"That is disappointing," Henley said, but smiled at the pretty young woman. "We will be back to see her soon. However, in the meantime, perhaps you could help us."

Evangeline smiled. "I will if I can, Mr. Henley."

Fiona sighed. God, it was just short of simpering, even for Evangeline, such a sophisticated young woman. How the ladies loved him and it did get tedious but Fiona supposed having a man that looked like Henley made things easier, and not just for investigating.

Henley cast a glance around the shop, where hundreds of goods hung from racks and were displayed on counters and in cases. Quite a few items were in glassine bags or stoppered and waxed glass bottles and vials with labels in French and English, and quite a few were clearly dried herbs, seeds and in some cases tinctures. Marie had a better selection than any of the other establishments they had visited today.

While Henley chatted with Evangeline, Fiona wandered around, noting the names on the packages and vials. Most she recognized immediately, everything from cinnamon to cilantro, but there were a few she'd never heard of before. This wasn't surprising, since she'd never really paid attention to this area of knowledge before. In addition, there was a shelf of books, and some were herbals, compendiums of plants and remedies and dictionaries of the same. She considered buying one, but then thought back to the books in Saint Germain's laboratory. One or two of these looked the same, so she could just borrow one of those instead, if she needed to know more.

Evangeline and Henley passed her and went through a beaded curtain into the workroom behind the retail store, Henley jerking his head to follow. Late afternoon sunlight streamed through the high windows, illuminating the long narrow room that reminded Fiona of Saint Germain's lab, tables full of mortars, pestles, charcoal burners, knives and marble cutting boards. It held none of the more sophisticated equipment she'd seen at Saint Germain's, but was much better equipped than the other establishments they'd seen today.

"So your main suppliers are local, then?"

"Yes, most of them live close by, upriver or some even here in the city," Evangeline said. "Some of the more specialized and hard-to-find specimens come by ship or train from the north."

"Is that usual?" Fiona said.

Evangeline smiled. "For us, yes. I cannot say for others. Madame is somewhat specific in many of her needs."

I'll say, Fiona thought. *God knows what's in some of those bottles out there, and likely worse hidden in here, not for public knowledge or consumption. Still, likely not what Saint Germain is looking for.*

"Ever buy from a Frenchwoman named Annette?" Henley was clearly through with subterfuge this afternoon.

"It is possible, monsieur Henley," Evangeline said. "But it is only for Madame to know. I do not concern myself with that aspect of the business. Sadly, she is not here." She smiled blandly and brushed away invisible specks from her pristine white skirt.

"Yes, so we heard," Fiona said. She was getting increasingly irritated and it felt as though the walls were closing in, redolent with the smell of cloves and some other aromas she detested. She grabbed Henley's arm and her fingers were not gentle. "Thank you for your time, Evangeline. We will be back next week to see Marie."

Outside, hurrying a block down, Henley pulled her under an awning. "What the hell is wrong with you, Fiona?"

Fiona shook her head as if to rid it of some lingering miasma. "Ah, Christ man. I don't know. It's too warm, I'm tired, there was that smell in there, and all that peculiar stuff stashed away. I swear to God Marie's got St. Patrick's eyeballs in a jar on a back shelf and likely his prick in a drawer somewhere. To top it off, of course, pretty little Evangeline is a rotten liar."

Henley stared at her for a second and then laughed, pulling her close. "I don't know what I'd do without you, Irish."

"For now, take me home and ply me with wine and cake. Tomorrow's another day."

11

Fiona stared up at the four-story white brick building that housed Tulane's School of Medicine, an imposing structure by any standards. The entire campus was comprised of similar buildings, gleaming like polished ivory among the lush green tree-covered grounds, and foundations were being laid for more. She grasped Henley's hand as they passed under the archway entrance and onto the long hallway that seemed to run forever down the center of the huge building.

"Reminds you of a church, especially Irish stone ones, doesn't it?" He squeezed her hand. "We won't take long."

He knew her well. She hated to admit weaknesses and she'd conquered most of them, but something about this place reminded her of St. Hilda's, the orphanage and church where she'd grown up and been married at fourteen to a brutal man. She'd long escaped that fate and had made herself into a different person, but the memories, when they surfaced, were disconcerting.

"Want to wait outside?"

Fiona shook her head. She'd found that the only way to

conquer fears was to face them. There had been occasions when that hadn't gone well, but since she was still breathing, she supposed they'd gone well enough. Besides, what could be so frightening about a medical school?

They entered the Dean's office. A clerk looked up from where he sat behind a large desk. The nameplate read 'Mr. Rafferty'.

"Good morning," Henley said, with a genial smile. "We've come by to see if we could have a brief chat with the Dean and perhaps a visit to the botanical lab."

Mr. Rafferty sniffed. "No appointment then?" He did not seem welcoming, running a hand over his brilliantined hair and straightening his tie.

"No, but this isn't a complicated matter," Henley said, handing Rafferty his card. "It won't take long. Is he in?"

Nonsense, Fiona thought. *Officious condescension wasn't frightening but it certainly was irritating. They didn't have time for this.* Fiona leaned over the desk slightly, but enough so that her breasts on the low-cut dress she wore came invitingly into view, and smiled at Rafferty, her tongue flicking quickly on her upper lip as though he was a frosted cupcake she wanted to nibble on. "You seem like a young man that's going places," she said. "I hope Dean Beaufort appreciates your abilities."

Blushing, Rafferty nodded, wordless for the moment. Fiona gently put her hand on his. "So, I'm sure he will be grateful to you for telling him we're here."

Nodding as though he were in a trance, Rafferty walked to the door behind him and knocked softly before entering. Henley shook his head and grinned at her. "I don't know how you do it, Irish. It's like a magic trick but one I love to watch."

Fiona gave a very unseductive snort. "You know exactly how I do it, darling. You just saw it."

After a few seconds, young Rafferty motioned them inside. Dean Beaufort stood up and held out his hand. "Lovely to see you both again. That certainly was a lovely masquerade you two hosted. I'm looking forward to next year. What can I do for you?"

In the end, it was a fruitless visit, despite the thorough tour. The labs were superb, very well-equipped and full of intent young students and doctors busily conducting experiments and rushing about with their hands full of glass tubes, tongs, and other things neither Fiona or Henley had ever been privy to before. Even so, no one seemed to have any answers as to a Frenchwoman botanist or any other botanists besides themselves, for that matter. Even a visit to the university's supply warehouse didn't provide any answers, just a myriad of possibilities, vendors and companies. There were so many, a great deal of them not even in Louisiana.

Back on the streetcar, Fiona sighed. "Listen, this is going to take years the way we're going about it so far. I want to study some of the herbals and books Saint Germain has up there, and learn a great deal more about plants and whatnot. While I do that, you might chat up some of the less visible types that supply all sorts of things around here. Maybe you'll stumble across something that leads us somewhere."

Henley shrugged. "Agreed. I have a feeling Marie may be of help, but we've got to wait on that, so your suggestions are good ones, Irish. Let's grab some sandwiches at Podreaux's. I can't investigate on an empty stomach."

"God forbid," Fiona said. "A hungry Henley is a dangerous creature."

~

Henley, well-fed and rejuvenated, was off to hobnob with the denizens of sin and iniquity that populated much of New Orleans's entertainment district, likely some of which Fiona knew he'd thoroughly enjoy. Fiona was back on Royal Street, and knocking on the door of the laboratory although she hadn't seen any sign of Saint Germain or Julius anywhere in the building, much less here. She unlocked the door with the key he'd included in the envelope. The large room was empty, shards of sunlight streaming through the skylight, dust motes moving in a slow minuet, a faintly acrid scent in the air.

"Saint Germain?"

Quiet as the grave, it was. Since he'd left the card for her, Fiona didn't think he'd mind if she was here, as long as she didn't disturb anything he couldn't rectify, although she had no idea what that might be. Still, life was full of chances, and she was eager to learn more about all of this. It was quite fascinating, and Fiona loved nothing more than garnering knowledge about things that piqued her interest.

When she'd first come to America, she'd found work as a lady's maid to Audrey Prescott, whose brother Joel had been the ship's doctor she'd come to know on the voyage, and she'd helped him deal with a cholera epidemic on the ship. Joel had been kind enough to help her through customs and obtain employment with his sister. Audrey had liked her on sight, and encouraged her to use the vast library in the Park Avenue house whenever she had free time, and Fiona had spent every spare moment reading every book she could find the time to do so. A vast and hungry appetite for knowledge had been kindled and today, in this odd room, it was ignited once again.

Fiona remembered the pile of books she'd seen, especially one with its pages open showing a drawing of a plant and its roots, and headed for that table on the other side of the room. She sighed with satisfaction because there it was, just as she'd last seen it. She sat down at the table on one of the room's high work stools and pulled the book towards her.

Many of the words that accompanied the drawings of the plants, including their flowers, leaves and roots, were in Latin, and occasionally what she assumed was Greek, along with some English, which was an odd mix. The details included the plant's uses, toxicities and occasionally, some growing instructions, such as "not a saturated soil", or "does best in a well-drained sandy bed" and things of that sort. They also included planting instructions, especially harvesting instructions, usually at what time phase of the moon it should be done, as in "at the dark of the moon" or "only at the peak of the full moon".

It was fascinating and Fiona found herself somewhat bereft as she turned the last page of the first herbal. She took the next book from the short stack, and looked at the bookcase shelves above to see what treasures she might've missed. There were quite a few that looked enticing, but she noticed a leather satchel nearly hidden on a small top shelf of the bookcase. It looked very old and she hesitated even as her fingers touched the worn straps, but curiosity prevailed. She flipped open the flap to disclose only a few pages of what looked to be another herbal, although they were not bound into a book. Curious as always, she pulled them out.

There weren't many, perhaps only twenty or so, and they looked to have been somewhat raggedly cut from a larger volume. Quite different from the sketches in the other volumes, the loose pages held luminous drawings of the plants, extremely detailed on each leaf and root, the paint looked as though the artist had drawn it yesterday. The script was in a language Fiona couldn't identify, some words similar to Latin, an occasional word in French or English that someone had written in, but for the most part, the words were indecipherable, at least to her. It was most peculiar, especially because some of the plants were not like any she'd seen before, either in reality or in the other books on the table, a few that she consulted to no avail.

Fiona knew full well her education was spotty at best. Anything remotely advanced or of a cultured or artistic level was not something she'd been taught at the orphanage school.

The time she'd spent in Audrey Prescott's Park Avenue library, and Julius's house in Chicago, had been her introduction to literature, history, philosophy and anything else she could glean. That she was what people termed "smart" or intelligent was a given, or she'd never have survived her younger years, but that was far from enough.

Now, she haunted bookshops in New Orleans in her off hours, buying books and reading into the wee hours many nights. Henley supported her efforts completely, one of the many reasons she adored him. The world was so vast that sometimes Fiona would fall asleep and dream of a universe spangled with places, people and wonders she'd never seen, or even read about, but knew were there, if not on this plane of existence, perhaps ones that existed elsewhere, waiting to be explored when people discovered how to do so.

Sitting at this laboratory table, staring at these unusual pages, a tremor of excitement ran down her spine. These pages were not those of your typical herbal compendium and she knew it just as assuredly as she knew every line Shakespeare had ever penned for Juliet. She opened a few of the other books and spread them out on the worktable, and began to cross-reference every plant that seemed remotely similar to the ones on the cut pages.

"Perhaps a better light would be helpful, *n'est pas?*"

Fiona nearly fell off her stool. "Christ Jesus." He was as silent as a ghost.

Saint Germain stood beside her, a smile flickering on his lips, his hands reaching out to steady her. "Apologies, Miss Shanahan. I did not mean to startle you. I am delighted you accepted my invitation to visit the laboratory. Please, continue with your work."

There was a distinct scent of sandalwood she hadn't noticed before. Fiona gave a small shaky chuckle. 'Don't have a concern, sir. I have been so absorbed in your books here I didn't notice the length of the sun. It is indeed quite dim in here."

"Not anymore." Saint Germain languidly waved his hand and she found he was quite right. The many gaslights in the room were lit, something he'd apparently accomplished while she'd been so absorbed in her studies, not even noticing the waning of the light.

"I am grateful," Fiona said. "Not simply for the ample light, but to be able to read these wonderful books."

"Of course, what I was hoping for when I gave you the key." He bent over her shoulder, the benevolent teacher. He stiffened when he noticed the cut pages she'd pulled from the leather satchel. "Where, might I ask, did you find these?"

Fiona swallowed. The steely tone of his voice made her uneasy. "They were in the leather bag on the shelf. If they are special, I was not aware. I was just cross-referencing them the last couple of hours, but oddly, I haven't found anything similar to the plants shown on those pages. I apologize if I somehow overstepped."

She ran her hand over the ribbon on the pocket of her corselette where she kept her razor, just to reassure herself. Surely any friend of Julius's was someone to be trusted, but she couldn't ignore the frisson of unease his attitude invoked.

Saint Germain stepped away and sighed. "Julius cautioned me about you. I should've listened but it has been a long time since I've had the opportunity to find someone like you, Fiona Shanahan. On this day, our journey together has taken on a different aspect than I'd envisioned. I believe I shall have to be a bit more forthcoming. Please indulge me."

He took her hand and gently led her to a set of two comfortable-looking leather chairs at the back of the laboratory. She didn't object, not simply due to her usual curiosity but from an innate sense that he wouldn't harm her. They settled in and Fiona leaned back against the down-filled cushion, a welcome respite from the laboratory stool. A small table sat between them, and from the panel below, Saint Germain pulled forth a green bottle of some white wine and two crystal glasses.

"Allow me to tell you a tale, my dear, not simply of those pages you have been busily perusing, but of their provenance. I believe you will find this story," he smiled in his charmingly oblique manner, "intriguing."

12

MANY YEARS AGO, EASTERN EUROPE

Maria de Medici tossed her embroidery into the cavernous fireplace, smiling with satisfaction as the flames consumed the fine linen underneath the colorful thread she'd pretended so assiduously to create with her needle. Gasps were heard but she ignored them and their vapid issuers as she always did. More whispering and tsking followed behind hands and fans, silk skirts rustling in outrage as though even the fabric was appalled. Maria wished them all skewered on a Turkish lance. She eyed her ancient lady-in-waiting Alana, whom she suspected of being a spy for the Countess. Alana would make a better offering than the linen but she was such a boney juiceless old shrew it would hardly be worth the trouble. Even the fire would be as bored with that as Maria was.

If only Francis would return from his latest fruitless campaign against the Hapsburgs. Maria was not well-versed in politics or warfare, but she was astute enough to know her lover, Francis Rakoczi II, the Prince of Transylvania, was obsessed with his years-long wars. She wished he'd learn chess, stay at the castle and play out his games on a board before the fire, rather than a frozen field on the steppes. Russia was supporting him now, and in tandem with Poland, had twice offered him the crown as king of Poland, but Francis had declined, wanting it all or nothing. She had made her choice with Francis twenty years ago, both of them mad with love. She had come to learn that being the mistress of a prince was far different than being his wife, especially in this godforsaken backwater. In France or Italy things would have been vastly different.

Their son, the sixteen-year-old illegitimate favorite of the prince, was the only reason she stayed, both of them awaiting the future and fortune Francis would bestow upon his darling bastard boy. His devotion had become nearly meaningless to Maria, what with Francis's constant battles and absences. For all she knew, he could be killed by a random arrow or swordstroke and they wouldn't know of it for weeks, and then be banished to some cowshed at the whim of the Countess. Meanwhile, Maria was trapped here in Hungary in his court, ruled in his absence by his cow-like Hungarian Countess, who despised Maria and her son, Claude-Louis. Only the threat of Francis's wrath should anything slightly untoward or worse befall either Maria or Claude-Louis stayed the Countess's vengeful hand.

Maria had written to her brother, Gian Gastone de Medici, the Grand Duke of Tuscany, to secure a place at his court for herself and Claude-Louis, in spite of the difficulties with the Hapsburgs and Rakoczis. No one there would have to know who Claude-Louis's father was, especially under the care of his Medici uncle. Maria could say she was the widow of a Transylvanian noble and they would be respected as members of Gian's court, privy to all the wonders and privilege of Tuscany and Italy, ancestral home to the Medicis. They could not afford to molder here under the thumb of Countess, and the very occasional visit from Francis. The landscape, the food, the weather and the company were all pallid and tasteless, none of which Maria any longer found of any interest.

In truth, she felt no desire even for the lover of her youth anymore, the lover who had put his rich wife and military ambitions ahead of Maria's well-being. She might learn to accept it if it was just her alone, but Claude-Louis's future was at stake, perhaps even his life, if the Countess considered him a threat to her dull brats, because darling Claude-Louis was anything but dull.

At sixteen, his mind was as sharp as Francis's favorite saber, and Maria knew he entertained both noble ladies and willing servant girls in his chambers nearly every night. Mother and son both needed more opportunities and entertainment than the Rakoczis could offer, stuck in this rundown and drafty castle in a backward and uncultured country. Maria had grown up in Italy, and Claude-Louis deserved to experience the educational and cultural wonders Italy could provide. All that was true and also this: Maria could not abide very many more dinners of overcooked mutton, mushy carrots, rutabagas and turnips and sour wine before she decorated the walls of the dining hall with said sorry victuals, starting with throwing them in the face of the Countess Eleni Rakoczi.

If she did not receive a response from Gian in the next few days, she would have to take matters into her own hands and assume they would be welcome. She certainly had enough jewels to pay for the journey, and just to be certain they never wanted for anything on the way, a copy of the keys to the vault and the tax monies Francis had levied to pay for his endless military forays. She and Claude-Louis were owed that and more. Francis likely wouldn't notice if some money was missing, as the only details he usually noticed were the shine on his boots, the honed edge on his sword, the softness of her skin and the perfect curves of his luxuriant mustache. Maria would be delighted to never see or hear about any of it again, particularly the overgrown mustache which had left a nasty rash on her thighs the last time he'd graced her bed.

~

CLAUDE-LOUIS GALLOPED AHEAD of the perfumed and lumbering coach, while only one footman mounted on the usual stable horse struggled to keep up with Claude-Louis's stallion. The other three guards stayed with the coach, shrugging their shoulders. The young prince always took care of himself.

The young prince, for his part, was delighted to be out in the fresh spring air, the road ahead clear and seeming to go on endlessly, much like the rest of his life, one he could now explore, finally free of Transylvania.

"Your highness, please. Have a care," the breathless footman pulled up beside Claude-Louis at last. "Your esteemed mother would have my head if anything befell you."

"I am sorry, Janos," Claude-Louis laughed. "I have been thoughtless, but I am so happy to be leaving, I cannot wait to cross borders, rivers and boundaries. I believe even you will love Tuscany and all of Italy."

"I'm sure you're right," Janos said. "Perhaps we could continue on a bit less quickly though."

"Of course. Besides, Janos, you do not have to call me a prince or your highness anymore. I am a bastard, as everyone knows, although I appreciated the sham of the title when I had to live in the same castle as my father's fat wife. Now there need be no more pretense."

"You will never be a bastard to me, your highness, and I hope you count me as a friend."

Claude-Louis grinned and held up a gloved hand, and Janos met it with his own and a smile. They were of an age, both pretty young men, sophisticated by the rustic standards they knew yet naïve in the ways of the outside world, and both needed a friend now they were venturing into unknown territory. They trotted on, with an occasional canter, chatting as the morning wore on. They were three weeks away from Transylvania's borders, and the journey had been uneventful which meant free of bandits seeking to cut their throats in the night, if not always as comfortable as his *mother Maria would've liked. They would reach Venice soon, journeying south to Tuscany and his uncle. A new world awaited and no one was more eager to enter it than Claude-Louis. He knew he would be an eager pupil, not just of lovely women, fine food and wine, but of the things he knew made up a life filled with the advantages that only sophistication and knowledge could bring. It wasn't simply the paintings, palaces and privilege that advanced a man, but the ability to appreciate the wonders that he would be exposed to.*

There are times in your life, he would reflect not much later, that are considered watershed moments, awakenings or epiphanies, but in his case the next few weeks were all of those things, wrapped into a book composed of shock, revelation, yearning, repulsion and desire. The ability to endure and learn from those reactions was called sophistication, but if not harnessed with taste, kindness, compassion and education, could descend into vulgar hedonism. Claude-Louis was fortunate to have those who supplied those traits beside him. His uncle, Gian Gastone, had most emphatically not been so lucky or discerning.

"Do not even consider attending Gian's masquerade ball this evening," Maria said to her son as they rode out of the palace walls towards the Plaza. "It will be nothing but a pageant of the dissipated wretches he surrounds himself with every second of the day." She urged her white mare into a trot and Claude-Louis followed suit on his glossy bay.

"What has become of the companion of my youth? He has transformed himself from a sweet kind boy into a libertine that indulges in every despicable habit from flatulence to gluttony to sodomy and revels in them like a pig in a sty." She sighed. "It is no wonder his wife has left him, as he will never get an heir on her, avoiding the bed of any woman like the plague. Leaving is what we must do as soon as I receive the deeds to the house in Siena, and the guaranty of income. At least he is still considerate and responsive to my needs, and for that, I am grateful, but I fear time is paramount,

as his whims and his mental condition vary wildly from week to week. Surely the King is not unaware."

While Claude-Louis loved nearly everything about Tuscany – Vivaldi's music, the paintings and sculpture, the magnificent palaces, one of which he lived in, the luxurious clothes his uncle had supplied him with, the libraries, museums and churches whose architecture made his heart soar, even the food and the chefs who made even the most humble vegetable into a meal worthy of a king, he agreed with his mother about his unfortunate uncle Gian Gastone. The man was hopeless. For Claude-Louis's part, he was waiting on an invitation to study at the Collegio Romano in Rome, renowned as the center in which to pursue his interests in science, alchemy and medicine, with a library they say rivaled even that of fabled Alexandria. He would happily pass years in that sacred and wonderful place, given the chance.

And so it came to pass that he did receive that invitation. A week later, he kissed Maria goodbye and set off for Rome, with Janos in attendance, two young men once again eager for new experiences. Rome and the Collegio Romano were everything he imagined and much more, and the years seemed to fly by while he immersed himself in his studies, particularly alchemy, but fully engaging in an active social calendar with the rest of the young nobles who studied there. Two things happened to end that idyll. One was the increasing pressure of the Hapsburgs and the Holy Roman Empire. Any connection to the Rakoczis or even the Medicis was problematic, even dangerous. He changed his name to Saint Germain but became increasingly uneasy. France could be a safer place to re-establish himself, in a country that valued the arts and the lifestyle he was used to, but one that was independent of the squabbles of the Italians and the Hapsburgs. His uncle had made sure Claude-Louis was well provided for, and his late mother had done so as well.

The other was the discovery of the book.

13

Saint Germain refilled their glasses. "So now, dear Fiona, you see it is not simply Annette I am seeking out of a fondness for reliving past memories or the hope of rekindling a romance, but rather a certain book stolen from me long ago, a much greater treasure and a much greater loss than that of jejune unrequited love. I believe she took it and has it still in her possession." He gestured towards the pages that lay on the worktable. "Those few pages are all that remain as an essential piece of my life's work and those pages are not enough."

Fiona sipped her brandy. "How did this unfortunate loss come to pass?"

Saint Germain smiled. "Ah, that is the story, is it not? Through my own foolishness, of course, a historical event or two that greatly affected my ability to travel, but most of all, my trust in someone I should have known much better than to believe. As Lysander says, 'the course of true love never did run smooth' and I was a bit of a naif in those days."

"Well, that phase definitely seems to have passed."

Saint Germain laughed out loud, the first time she'd ever

heard him do so, belying the restrained and refined gentleman he portrayed.

"Julius said you were a treasure, my dear," he said and held up his glass. "He wasn't wrong. To enlightenment."

Fiona met his glass with her own, the fine crystal chiming in agreement.

"Tell me more about the book."

"Yes, therein lies the tale," Saint Germain said. "As I said when I studied at the Collegio Romano and the Vatican library, I ran across a very special book, quite by chance, really. I was researching, with the help of my tutors and the librarians, early botanical encyclopedias and scientific treatises from ancient times up until the 1600s, and one afternoon, the clerks brought me my usual selections for the day. Buried among the heftier tomes, was a smaller raggedy leatherbound book with vellum pages. It didn't look worth pursuing, but when I opened it and saw the first pages, I knew immediately this was a book of profound importance.

"As you have seen from the few pages, the illustrations are masterful but the entire manuscript is encoded with a cypher or language I'd never seen before. Remember, at this time I'd been studying there and using my own laboratory on the Via de Longario next to my lodgings in the old Medici house for some years and had become quite adept at decoding and using botanical and alchemical recipes I'd discovered in this very library. I daresay I was one of only a few scholars on the planet that could've solved this puzzle. It was clear from notes on the margins that others had tried but failed. I did not fail." He didn't boast, but said it matter-of-factly and that alone let her know how important it was.

Fiona gazed at him over the rim of her glass. "You had the book, then, for some time. How did Annette manage to take it?"

"I left it in my chateau in the Loire valley when I was forced to return to Paris, as things were in a great state of unrest, thinking it would be safer there, under her regard. For insurance, I took those few pages you saw tonight, thinking I had the essentials of the formulas I most needed, but time was short and I was careless. I found that I was missing a few key steps and ingredients that can only be found in the book itself. So, you see, finding Annette is crucial to my continued. . . success and experimentation."

Fiona leaned forward. "Not that I have the slightest care for the Church or what they may or may not have in their vaults and rooms, but I assume that book somehow never found its way back to its dusty shelf, even as a copy? Of course, no one could read it anyway. Likely it found a much better haven with someone who could put it to good use, I believe."

Saint Germain smiled. "You are a very practical person, Miss Shanahan. We will make an excellent team."

"I quite agree, Comte. Now, you must excuse me. I am meeting Mr. Henley for an early supper and I don't want to be late. I will share our discussion with him, if you have no objection. We share most everything in our lives together."

Saint Germain stood up. "Of course, I expected you would do so. I look forward to seeing both of you in the days to come."

14

Saint Germain sat back down in his chair and poured another brandy. Although he thought about the book often, he tended to avoid thinking of Annette, his life in Italy, Prague, France and other faraway lands, and the disastrous events that had led to this very moment. It had become crucial to him now that he acquire the book at any cost. He sipped his brandy and leaned his head back on the soft damask of the chair. It had been a long while since he'd relived that painful night but talking to Fiona had brought it all back. He hoped he hadn't divulged too much information that she could use against him or decline to help him in his quest. She was a remarkably intuitive young woman.

LOIRE VALLEY, *France*

He had left it too late, but he already knew that. There was nothing for it because without the book and the reserve vials, he was doomed. He'd sent Annette a message but from the turmoil he'd seen in every village and on the roads, she may not have received any of his letters or any messages in the last year. After the queen and king had met with Monsieur Guillotine, France had become a charnel pit, mobs descending on friend and foe alike, but certainly anyone who looked to be an aristocrat, even if by so much as a lace cuff, a feathered hat or a misspoken word.

Saint Germain had been in prison himself for three months before the royal executions began, before resorting to bribery and a smuggled dirk after realizing no lawyer was ever going to plead his case to any just authority. Since the night he'd escaped, he'd lived like a cornered rat, afraid to stick his head out of the woodpile except after dark, stealing food or paying a street urchin to bring him some. After a week of that, he sneaked into his townhouse on the Rue de Dauphine, to find it ransacked, the furniture smashed, the silver and paintings gone, and excrement smeared on the walls. What he knew that the mob did not, however, were the secret hidden compartments where he'd stored money, jewels and notebooks in a leather satchel -- two in the drawing room fireplace bricks and one in a niche in the library, opened with a secret latch behind the bookcase. Securing these treasures, he traveled some miles from Paris and bought a horse from a farmer who didn't question who was purchasing his nag, since the buyer looked and smelled as downtrodden as he did, because Saint Germain was still wearing the same clothes he'd worn the day of his arrest, his only ablutions the streams he ran across on his journey. If being clean meant discovery, he was happy to stay dirty.

He traveled at night, resorting to the light of the moon and took to the woods at dawn, when the roads were a mix of refugees and those who would detain and prey upon them given the chance they sought. He saw farmhouses of size burning, and the occasional chateau, the dark streaks of soot on the white bricks of their once pristine towers, foul evidence of the destruction within. He ignored the cries for help or shrieks of despair that drifted through the trees at all times of the night and day. Much as he detested himself, that way lay doom.

When the towers of Chambord came into view, he sighed with gratitude since there were no such marks on them. Still, he approached warily, even though the countryside he'd passed through on the last day had been quiet, only the lowing of the cows or the chickens scratching over their food. He tied the horse to a tree with abundant grass below it and crept cautiously to the kitchen door, opening it cautiously and peering within.

Marcelline, his cook, stood at the table, chopping vegetables and gave a start, dropping the knife as he stepped inside. "My lord, we have been ill with worry for you. Where have you been?"

"Places you do not wish to be, my dear." He sank down on a wooden chair before the fire. "How are things here?"

She rushed over to the table with a bottle of brandy and a glass in one hand, and a hunk of freshly baked bread in the other, both of which he wasted no time in utilizing. Her plump face was full of concern but Saint Germain did not have the luxury of being comforted at the moment.

"I will fetch Bernard," Marcelline knew Saint Germain well, wiping her hands on her apron. She fairly ran out of the kitchen. Before he could finish another piece of bread, she was back, trailed closely by a large man in work clothes, a welcoming grin on his face.

"My lord," he said, and undeterred, enveloped Saint Germain in a bear hug. "We were worried."

"Yes, yes, my friend, I understand," Saint Germain said, disentangling himself while patting Bernard on his hefty shoulder. He knew his staff loved him and Chambord had never been an estate that ran on formality but equality, both unusual and likely the reason it was still standing, however he wasn't generally comfortable with physical touch.

"Sit, Bernard, and you as well, Marcelline, and bring two more glasses, and we shall share our tales."

He poured more brandy and sat back, realizing for the first time how tired he was, his hand trembling on the glass he grasped. "The

Bastille is not a nice place to spend the summer, and that is my story, now that I have escaped it and am here. Many others were not so lucky. Unfortunately, I cannot stay. I don't think they have forgotten about me. A day or two, and then to the coast and a ship. Have you been safe here? Is Madame in the East Tower?"

Bernard and Marcelline exchanged glances. Bernard finished his brandy and put the glass down. "We have been safe, although threatened by some roving mobs now and then, as well as a troop of horsemen that said they were the government and the chateau belonged to them." He shrugged. "We gave them a home, since they insisted. They are buried in the apple orchard."

"And Madame?" Saint Germain was getting a bad feeling.

"She is gone, Comte. She left five weeks ago." Bernard glanced cautiously at Saint Germain, his eyes like a puppy who knew he had transgressed. "I tried to tell her she was safe here and that you would return, but she would not listen, nor would she tell me where she was going. I am sorry I was not up to the task."

Saint Germain finished off his own brandy, and poured them all another. "Do not blame yourself, Bernard. Annette du Chambord is her own woman, a fact no one knows better than I do." He sat back in the hard chair, exhausted. "And I never in this world or any other should I have trusted her, fool that I am. Better men than I have fallen prey to beauty but that is a feeble excuse."

He waved off any more conversation on that front. He asked about the state of the vineyards, the farms and the stables, where he was breeding magnificent Arabians, to be told all was well, which was what he wanted to hear, no matter how improbable it might be in France of 1794. He instructed Bernard to have the staff leaders join him that evening. For thirty years, Saint Germain had done the improbable. He had allowed those who staffed and worked Chambord to share in its profits and rewards, even putting it on the deed, which he doubted any French noble or any other European one he knew of, had ever done. He alone knew how effective it was.

His wines, horses, and farms were the most productive in France and those who shared in their success would defend it, as would their descendants. No matter if the country was run by aristocrats, merchants, a monarchy or a republic, Chambord was safe from their political depredations and supported by those who lived there, and would defend their cherished and hard-worked-for independence. He had faith that France would stabilize itself even if that would take years. Major changes always did.

"Now, I must go to the East Tower laboratory, my friends," Saint Germain said, standing up. "I can only hope she didn't destroy anything." He was a bit dizzy but he knew he'd be fine once he began moving.

Bernard took his arm anyway, ever vigilant. "I cannot say, my lord. Only you and she have the keys and the door has been locked since she left."

"Thank you, my friend," Saint Germain said. He made his way alone up the long staircases to the East Tower. At the top, its sturdy oak door barred his entry, until he took the keys he'd retrieved from his desk downstairs and inserted the large iron one in the lock. It opened silently, the hinges well-oiled, and he entered his sanctum.

Morning sun streamed through the stained-glass windows, dust motes floating in the golden light, to reveal a spacious stone-floored room that had been transformed into a working laboratory, with even a sink fed from the cistern on the roof that he'd installed to have fresh water when he needed it. Long wooden tables were filled with glass beakers, racks of vials and pipettes, while another held an elaborate orrery, a display of large solar charts hung from the high ceiling and telescopes, pointed at the glass ceiling above it all. Yet another worktable held charcoal burners, another assortment of glass vials in wooden carrying crates, a huge armoire full of hundreds of small drawers, each labeled with a different herb or substance, and a large assortment of marble mortars and pestles, a shining rack of knives beside them with copper pots of all sizes hung above. A bookshelf rising from the floor to the dizzying high ceiling was crammed with books of all sizes, shapes and bindings, a spiral moveable iron staircase immobile in its middle.

He breathed a sigh of relief. She had left it untouched. All seemed normal, but he was not convinced. Not yet.

He made his way to the spiral staircase, positioning it somewhat more to the left, climbing up to the sixth shelf and chose a book from the shelf, its green leather binding reading "Ars Semantica". As he pulled it towards him, there was a faint whirring sound and the remaining books on the shelf slid inside, revealing a small metal-lined cavity. It was empty. There was no book, no small wooden crate of glass vials, nothing, not anymore. Saint Germain felt every ounce of breath leave his lungs. How could she do this to him?

At that moment, he vowed to find her, no matter how long it took, to whatever place on earth she had chosen to hide herself in. It didn't matter, because he had no choice. The world became grey, then black. He remembered hearing Bernard's voice and felt his strong arms support him but then nothing. He did remember smiling, incongruously enough, grateful for the people he'd nurtured and who now returned that care to him, the man who never thought he'd need it but grateful beyond measure that he did.

∼

WHEN HE NEXT OPENED HIS eyes, it was twilight, and Marcelline herself was setting a tray of silver-covered dishes on the table beside his bed. He was ravenous and the aroma of the chicken in wine sauce with pears nearly made him faint with anticipation. She set about propping him up with pillows but he shook his head.

"At the table. I am no invalid, just a half-starved and weary man," Saint Germain said, "and one badly in need of a bath."

Marcelline gestured towards the hearth, where water steamed in a large copper bathing tub. "First food, Comte."

"You are too kind, always anticipating my needs."

Marcelline snorted. "There has been no mystery about any of your needs today, my lord."

He smiled and shooed her away, wanting no witness to his repast and ablutions. He was too hungry to worry about fine manners. Within an hour, he had demolished all the food on the tray, was bathed, groomed and attired for the first time in months in clean well-tailored clothing from his own wardrobe. He smiled as he entered the front drawing room, where those he'd appointed as managers on the estate greeted him warmly.

Marcelline was there, with three of her housekeepers, as was Bernard of course. Francois the stablemaster, sleek and polished as were the Arabians he supervised, stood nearby. Gaspard the head vigneron, his hefty belly and grin as happy as the delectable grapes he cultivated with Andre, the chief winemaker, were present, and of course Denis, the head gardener, whose celebrated vegetable fields supplied half the markets and restaurants in the Loire, was seated near the fireplace. Fifty other people, give or take, lived and worked at Chambord, but it was these few Saint Germain depended upon. Bottles of Chambord wine and glasses gleamed on the sideboard, and when Saint Germain had poured his own glass of Chambord's Melon de Borgogne 1780, everyone followed suit, pouring either the new Melon, the renowned Pinot Noir or the famous Cabernet Franc, which had, sadly, been the favorite of Marie Antoinette. The three varietals were renowned throughout Europe, and even during France's turmoil, were being produced and shipped around the world, even now to America.

"Mes amis." Saint Germain held up his glass, the golden Melon yet untasted. "It has been, and will continue to be for some time, sad times for France. We must have faith, safeguard Chambord and our loved ones, and remain vigilant in our care for this place and each other. It will return our care tenfold. To Chambord."

"To Chambord!" echoed throughout the room and everyone drank.

"Nothing will change about our arrangements here at Chambord, and I will next meet with the six of you who are my mainstays. As I'm sure you are aware, I have been a reluctant guest of the flea-ridden hosts of the Bastille and must soon depart to ensure you and everyone at Chambord are not put in danger because of me. How long I will be gone is impossible to say, but I know it will likely be years, and not months, before the Terror subsides and some sort of normalcy and sense allows the citizens in Paris to establish a steady government. I am not only in danger myself, but being arrested again will be difficult for you so we must wait.

"Until then, Chambord is yours, as it really always has been, according to the agreements we have made years ago. It might be best to keep the authorities unaware of how we do things here. For all their talk of equality, so far I have seen little to support anything but their own greed and revenge."

Murmurs of agreement followed this remark, for which he was grateful but not surprised. If there was a traitor in this group, there was little he could do about that now. Bernard came around with a bottle of Melon and refilled Saint Germain's glass, along with others, for which Saint Germain was even more grateful, finding his throat dry with the unaccustomed talking. It could have been apprehension as well, but he was determined to ignore that.

"Where will you go?" Bernard said.

Saint Germain shrugged. "I had thought London, but I hear there are French agents capturing aristocrats for a bounty and returning them to the hungry arms of La Guillotine and I have no powerful friends there as yet. I think Rome will be my first stop, on a fast ship rather than a slow carriage overland. Le Havre?"

"Non, non, Comte," Andre said. "Le Havre is not safe. More government troops are scouring the docks for aristo refugees than sailors to man ships. That is a death trap."

"What do you suggest?"

Denis smiled. "I take wagons of courgettes, potatoes, cucumbers and tomatoes to San Malo every week, my lord. There is no one there anymore but the people, restaurants and fishermen who like fresh food for their week at sea. You will be my assistant. I know a captain who travels much further than France. He is waiting tomorrow for my produce and other shipments although those suppliers, of course, I know nothing about."

Saint Germain nodded. "I will be at the stables at dawn, Denis. I fear there is no time to waste and even now I keep thinking I hear horses arriving."

Bernard jumped up and peered out the tall windows. "There is no one."

"Of course not, it is just my imagination and a bad case of nerves," Saint Germain said. "Still, let's finish our business. Au revoir to everyone except you five," he gestured at his chiefs. "I cannot say when I will see you again, but believe me, I will. For now, I will keep in touch and all is in place with the lawyers to assure our operations run smoothly and the contracts are secure."

The six of them talked for another hour and Saint Germain found himself unaccountably weary, having difficulty keeping his eyes open. It wasn't surprising, given the turmoil of his journey and the last few weeks. He wished everyone good night and arranged to meet with Denis in the morning, although it was nowhere near dawn when a firm hand shook his shoulder.

"My lord, there are armed men in the courtyard. I have your bags and some food from Marcelline. Denis is waiting below at the secret staircase with the produce wagon. We will make such a racket confronting them they will not hear you leave." He was right. Saint Germain could see the burning torches and heard the pounding on the doors.

Could there be no peace? Saint Germain raced down the staircase. Before they reached the outer door, they heard shouts and shots. Only when he was quit of France would there be peace for him, it would seem. What a coward he felt like, running and hiding like this from his beloved adopted country, the friend of kings, but he knew it was best. If they discovered him here, they would not only kill him but punish everyone at Chambord. He scrambled *aboard the wagon, watching Bernard bury his precious bags deep under the mounds of cucumbers as Denis silently urged the horses away into the night. France and Chambord must be left to their own fates, while his future lay in the city of Prague and the estate of the Rakoczis, his past and future sanctuary.*

15

Henley took her arm as they strolled through Jackson Square, reveling in the quiet. The white façade of St. Louis Cathedral glowed in the moonlight and a light breeze stirred the trees, the air carrying the scent of spicy Creole gumbo, a dish they'd just enjoyed at a small restaurant on St. Charles. She'd told him most everything Saint Germain had said earlier over supper and Henley hadn't had much to say. It was quite an extraordinary tale, to be sure.

He stopped and gently turned her around to face him. "Fiona, listen." Even in the dim moonlight, she could see the frown on his face and sense the anxiety in his rigid stance. "I don't like this case. I don't like anything about it, especially the Comte Saint Germain and I haven't from the first second I saw him. I understand that he's Julius's friend and because of that I've tried to keep an open mind, but I will tell you I've known Julius a long time and he has had many a peculiar friend or two, but no one quite like this."

Fiona took his hand and led him to a seat on an iron filigreed bench. "I know. I am uneasy as well, my love. Every once in a while when I'm with him, it's as though the mask slips just a touch and he seems like someone far more ruthless but then in a blink of an eye, he's all charm. I keep thinking it's just a fancy of mine but now that you have noticed it as well, I realize it's not. Even at that, I like him, find him quite fascinating because there's something infinitely sad about our mysterious Comte."

Henley lit one of the thin little cigarillos he favored and leaned back. "What to do, eh?"

"Indeed. I think we're in a bit of a pickle here. Julius is depending on our help with finding this woman, or this book, or who knows what. He'll be furious or at least extremely unhappy if we say no, and frankly, we'll sound like scared little children. 'Oooh, he's weird and he scares us' is downright silly."

Henley snorted. "Understatement, Irish. We're hardly innocent lambs in the meadow. We've been known to specialize in burial shrouds ourselves now and then so when it comes to sinister we're in proper company."

Fiona gently took the cigarillo from his fingers and took a puff, the smoke curling in the light of the moon. A minute passed. She took another puff and stood up.

"Well then, we've reached a consensus, I believe. Number one, Saint Germain is strange and we are not certain about him. Number two, Julius has asked emphatically that we help with this problem and things could become difficult at best if we don't. Which brings us to number three: we find Annette and/or the book as quickly as possible and wash our hands of the whole affair."

"Excellent deductions. And once it's done, we go visit Heart's Ease and never think about it again," Henley said, taking her hand. "Glad we had this chat, Irish. We have a busy day ahead of us. Now it's time for bed."

"I am a bit sleepy," Fiona said. Henley's hand was warm and comforting.

"Sleep's not exactly what I had in mind."

"Ah. What a surprise."

"I've found you're hard to surprise but I'm working on it."

"Intriguing. Walk a bit faster."

"Psst. Miss."

She'd been hearing him for some time, like the persistent buzzing of a mosquito in her ear. Until now, she'd been quite good at ignoring him.

"What, Nico?"

"Marie is back. She knows you wish to see her."

Well. That was good news. "*Merci*, my little friend. Tell Raphael I said to give you breakfast."

Soft laughter. "He will not believe me. No worries, I will steal it. Raphael needs to move faster."

She opened one eye. It was still far from sunlight and Henley snored softly beside her. Marie could wait. She slept again.

Two hours later, Fiona and Henley entered the garden and took the path towards Bourbon Street. The morning air was fresh and clear while dew still glistened on the trees. They rounded the corner into one of the sitting areas to find Julius and Saint Germain having coffee and beignets.

"Ah, good morning, gentlemen," Fiona said, recovering first. "Hope you're enjoying your breakfast. I see you're up early too."

Both gentlemen rose as was polite and Fiona motioned them back to their seats as was also a courtesy.

"Where are you off to?" Julius said. "Hot on the trail of a clue in our elusive search?"

"Exactly," Henley said. "Not a moment to waste with such an engrossing case, I'm sure the Comte would agree?"

"Indeed, Mr. Henley," Saint Germain said, sipping his coffee. "I'm gratified to see my team of investigators working so diligently." He glanced at Fiona. "You look fetching this morning, Miss Shanahan. Lovely hat."

"So kind," Fiona said. "I do try to dress for the occasion. We must be off."

They didn't speak another word until they turned east onto Bourbon Street and both blew out a breath of relief,

"Christ Jesus, that was awkward," Fiona said. "I was waiting for one of them to ask us where we were going after which I'd have to make up a lie. I have a feeling Marie would not want to be known as being entangled in this endeavor."

Henley took her arm and they walked more briskly down Bourbon. "I agree. Convincing her to help even you and me may not be easy. Best to leave them out of it."

Evangeline looked up and smiled as they entered the voodoo shop, the little brass bell tinkling on the door. "*Bon jour.*" Today the shop smelled of cloves and lemongrass, the two scents sharp and at odds with other, but somehow blending into an enticing mix. Fiona always looked forward to coming here.

"And to you, Evangeline. You look lovely this morning. Is Madame receiving?" Henley said.

"Only you two," she said, and led them to the staircase in the back. "Just knock on the study door, she knows you are coming."

The door was ajar but Fiona knocked softly on the frame as they pushed it further open. Marie looked up from her writing and motioned them to the chairs in front of her desk. The drapes were closed and the room was dim, the lamp on the desk the only illumination.

"Sit, my friends." She finished writing in the journal in front of her and closed the cover. "You two have been busy little birds lately, have you not?"

"We are always busy little birds, madame. It is in our nature," Fiona said.

Marie Laveau smoothed a few errant hairs from her temples and secured them under her tignon, today a bright silk turquoise. "Perhaps I should have said, nosy little ferrets this time."

She sounded displeased and Henley nudged Fiona's toe, clearing his throat. "Have we overstepped somehow, Madame?" He disliked coming here.

She sighed. "You wouldn't have known, of course. You've been asking all around about botany, herbs, gardens, potions, that sort of thing, and there are those who wonder why. Is that not so?"

"Yes," Fiona said. "We would've come to you first, of course. In fact, we did but you were not here, so we asked others in the meantime. It has been a fruitless enterprise, but we never presumed one that would cause any harm."

Puzzled, Fiona glanced at Henley, who was now on high alert, like the guardian wolf he sometimes resembled.

"To be truthful, I am at a loss," Henley said. "Please tell us exactly what you are concerned about."

Marie put her hands firmly on the desk and stood up. She began pacing back and forth across the room. "I walk a fine line here, between those who would see me arrested, and those who wish me to be branded a witch and burned in Jackson Square in front of the cathedral, and those who value my continued health. It is only my connections with those I have aided, or provided entertainment and services for, that keep these forces balanced and at bay, and allow me to practice my own religion and live the way I wish. New Orleans is a city that follows its own rules and those rules are fragile, especially when the rest of the South finds itself falling into the old hateful patterns of the past."

Fiona and Henley knew that only too well, and fighting against those prejudices was one of the reasons they were in

New Orleans, working for Julius, who championed those who had suffered under them.

"The problem," Marie said, stopping her pacing and staring at them, "is that your search is focusing on areas of interest to me. I have a small plantation out on the River Road where I dabble in botany myself, and herbs in what would be called a poison garden, for the ignorant, or if you wish to be dramatic. It is useful farm for all the botanicals and herbs I sell in the shop. I also grow an herb out there for voodoo practice, but it is one associated with the old Haitian zombie cult, which is nonsense, of course, but one that frightens the gullible. The world is full of gullible and those eager to impugn those who are different. You are both very aware of that."

"We are so sorry," Fiona said and she meant it. To do anything to alienate their dearest ally in the city was the worst action imaginable, and one they would never undertake. As far as she was concerned, Saint Germain and Julius would have to find someone else for this task before any more damage was done. "We did not know this, and would have been more discreet had we known. What can we do to alleviate this? Henley and I consider you a treasured friend and would never knowingly do anything that could hurt you."

Marie gazed appraisingly at both of them for a long minute. "I believe you."

She sighed again, heavily this time. "However, there is more and I feel it is connected somehow. All of this chitchat has created a ripple, *n'est pas?* I don't like ripples, for various reasons, but this time the ripple may have brought other predators to the surface, from what I am hearing. There are noxious rumors of vile practices upriver, undertaken by those that are perhaps interested in your efforts, and who are definitely not friends of mine. I doubt they are anyone's friends. The second ripple is closer to home and I do not see the connection yet, but it will become clear why the Cassini Brotherhood is rumored to be in New Orleans once I connect the two."

Clearly frustrated, Henley stood up and began pacing himself, while Fiona sat quietly as a mouse on her cushion. "I have never heard of these people. Who in bloody hell is the Cassini Brotherhood?"

Marie stared at him and shook her head. "So you do not know of them?"

Fiona hardly dared breathe. It was a good thing that Henley looked like a charmingly bewildered boy, running his hands through his hair and even more so that Marie had always liked him.

"Oh my dears, you must be more careful."

"I always endeavor for carefulness, Madame, but I can hardly do so when I do not know the parameters of the game," Henley said.

Marie gave a snort or what came close to one for a woman so elegant. She sat back down heavily on her chair. "Sit down, knight errant. If you did not know what fire you are playing with, it is time you did."

"I do not see how any inquiries we have made could have interested the Cassinis," Fiona said, her voice low but steely. "There is nothing here for them."

"Oh, then. So you know of them?"

Fiona sighed. "Long ago, at St. Hilda's orphanage when I was a child, there were ghost stories and fairy tales the older children would tell of the Cassini Brotherhood. They came from the Vatican itself, like the guard dogs of Rome, sent to sniff out heretics. If you were not sufficiently penitent, or if your sins were too dark, they would come to take you away, the Cassinis. They wore the long black robes similar to the Jesuits, but they were not there to absolve you."

Fiona felt as though fear was squeezing her throat shut as it had when she was seven years old and first heard these stories.

All of the younger children had nightmares for weeks. "If they came for you, that meant you were beyond redemption, so the stories went. You were an affront to God himself and you would be purged from this world and the one that came after, even purgatory. No one could stop them, not priests, nuns or the Archbishop himself. The Cassinis would take you away and burn the evil from you." Her voice broke and she shivered in spite of herself.

"Holy Christ, Fiona," Henley said, taking her hand. "The church lets children listen to this rot?"

Fiona looked at him and shivered. This talk had triggered memories she thought she'd forgotten many years ago. It wasn't pleasant to have them back. Although she no longer believed in any teachings of the Catholic church, thoughts like this threw her back into those terrible times before she'd left Ireland.

"I haven't thought about them in years," Fiona said. "I never thought they were real anyway. I dismissed those fears along with everything else I left in Ireland."

"Ah, but they are real," Marie said. "They have been here before, in my mother's time. She banished them, or at least she thought she had. Now, I hear rumors they are back again, possibly drawn by talk of this elusive Frenchwoman you are seeking. One was seen in Jackson Square two nights past, according to my sources."

Fiona's heart sank. They had mentioned Annette Chambord's name at the beginning of their quest. How foolish they had been. Then again, how could they have known?

"This is ridiculous. Why would they have any interest in her?" Henley said. "We were given her name in our search for a local botanist by an old friend of hers who wishes to reacquaint himself after many years, as he said they had lost touch. Surely there is nothing sinister in that?"

Marie stared at them, her gaze direct and piteous. "Because, my little lambs, according to some historical records, Annette

Chambord, if she truly existed at all, was the botanist poisoner who dispatched many French revolutionaries some one hundred and ten years ago. Perhaps you are looking for her great-granddaughter? Or someone with a peculiar sense of humor?"

Fiona felt a shiver snake down her spine and she squeezed Henley's hand so hard he winced, although Marie didn't seem to notice.

"How odd," Fiona managed. "Perhaps we misunderstood the name."

Marie smiled coldly. "You may have misunderstood more than a name, Fiona Shanahan. There has been a strange presence in this city since the dawn of the new year. You would do well to either expand your investigation quickly or drop it altogether."

Henley put on a dazzling smile and dropped her hand. "Marie, I assure you we will do our best to remedy this entire situation, which seems to have arisen from our own ignorance and clearly what has been an historical error from a source we thought credible. Your candor has been invaluable in helping us and please know that we would never intentionally bring any trouble to your doorstep."

"Once again, my dears, I believe you, although you are trying my patience. You may let yourselves out. *Au revoir.*"

16

"You want to have lunch somewhere?" Henley said, trying to keep up with Fiona who was practically running down Bourbon Street.

"Hell no." Fiona flung the words over her shoulder and sped up. "How can you be interested in food? We need to go home where it's safe and figure this out."

He increased his stride and grabbed her elbow. "Irish, we'll be fine. I've never seen you like this. Calm down."

She stopped, looking around at the street where a lone carriage passed by, the horse's hooves flinging mud in his wake. No one else was nearby. "This is bad, Henley. You don't know."

"Well, maybe I don't, but running like crazed rabbits down Bourbon Street isn't going to enlighten me much. Take a breath, love."

Fiona did so. Then she took a few more, standing very still for the first time since they'd left Marie Laveau's.

"She's not wrong, you know."

"About what?" Henley said, taking her hand.

"The Cassinis."

He snorted. "You said it yourself, Irish. They're a fairy tale to frighten children. Even if there's a shred of truth in that myth, there's no reason for them to be in New Orleans of all places. Don't these people live in the Vatican basement or something, likely in spider-webbed tombs and only come out at night? We could probably smell them coming from blocks away."

"It's not funny, Henley."

Clearly exasperated, he pulled her into Oscar Byrne's oyster bar, where the bartender had just opened the floor-length shutters. "Food, perhaps later. Brandy, my dear, right damn now."

They were the only patrons at this late morning hour. Ensconced in a booth near the back of the place, Fiona downed the first snifter before saying another word, and at Henley's signal, another swiftly appeared before her. She wasn't sure why she'd panicked, something she couldn't remember doing before in her entire life. There had certainly been instances and situations where she could or should have, but she'd never felt anything like this before that she could recall. The only thing she could think of was sitting in Marie's somewhat macabre dimly-lit chamber when the woman said the words "Cassini Brotherhood" and the childhood fears had flooded in like a tidal wave. It was silly, really, completely out of character for the dangerous and capable woman she had since become.

Silence reigned in the dim bar, only the sounds of the bartender attending to his opening tasks, the pleasant scent of fresh-cut lemons and limes wafting through the air.

Fiona took a sip of the fresh brandy. "Can't say quite what came over me, love, but we do have a situation here. You can't be denying that now."

"That is certainly true," Henley said. "We've managed to upset Marie, and that is not something we can afford to do if we have any future in this city in this business. It also seems we have some information from Julius and the Comte that isn't quite accurate, for one reason or another." He chuckled dryly. "Calling them out is another something we can't afford to do if we have any future in this city in this business, since Julius is our patron." He drank some of his brandy. "What was that poison garden business about, you think?"

Fiona waved her hand. "Oh that, 'tis nothing to speak of. Isn't quite as innocent as she made it out, though. She uses datura in some of her rituals, I've no doubt about that. She as much as told me that a year ago. It's some temporary paralyzing herb. It isn't really dangerous if used correctly and she knows what she's doing. I had no idea she had a place out the River Road but it makes sense, now that I'm thinking on it."

Henley gulped the rest of his brandy and stared at her, eyes wide. "What the hell are you talking about, Fiona? Why did you not tell me this before?"

"Jesus, man, calm down. People are different, I'm thinking. It's a voodoo thing these people do, and no business of mine. It was just a conversation between women we had and no need for it to go further. As far as I know, it's just a temporary thing, but as I said, no business of mine."

Henley started on his second brandy. "Sometimes I forget who I'm dealing with when it comes to you, Fiona, God love me for the fool I am."

She stroked his hand. "Henley, you are no fool and you know it so. We've had a bit of a shock, but let's not get dramatic. I know that game better than you."

She finished off her brandy and grinned. "I'm feeling very much better."

He glared at her, as much as Henley could ever glare at her. "The appearance of an elfin Irish princess, with the mind of Attila the Hun. My fate was sealed from the minute I met you."

Fiona rolled her eyes. "Spare me, MacBeth. Come, we have work to do."

Henley held her arm as they left Byrne's, as neither of them was as steady as they could be. Fiona hoped Raphael had extra beignets still, as her stomach was rumbling. Traffic had picked up as they headed down Bourbon to their block. Horses, carriages and delivery wagons vied for space on the muddy street, and now the boardwalks were filled with people shopping or on their way to do business or one sort or another. Just before they reached the entryway to their garden, Fiona felt uneasy. She turned and glanced behind her. A tall figure in a black cassock and a biretta hat stood a block away in front of an art gallery, but his eyes were not on the display in the glass window, but fixed on her.

She jerked on Henley's arm. "Do you see him?"

Henley turned and just as he did, the figure abruptly disappeared, likely into an alley.

"Stay here, Fiona," Henley said, and ran back down the street. There was no alley, no doorway and no one in a black cassock on the street anywhere behind them, in this block or the second one behind.

Fiona hadn't moved since Henley had sprinted off and was still standing in the same spot when he returned four minutes later, panting slightly. "Didn't find him, did you?"

"No."

She nodded and opened the gate to their block. "Cassinis. Tricky bastards, so the fairy tales go."

"We're talking to Julius," Henley said, "I've had enough of this mysterious nonsense for no apparent reason. There's more to this and we need some answers."

"You look agitated," Julius DeMonte said. "Can I assist?" He ushered them into his private drawing room on the second floor, the balcony shutters closed on the bustle of humanity below on Bourbon. He was alone, the sisters off shopping, no doubt. The troupe couldn't wait to get to New Orleans in the fall to indulge themselves with all its treasures and entertainments. Clothing, hats, perfumes, absinthe, music, shows. The city was a cornucopia of delights, especially when you'd been sequestered on a showboat coming down the Mississippi for six months, only stopping at little towns.

"I hope so," Fiona said, eyeing the pralines among the pastries on the tea tray Raphael had deposited on the low table between them. "We have questions. Things are becoming a mite complicated on this Chambord woman and her botanical farm or shop or what have you, search." She sighed and gave into her appetite, biting into a praline and feeling the sugar melt in her mouth.

Julius sipped his tea and raised one aristocratic eyebrow. "Oh dear."

"You don't seem surprised," Henley said.

Julius brushed his long silver-blonde hair back onto his shoulders and put his cup down. "I was hoping this would be a fairly routine matter, finding Annette. I should've known better because it's been such a long time since she's taken to ground, so to speak, so she's been more capable than we would've thought."

"We?"

"Claude-Louis and I, although to be truthful, I've never met the woman myself."

Fiona glanced at Henley. "We heard that in fact, we are likely searching for her granddaughter or some close relative, since there was an Annette Chambord active in France during the Revolution."

Julius flung one arm casually over the back of the settee. "How odd. I guess the Chambords are one of those families that likes to use the same names generation after generation. I know it's true of mine."

That was true, Fiona knew. Julius's father was the Duke of Sandford, another Julius, who had banished his wayward younger son to the Americas years ago to pursue his theatrical bent without harming the family reputation any further than he already had.

Henley looked dubious. "I suppose we'll have to assume that's true. Should we speak with the Comte? He might provide us with more information."

"I don't think that's necessary," Julius said. Even as good an actor as Julius was, Fiona suspected he was lying. "He's as much in the dark as we three are. All he knows is she is said to be in Louisiana, in or near New Orleans. I apologize I can't provide you two with any more information than that. I will mention your difficulties, of course, even though he is very busy. Perhaps he might have some advice."

"Not to worry," Henley said. "We'll find her."

"Excellent." Julius stood up. Clearly this chat was over. "I am hoping you'll join me for dinner in the next night or two. You are my two favorite people in the world and we haven't spent as much time together as I'd like so far this season. We shall have to remedy that."

Fiona took Julius's hand as she rose from her chair and smoothed her skirts. "Just one more thing. Why would the Cassinis be interested in any of this?"

"What did you say?" Julius's voice modulated from silken to steely. "The Cassini Brotherhood? That's an old myth to frighten unruly children. They aren't real."

"One of those myths followed us down Bourbon Street this afternoon," Fiona said. She was growing weary of lies. "He looked goddamned real to me."

You had to give him credit, Fiona thought. Julius threw back his head and laughed his best mad Hamlet. "You two have to stop drinking absinthe at lunch. You're off with the fairies, Fiona. All will be well."

"It will be well, because we'll make it so," Henley said with a grim smile. "There is nothing amusing about this. I saw him too, Julius. He was no fairy tale." He took Fiona's hand firmly in his. "We'll talk further soon."

Fiona glanced back before the door closed. Julius sat on the settee staring at his clasped hands between his knees as though he was searching for answers to all the mysteries of the world to no avail, his hair shadowing his face. It hurt her heart to see him so, this incredible man they all loved. They had to find answers.

17

REGENCY ENGLAND

Julius Cargill inspected himself in the full-length mirror, turning to and fro to ensure there were no unwanted creases or the slightest sag in his bespoke suit, from waistcoat to the slim trousers. Black leather boots reached his knees, adorned with front tassels that twitched coquettishly with each step. He smiled at himself with satisfaction. Yes, darling, you are gorgeous.

"Nigel," he called. "Come help me with this damnable cravat. My fingers are not cooperating this evening. I want a Corinthian knot and you're so good with those."

His valet appeared at once, carrying a cloth and an opened bottle of champagne. Julius had inherited Nigel's services from his father when the Duke decided to spend most of his time at Sandhurst, viewing the debauched society of London with disdain, detesting his youngest son's behavior in particular, but sending Nigel to shepherd him because he knew Nigel would be needed. Julius was well aware of Nigel's place in his father's scheme, but he trusted him implicitly anyway.

"Ah, you remembered the champagne for boot polish. Brummell says it brings a particularly lovely sheen to black leather."

"So I hear," Nigel said. "Beau Brummell has a great many ideas."

Julius glanced quickly at Nigel's face but couldn't detect any lip-twitching or eye-rolling, things Nigel had learned to hide when dealing with subjects he found nonsensical. The Duke wasn't the only person with a goodly portion of disdain, Julius had found. Still, Nigel was loyal, kind, and one of the only people in this world Julius trusted fully. Occasionally, Nigel's observations were remarkably on target, and his care for Julius's overindulgences were legendary. At White's and Boodles clubs, they knew to send for Nigel when Julius's behaviors became more than they could deal with, no matter the hour of the night. The young aristocrats, heedless of society's rules, overindulged themselves. Their lusty appetites for gaming, food, alcohol and women often placed them on paths no sane person should travel. There were no guides, but if they were lucky, there were the Nigels of the world to lead them out of those dangerous woods.

Impeccable fashion was the kindest of those indulgences, mostly thanks to one Beau Brummell, more or less a nobody who had a fantastical aptitude for style and the clothing at its foundation. He had first ingratiated himself into the Prince Regent's circle, and before anyone could blink an eye, was its unofficial fashion ruler. Designing clothing that complemented the male body rather than that which frequently made the wearer look like a circus performer was Brummell's skill. Silks, satins, laces and pastel colors, short pants, stockings and buckled shoes became laughable, replaced with sleek suits, tight trousers, boots and impeccably tied cravats with a myriad of styles and knots, the very thing Julius now needed Nigel's help in tying. The yards-long tie of starched linen was slippery in his fingers tonight.

Five minutes later, Nigel tied the last tie and stepped back. Julius looked in the mirror and smiled. "Nigel, you've outdone yourself once again. Let's get to the boot champagne and I must be off. Prinny's coming to Brooks's tonight with some Frenchman he's pimping about, loves his music or some such. One must ooh and aah with the best of them to keep those invitations flowing, don't you know? Otherwise I'll end up back at Sandhurst for the summer, swiving goose girls for entertainment. Not there aren't some pretty ones, but I'd rather bed a woman that smells of perfume than bird shit."

Midnight found Julius at Brooks's, fairly drunk and still waiting, as were his companions, for the arrival of the Prince. Prinny was notorious for tardiness and occasionally never showing at all and Julius was growing impatient, despite the brandy.

"Chef just sent a messenger. Delilah and the other two girls are in place. Dessert is served, my man," the Marquess of Denbrook, Julius's best friend, whispered in his ear. These two were renowned for their antics, even among the fastest set. Twice before, they'd come up with the now-famous Dessert idea and it had become a favorite. Half a dozen young men were signaled and followed the guide down a quiet well-carpeted hallway to a large set of double doors. The guide flung the doors open to a cornucopia of delight, discreetly shutting them as he left.

Three beautiful and naked young women lay spread out on three tables, their bodies covered in mounds of whipped cream. Artistically positioned pastries, tarts, and cleverly decorated tea cakes were invitingly placed in strategic areas of their bodies from the neck down. Delectable slices of peaches, pears, apples, and strawberries were arranged to complement the entire tableau from their lovely faces to the tips of their toes.

Delilah, Julius's favorite courtesan, smiled at him from where she lay on the center table. "Are you not eager for something sweet, milord?"

Before he could move a foot or open his mouth, the doors behind him opened. "Faith, Cargill. Could you not wait for your Prince? Dessert is my favorite."

Beside Prinny's large presence stood a slender man, his black suit stylish, dark hair reaching his shoulders, unrestrained. His eyes landed on Julius and he gave a faint smile. "In truth, it is mine as well. I see we have arrived just in time. Music shall wait for another venue that I fear will not be as delectable as this one."

~

JULIUS AWOKE, staring at the familiar plaster cherubs on the ceiling of his bedroom and tried to sit up. He could not, his arms pinned to the silken softness of the bed beneath him. He felt an instant of panic, turning to his right, to find Delilah's golden head of curls resting on his arm, breathing softly. Ah, yes. Memory surfaced as erratically as a morning tide and he turned his head to the left. The Comte de Saint Germain rested on his other arm, his breath sweet as the whipped cream they'd indulged in the night before, his bare torso sticky with the stuff. Julius lay back, surrendering to slumber filled with the delights of the evening before, his thoughts swirling. Nigel had done his work well, rescuing not just him but his companions from what he considered Dionysus's rites. Julius thought a moment before sleep overcame him. He'd have to work on that. Bacchanal at Sandhurst was a stupendous idea, if only he could persuade his father to absent himself for a week. The goose girls would be an additional asset.

When next he woke, afternoon light filtered through the silk curtains and the bed was empty but for himself, Nigel rousing him to sit at the table before the fire and a silver tray filled with a pot of chocolate and cinnamon buns glistening with sugar.

"When you're ready, the bath has been prepared," Nigel said, with only a faint wrinkling of his nose. Julius ignored him and poured a cup of chocolate, the rage these days. He quite adored it. A heavy cream-colored envelope sat beside the tray and Julius broke the seal and opened it.

"Thank you for a delightful evening. Please know you are welcome at any time. Six-eleven High Street. SG."

For the next months, Julius indulged himself in every amusement he could find, and through Saint Germain, found many new ones, even some cultivated through the ages that engaged his senses and his body in ways he could've never imagined. Pleasure and inconsequence ruled in methods he had only dreamt of. They were both devotees of the theater as well, seeing plays constantly, and knowing every line before the actors ever spoke them, from Shakespeare to Dante, often hosting half the cast after the curtains had closed. There were no limits. Saint Germain's music was incredible, played at many venues – the theaters, concerts, royal performances and even taverns where it was acclaimed by aristocrats and the hoi polloi alike.

Julius had found the companion of his dreams in Saint Germain. Every once in a great while, usually spurred upon Nigel's clear disdain, he questioned his adventures but it only took a sip of absinthe or an enticing caress to put those nagging thoughts at bay.

His father had been sending missives that Nigel insisted on bringing to him, and Julius threw them all into the fire without breaking the Sandhurst seal. Life was short and he had no time for unnecessary repentance, the folly of the gullible.

Winter arrived with the London season, with no letup in its round of balls, galas, parties and fresh debutantes to defile, a challenge to all the young aristocratic rogues who filled the ranks of the most invited gentlemen, the chaperones and hopeful mamas ignorant of their true natures. The girls were hoping for husbands, but predators abounded in the list of eligible bachelors.

"An exhausting business, most of these young ladies," Saint Germain said, sipping his wine, a delectable Bordeaux. They sat in front of the fire redolent with the scent of applewood in the Sandhurst townhouse, relaxing after an evening at the theater, one that hadn't provided further entertainment aside from a well-done MacBeth. "Occasionally you find one that's been messing about with their grooms in some hay-filled barn and knows the way of it, but more often than not, it's some prissy little snit that regrets her choice in mid-action and you end with sniffles if you're lucky, rather than a screech. Such a bore. Christ spare me."

Julius nodded. "Couldn't agree more. We need to be more careful. I find it's in the eyes, that's how you can tell."

"True," Saint Germain said. He sipped his wine, staring into the flames. "You know, Julius, you're young but one of the most amusing companions I've encountered in a long time. I'm going to have to leave England in a short while, but I'd like to think we may meet up again in the years ahead, and you are one of those people with an interesting mind that begs an incredible future. Perhaps I can assist with that, my dear friend."

Julius gazed at his friend. "How would that be, Claude-Louis?"

"Just so." Saint Germain produced a small vial of golden liquid from his vest. He opened the cork and sent two drops into Julius's glass of Bordeaux.

"Drink, mon coeur." Saint Germain's dark eyes reflected flickers of firelight.

Julius raised the glass to his lips, and staring at Saint Germain, drained it to the dregs. He sat the glass gently on the table between them.

"What was that?"

Saint Germain smiled. "A touch of immortality."

18

"Rise and shine, Irish. We've a busy few days ahead."

"Have I mentioned that there are times when I truly detest you, Henley?" Fiona flung his hand from her shoulder. "This is one of them. Take note."

She detested being woken by anyone or anything that wasn't her own will and he knew it. There had been too much of that in her life. She squinted at the sunlight making patterns on the white silk coverlet. Too early, as she suspected. She pulled the pillow over her head and closed her eyes.

"I'm serious, love. We're going up the river in search of our mysterious botanist."

Fiona lifted the pillow an inch or two. "What makes you think she'd be living on the River Road?"

"Just a hunch. That's what investigators do. We investigate hunches," Henley said. "I certainly haven't developed any roaming around the city. Besides, a botanist needs space to grow plants, wouldn't you say? Like a field or two? Marie as much as told us so."

Fiona pulled the pillow back down. "Christ Jesus. You are delusional."

"Hardly." He threw her pillow to the foot of the bed. "Up, Fiona. I'll have Robert get the carriage and I told Mrs. Acante to pack us a lunch hamper. With a pack of ice and two bottles of Piesporter."

Fiona moaned softly. "And chilled shrimp salad?"

"Of course, among other of your favorites."

"I still hate you."

"Of course."

An hour later, washed, dressed in cool white muslin, her hair piled under a large sun hat, Fiona sat in the carriage beside Henley and finished off her almond croissant and coffee. By the time they left the city limits and were trotting up the River Road, she was smiling.

"It's a lovely day."

Henley grinned. "Indeed it is."

Their first stop was Belle Fleur, once a flourishing cotton plantation before the war and now a rather run-down farm, although still growing cotton along sugar cane and a large variety of vegetables. Jacque LaSalle came out on the portico to greet them. They'd met him many times at meetings and events in the city. He was a white-haired Confederate veteran, a former cavalry Colonel, with a limp from the battle of Antietam, quite a charming man who endeavored to take care of all the people who lived in his domain, family, workers and ex-slaves alike and all treated the same. He'd known Julius for years.

"What a pleasant surprise," Jacque said, running a hand over his trimmed white mustache. "Y'all come on in and have some breakfast. What brings you by this fine mornin'?"

"Well sir, we're mostly on a pleasant ride, hoping to look up an old friend," Henley said. "Your offer of breakfast sounds wonderful."

He tied the reins of the two matched bays to the post outside the portico and helped Fiona down from the high seat.

While the house itself still bore bullet holes and other scars of war, threadbare carpets and worn furniture notwithstanding, the large kitchen and its big wooden table was filled with people and a great deal of delectable food. Warm biscuits, sausage gravy, pancakes, eggs, biscuits and sliced peaches in bowls of fresh cream were in a surplus and after greeting people they hadn't seen in a while and some that were previously unknown, Henley and Fiona wasted no time in sitting down to a delicious breakfast.

"I think I'm never going to eat again," Fiona said, after they'd sat back down out on the verandah. "Mrs. Acante needs to get more creative in the kitchen. Thank you, Jacque, that was delicious."

"Anytime, my dear, it's just simple country food," Jacque said. "So what really brings you two out of the city?"

"We're hoping to locate an old friend," Henley said. "Have you ever heard the name Annette Chambord?"

"Can't say that I have," LaSalle said, his brow furrowed. "She have a place out here?"

"So I heard, but maybe it's been a while," Henley brushed a croissant flake off his trousers. "She's a botanist, so she needs more than some little space for her plants and workroom and that. I know there's sadly been land going fallow out here for some time, with no one to work it or lost due to taxes and all, and we thought maybe she may have found one of those."

"A possibility, yes," Jacque said. "However, nothing comes to mind, far as I know. Most of the old families are gone." He shook his head. "Damn Northerners and scalliwags came in and took over for nothin' more than back taxes, but y'all know that sad story. Song of the South, eh? We'll get it back, have no mind. This time the right way."

"I know you will," Fiona said, patting Jacque's shoulder. "You've brought this place back to life and haven't lost an acre."

Jacque laughed. "The fields look good, that's for sure, and

we've even had some profit in the last few years. The house is a mess, as you've noticed, but the priority here has been on people and planting, not gewgaws and whatnot." He pulled at the shabby pants he was wearing and shrugged. "Not going to a ball any time soon, so they'll do."

"Your priorities are right on the money, Jacque. You're doing a remarkable job," Henley said. He stood up and shook Jacque's hand. "Thanks again for breakfast, we've got a long day ahead of us."

"You're welcome, stop by any time," the older man smiled. "Good luck with your search. I'll let you know if I run across anyone that's heard of this Annette."

"We'd appreciate it," Fiona said.

Back out on the River Road, they pondered their next stop. The plantations and farms up and down the river were a mixed bag since the war ended. Many had fallen with their owners, the men killed in the war and the families gone to live with relatives elsewhere. A few had been reclaimed, like Belle Fleur, but most were not flourishing, the big houses derelict and sometimes empty due to the cost of maintaining them. There were exceptions, and they decided to head for one in particular.

Oak Alley was originally built as a gift by a Creole gentleman, one Jacques Roman as a gift for his beloved wife Celina. Its Greek Revival façade with its second-floor balconies that surrounded the square house was timelessly magnificent, its twenty-eight white pillars matching the twenty-eight massive oak trees whose branches created a welcoming bower over the long brick walkway leading to the front door. It had been the showcase of the plantation homes, even eclipsing Belle Fleur, before the war and had been restored, although its previous owners since then hadn't had much luck with their crops, among other things.

Oak Alley had been the home of spectacular pecan groves as well as sugar cane but fell into disrepair after the war.

Owners had come and gone, but last year, a man called Andrew McDade purchased it and from all they'd heard, had begun to set it to rights once again. Truly the place did seem cursed and rumors had flown for years as to why that was so. Would it resent any owner that was not French Creole? Was it because Union soldiers had been bivouacked in those abandoned sugar fields? Were the spirits of the many slaves that had lived and died here seeking vengeance?

Many tales were told, but no answers had provided information of a factual nature, only rumors that continued to propel the myths. Fiona and Henley had met Andrew McDade at the governor's reception shortly after the Scotsman had purchased the much-maligned property, but had never discussed Oak Alley's history. Fiona had seen paintings of the place before and was thoroughly enchanted with the property and thought the stories about Oak Alley poignantly sad.

As they turned into the gravel road leading to the house, she could see the oak allee looming ahead, the massive green branches nearly obscuring the house beyond until one drew closer. She clutched Henley's arm. "The thing is, I almost don't want to see it, my love. I have fond memories of the painting done back in Jacques Roman's day, the one that hangs in Jean-Claude's gallery and no desire to sully that image. Perhaps I should just wait out here while you see Mr. McDade. Likely a fool's errand anyway."

Henley sighed. "Irish, you've been acting skittish for days. Your Gaelic weirdness is starting to worry me, to say nothing of the Cassinis and Julius's behavior. I need you with me on this, love. Your insights and instincts are better than mine, and we both know it."

Fiona took in a few deep breaths. She leaned over and kissed Henley on the lips, drawing away slowly with a slight smile. "Sorry. Not sure what's got into me. Whatever it is, I'm sending it far away in some blighted field near Ballyowen. It has no place here."

She grabbed the reins from Henley's hands before he could say a word, snapped them lightly but effectively on the bays' hindquarters, and down the lane they went. They tied the horses up to a hitching post in front of the house and were met even before they reached the wide verandah. A young black woman, a white tignon on her head in the old style, greeted them with a welcoming smile. Beside her stood a little boy in white livery, the wide grin on his dark face matching hers.

"Welcome, travelers," she said. "How may I help you?"

Fiona was a bit taken aback. The atmosphere was distinctively antebellum and Henley shot her a sideways look. He felt it too.

"Good morning. Is Mr. McDade in?" Henley said.

"I will see if the master is receiving," the woman said. "Would you care for some lemonade while you wait?" Her manner, while welcoming on the surface, was guarded.

"Thank you, that would be lovely," Henley said, and they sat down on two of the chairs on the wide porch. The woman and the boy disappeared into the house.

"Bit weird, don't you think?" Fiona whispered, not quite sure why she was doing so.

"Let's not jump to conclusions, love."

The house had recently received a new coat of paint, and the front grounds were well-manicured, unlike most of the plantations they'd passed so far. McDade apparently had plenty of money to spend. As for the fields, stables and outbuildings, there was not a sound of any activity that drifted near the house. The newly restored façade seemed just that, almost like a stage set.

The boy arrived with two glasses of lemonade on a silver tray. "Mr. McDade is very busy this mornin' but can spare some time shortly."

"Thank you kindly," Henley said.

"Well well, aren't we fortunate," Fiona sipped her lemonade. "Good lemonade, though."

Fifteen minutes later, lemonade drained, Fiona stood up. "This is a waste of time, Henley. Let's move on."

He couldn't disagree, and untied the reins. As he was helping Fiona into the carriage, a tall portly man with a bristly moustache and piercing eyes stepped through the front door. He was clad in white from his suit vest to his shoes.

"My friends, I apologize for the delay. Please sit back down. I'm Andrew McDade. I don't believe we've met before but I can spare a few minutes. How may I help you on this fine morning?"

Fiona was thoroughly irritated and McDade's demeanor wasn't helping. "How charming to meet you, Mr. McDade. I'm Fiona Shanahan and this is my colleague, Mr. Henley. We're here on a bit of a fact-finding mission, as well as visiting old friends on the River Road today. We were hoping to ask you a few questions, since you now reside in the area. Would that burden you?"

The man was full of charm, or so he thought. Fiona thought he resembled a villain in a stage play about to preen his moustache.

"Not at all, Miss Shanahan. I'm always ready to meet new friends in Louisiana. I'm from New Hampshire myself, had a good-sized operation there but the cost of labor, and too much government oversight was cutting into my profits. Besides, the winters are brutal. Down here, it's quite different in many ways. It's a new experience, but I'm doing my best to adapt to your southern ways and culture. Please." He gestured to the same chairs they had occupied earlier and took one himself. Apparently, they were not worthy enough to be invited into the house itself and from that oversight, it was evident Mr. McDade hadn't adapted to southern hospitality in the slightest. Manners in

New Hampshire, at least among his crowd, must be on a par with sitting on a hay bale in the barn, whiskey bottle in hand.

Henley sighed, taking her arm and guiding them back to the chairs they'd recently vacated.

"We won't take up much of your time, Andrew. I'm sure you're a very busy man. Oak Alley is looking quite well," Henley said. "It's wonderful you've taken such an interest in restoring it."

"How kind of you to say so," McDade said. "It's been an investment, I can assure you. I'm trying to replicate its former glory in every way but it is an ongoing process."

"I'm sure," Fiona said. "Still have the slave quarters?"

McDade laughed, clearly taken aback. "Well, yes, actually. Where else would the help live?"

Fiona smiled, showing her teeth. "Indeed, former glory and all." It was becoming abundantly clear Mr. McDade had never been an abolitionist.

Henley was growing agitated, Fiona knew, and with reason. They needed to get away from this cursed place. He put his hand on her arm.

"It's been nice meeting you, Andrew. Actually, we stopped by without notice today simply to inquire if you've had the acquaintance or any dealings with a woman named Annette Chambord who may have a holding in the area."

McDade cocked his head, as if to give the impression he was searching his memory. Then he sighed. "No, I can't think I've met anyone by that name. It seems you are on a fruitless search, my new friends. I will keep the name in mind, however. Do you have a card?"

McDade took the card from Fiona's hand and upon reading it, bowed stiffly, wished them safe travels, and disappeared into the house.

"Well. So much for adaptation, eh?" Henley said. "We'd better get going or the dogs will be let out next."

Henley took the reins and they left Oak Alley at a quick trot. Before they reached the end of the allee, the young boy from the porch emerged from the trees and held up his hand. Henley stopped the carriage.

"Please sir. Mirabelle sent me with a note for you. Things are not as they seem here."

Fiona took the envelope from his hand. "Thank you, we were fairly sure they were not," she said. "We will try to help."

The boy shrugged. "No one has." He ran back into the trees.

"Christ Jesus. Just when we try to solve one problem, we find another," Fiona said. "McDade is not only an ass, but a nasty piece of work."

Henley shook his head. "I have a feeling one problem may be related to the other, Irish. Marie may be onto something. Maybe this stop wasn't a complete waste of time. Read the note."

19

"Go see the voodoo woman in Vacherie.'" Fiona put the note in her reticule.

"That's it? That's all she wrote?"

"That's all we need."

Six miles down the road, they came to a tumble-down log and stone building that sat in a clearing among the sweet gum trees and boasting a hand-painted sign that read "Vacherie Store". Shaded by the trees, wooden stands outside the structure displayed crates of fragrant melons, tomatoes, peaches and other fruits and vegetables, while a few chickens pecked listlessly around the yard, hardly noticing as Henley and Fiona walked among them.

Inside, it was dim and cool, shelves of canned goods and burlap bags of staples stacked up haphazardly, and the smell of chicory and coffee hung in the air. Behind a wooden counter, a man turned his attention from arranging cans on the top shelf and stepped down from the short ladder.

"Mornin' to you, friends," he smiled. "How can I help y'all today?" Tufts of white hair formed a patchy circle below his shiny bald head and his blue eyes were warm and friendly. Fiona smiled back. It was a nice change from the reception at Oak Alley.

"Morning to you as well," she said. "We're just passing by and thought we might get a couple of peaches for a picnic later on."

"Nice little store," Henley said, looking around. "First one I've seen today."

"Thank you kindly," the man said. "Hiram Roundtree's my name. Wife and I been running this place for thirty years, give or take. Ain't much competition around here, so we make out all right, thanks to the good Lord. Fair trade and fair prices."

"You have your own gardens?" Henley said. Fiona left them to their conversation and began to wander around the store, perusing the merchandise. There was a glass case with small bottles, some with corks and others sealed with wax. She peered closer. Herbs and spices, according to the handwritten labels. She opened the cupboard and took out a bottle of angelica and another of sage. The sage bottle had a cork and she pulled it out, sniffed and nodded in appreciation. It was freshly harvested and well preserved.

"Yessir, we surely do," Hiram said, "and my nephews run the flour mill up Hillsdale way. I've been working on a sugar supplier that's local. Used to be over to Riverbend but no more."

"Is that so? Try Jacque LaSalle, he's got some cane in," Henley was running out of small talk but Hiram continued to tell him about his ventures. Fiona brought the bottles to the counter.

"These look wonderful, and the sage smells so fresh."

"Yes, ma'am, 'course it is. Grown right here in the river valley, Aunt Verna tells me."

"Aunt Verna?"

"She lives a ways out back of here, got her own place, she does. Handles that sort of thing," Hiram gestured to the apothecary case. "Makes tisanes and remedies too, if you're in need of something like that." He winked. "Love potions, even, so people tell me, but you two don't look to be in need of that."

Fiona smiled. "You're an observant man, Mr. Roundtree. So would Aunt Verna be a conjure woman?"

"Well, them would be your words, not mine," Hiram said. "I wouldn't want to be doing any harm to her reputation. That woman's the salt of the earth, she is. We all love her around here."

Fiona held out her hand. "Please don't misunderstand me. I ask because I do have need of a remedy for my father's gout, and I haven't found anyone in New Orleans that makes a good one. Perhaps we could stop in and see Aunt Verna. She sounds very knowledgeable."

Henley stepped outside and returned with two ripe peaches and a melon, setting them on the counter. "We need to be getting along, Hiram. How much do we owe you?"

Fiona put the herbs in her reticule while Henley put five dollars on the counter, Hiram handing him the fruit in a paper bag. "You want to visit Aunt Verna, you go up the side road to your left, it's about a half mile. You can't miss it."

True to his word, about half a mile up the grassy lane stood a little cottage, nestled in a grove of apple trees. It looked like a fairy tale house, built of rocks with stained glass windows and a crooked chimney. The rounded door was open to the morning breeze as were the windows, and it took them a minute to discover where the tinkling sounds originated. Shiny objects and little yarn and cornhusk dolls swayed above them in the trees, moving slightly in the wind. Bells of all sizes, spent shells, broken silverware, all manner of discarded objects had been polished and hung with nearly invisible fishing line from the branches, creating a delightful low-pitched symphony from the unusual orchestra.

The tiny woman who came to stand in the doorway hummed a tune along with her unusual instruments, the muse and conductor of it all. She smiled and gestured them inside, sitting down at a workbench beside the empty fireplace and waving Fiona and Henley to the two chairs on the other side. Her wizened nut-brown face looked almost too small for her big brown eyes and the wide grin she bestowed on them. Her hair was hidden in a calico tignon of the same fabric as the simple dress she wore. The cottage smelled of cinnamon and a darker, sharper scent that was quite pleasant.

"I wasn't sure you two would be here so fast as today, but here you are. Miss Fiona and Mr. Henley, I am Aunt Verna and it is pleasurable to meet you."

"How did you –" Henley started and both Fiona and Aunt Verna chuckled at the same time. "Of course."

"Word travels fast in these parts," Aunt Verna said, cocking her head like a little brown sparrow. "Mirabelle is my great niece and of course, another acquaintance of ours has let me know you could be by. Looks like we have some things to discuss. I have some raspberry mint tea steeping."

"And we brought lunch, if you would join us." Henley put the picnic basket on the table.

The shrimp salad was still cool, as was the wine and sliced cucumbers in dill cream sauce, while the round loaf of bread and the sun-kissed peaches were still warm. Fiona had thought she'd never eat another bite after breakfast, but that was long ago, according to her appetite, perhaps fueled by anxiety, more than matched by Henley and Aunt Verna who didn't hold back either.

While they enjoyed their lunch, conversation was at a minimum, but Fiona's eyes swept around the room thoroughly. The entire back wall of the cottage, aside from a curtained off sleeping area, held cupboards and shelves full of drawers, bottles, sacks and packages full of botanicals of all kinds. Drying herbs hung from the ceiling in bunches all over the room, scents from all them blending into the sharp aroma she'd encountered in the beginning. It was an herbalist's treasurehouse, putting Saint Germain's to shame. True, Aunt Verna's lacked the expensive modern equipment that he had amassed in his laboratory, but the sheer quantity and variety in Verna's little storehouse eclipsed his in great measure. Of course, hers was mainly medicinal and of the household variety, from what little Fiona could discern. Saint Germain's, on the other hand, ranged from exotic pain elixirs to ingredients in his search for the Philosopher's stone and who could imagine what else, from what she could discern.

Empty containers packed away, Aunt Verna lit up a small wooden pipe and leaned back contentedly in her chair. "Down to business, I expect."

"Yes, ma'am," Henley said. "What's amiss at Oak Alley?"

"Y'all get right to the point, young man. Which is a good thing. Truth is, I'm not 'zactly certain, as I've not seen it for my own self, but Mirabelle says there's something not right about the field workers over there. McDade's got them out in the old quarters and they's mighty quiet after a day's work. She's not certain they's even got any food out there, which is near impossible, but there it is. None of 'em talk to her or the other five or so servants in the house."

Fiona frowned. "How could they survive? That's hard work. Maybe they just cook for themselves and she doesn't see it."

"Maybe." Verna looked skeptical. "Maybe she don't see a lot of things, Mirabelle. She never been the most bright-eyed girl but still, they's something not right over there. She says they come and go at night sometimes too, and could be it's not always the same bunch as comes back."

"That's peculiar," Fiona glanced at Henley, who seemed as perplexed as she was. "Why in the world would that be?"

"Me, I don't know that, and Mirabelle can fancy things. But little Henry, her son? That boy is quick and I tell you what, that boy is scared. So I been givin' this some thought but I ain't quite sure enough to be talkin' yet."

"Any other places where odd things are happening?" Fiona said. "Seems you know a lot about the goings-on around here, Aunt Verna."

Verna smiled, clearly pleased. "That I do, miss. I heard some about a couple other of the plantations and farms. Not until McDade come out here and bought Oak Alley was there much on that kind of scale."

"How many workers does he have over there, you think?" Henley said, finishing off his wine. "Twenty? More?"

Verna snorted. "You don't know much about growing cane or cotton, do you?"

Henley chuckled. "No, ma'am, I do not, which is why I'm seeking your expertise."

"You need least thirty men or more to work any size field like Oak Alley. Lotta people seek my expertise, all right," Verna said. "Even the queen herself. You know she get some of her stores from me. She know I grow the best."

Well. That said a lot. Fiona got up and stretched, hands on her lower back. That damn Marie never divulged anything but let you figure it out for yourself. She could have sent them right to Aunt Verna but of course she did not. Still, they had found her.

"The queen has her own place up here, so I understand," Fiona said. "Did she get her plants from you?"

"You're a quick one, aren't you, pretty? Me, I give her some starts, you know?"

"Where's her place?"

"Out the road a piece. She have it for some time now. Le Petit Jardin, I think she call it."

Henley was growing restless and gave a small jerk of his chin towards the open door, the afternoon sunlight shadowing the entryway. Fiona wasn't quite ready.

"One last question? Have you ever heard of a Frenchwoman who has an herb farm similar to Le Petit Jardin out here? Perhaps named Annette?"

Aunt Verna abruptly stood up. "No. That name nothing to me. I think it's time for you to go."

"Verna, you've been very helpful and we are grateful. We will look into the situation at Oak Alley and see what we can find out. When you're ready to share your thoughts, please send word, can you do that?" She put their S&H Investigations card on the table. "We'll help if we can."

Verna peered at them both through a haze of aromatic smoke from her pipe. "I think you tellin' the truth. There's things you city people just don't know about life around here but that don't mean things can't touch you. Be careful, you."

"We will." Henley picked up the basket and they climbed into the carriage. Fiona looked back and waved at Aunt Verna who stood in the doorway, watching them go. She didn't wave back.

"Irish, I think we may been in over our heads on this. Dear Aunt Verna is lying, at least about Annette Chambord, and god knows what the hell she's on about with these field workers. That's a kettle of fish we don't need right now."

Fiona was silent for a moment. "You may be right. Only thing is, Henley, I think that kettle of fish is full of more than field workers. A visit to Marie's garden could be illuminating, if we can find it. I've got a feeling she hasn't got the only one. Saint Germain's herbals have been quite educational."

Henley groaned. "We're stopping back in at Hiram's, that's for sure. That guy is annoying, Fiona."

"Hello again, travelers," Hiram greeted them with a broad smile. "Guess you found Aunt Verna. What can I do for you so soon?"

"We need some advice," Henley smiled back. "First, how do we find a place called Le Petit Jardin?"

"Ah, that place. It used to be called Fox Run but the taxmen got it. Don't rightly know who's up there now. It's about ten miles up the road. Easy to miss. Look for two big live oak trees that mark a lane. There's a white farmhouse with black trim back in there a bit. They keep to themselves, though."

Henley nodded. "Understood. Think they'll shoot?"

Hiram laughed. "Naw, they real friendly. Anything else I can help you with?"

"Actually, yes," Fiona chimed in. "Is there an inn around here, in case it gets too late to get back to New Orleans tonight?"

Hiram cocked his head, rubbing his chin. "Heard tell of a place up near White Castle, but it's pretty rough...let me think."

A stout little woman in a white apron bustled out from the back room. "Hiram, don't be sending these fine people to that hellhole." She held out her hand. "Mary Roundtree, his better half. Pleased to meet y'all." They shook hands. "Now, the old Depardeau plantation is being fixed up and they say part of it's a hotel with a dining room and all, been so for a couple of years. It's near the old Fox Run place, if that's where you're headed. It'll be late afternoon by the time you get there, so it might work out."

"That sounds fine," Fiona said, "thank you so much. We'd better get moving, then, Henley."

They waved goodbye and hurried back to the carriage. Fiona rubbed her backside but climbed in. This day had been long but somewhat informative. She hoped the rest of it proved to be as well. They had a lot more to learn and still no Annette Chambord, that elusive and mysterious woman. She was starting to think Annette was a figment of Saint Germain's very active but faulty imagination. At least they hadn't run into a Cassini brother. He'd probably be as out of place out on Plantation Alley as they were. Especially with that black cassock and very unattractive hat. The Vatican had little fashion sense, and as far as Fiona was concerned, little sense about anything, having been a victim of the church's idea of benevolence herself.

20

The sun was reflecting low on the Mississippi by the time they came to the aforesaid two live oaks, the Spanish moss hanging low on both of them, a two-track lane winding away through the grass. Henley glanced over at Fiona and raised an eyebrow.

"Should we wait until tomorrow? Your call."

"Let's go. We need to get some answers and I don't want to come out here again unless we have to." She shivered. "I don't like this place, Henley."

He nodded in agreement. "Let's get it over with. Marie wouldn't be involved in anything truly evil, at least I don't think so. She's formidable, but she has her own set of rules."

As Hiram had described, a white farmhouse with black trim came into view before too long. As they pulled up the tired horses, a man stood up from a chair on the porch, cradling a shotgun in his arm.

"What you looking for?" He didn't look pleased at the intrusion.

"Le Petit Jardin," Henley said. "Are we in the right place?"

"Why don't you both come on up here." He motioned with the shotgun. "Things might become more clear."

"That could be possible, if you put down that shotgun," Henley said. "Doesn't seem all that welcoming." He looked at Fiona and she nodded. His hands tensed on the reins.

Instead, the man on the porch raised the shotgun. At the same time, Fiona pulled her pistol out of her reticule and before his finger pulled the trigger, she shot him in the shoulder. He screamed and dropped the gun while Henley whipped up the horses and they tore back down the lane, followed by shouts and a blast from the shotgun.

"Guess we had the wrong place, eh?" Fiona said. "Can these poor horses go any faster?"

Henley grinned. "They'd better. By the way, I put a rifle behind the seat. Might be a good time to grab it, deadeye. Longer range and all."

She leaned over, holding onto the seat as they raced down the path, rummaging around until her hand felt the rifle case, pulling it into her lap as she plopped back down. She took out the Winchester, checked it was loaded, and peered behind them.

"Nobody's following us," she said.

"That's because they'll be behind those oak trees coming right up," Henley said. "We walked right into the oldest trap in the book, God knows why."

Fiona's hat blew off but she tucked her hair behind her ear and sighted the gun. "You're going to have to slow down a little so I can get a good shot."

"Yes, dear." They were almost to the trees. "Besides, we have to turn out of here fast after you kill them."

"Of course. Might be best if you stop altogether."

Henley pulled back on the reins just as a man with a shotgun stepped out from behind the oak tree on their left. His shot went wild but Fiona's didn't, and he dropped to the ground without a sound. A moment passed, but the other tree didn't yield a gunman.

"Guess they were a bit short-handed today or we didn't look like much of a threat," Henley said, sounding disappointed. "East or west, darling?"

"Definitely east. Belle Fleur will be feeding us dinner as well as breakfast. Jacque will be fine with that." Fiona kept the rifle on her lap. "Hopefully he's got a soft bed for the night."

"East it is, love. Besides if we had actually made it to Mary Roundtree's kind recommendation without getting shot here, they'd have another opportunity to make sure we didn't have the most pleasant night's stay. We'll be back to deal with those two some other time."

JACQUE LASALLE POURED them all another a glass of the whiskey Henley had thoughtfully packed. He was amazing that way, and Fiona had stopped being surprised. Henley was a man that always thought ahead. They sat out on the south portico, the nightbirds calling, watching the bats flitting through the fields, after their own delicious dinners, courtesy of LaSalle again. The breeze off the river was soft on their faces, a calming delight after the hectic day, filled with the scent of honeysuckle and the sweet tang of ripe sugar cane. The tired bays were in the stables, well-brushed and enjoying Belle Fleur's oats and alfalfa.

"I've heard rumors," Jacque said, putting his glass down on the wicker table. "Probably should've said something this morning, but I didn't think it was anything that would interest you, since you were simply looking for some woman as you said. Now, though, after hearing what happened up the river today, I guess I should've. As you've heard earlier today, there's something not right. It's been on my mind, and quite a few others as well. It may be time for a reckoning.

"For one thing, Hiram Roundtree is a rum one, he is. He'll sell anything to anybody, far back as the war. Union, Confederate, carpetbaggers, you name it. Never lost so much as a crabapple, that one, while everyone else was digging for last year's potatoes. You wanted to buy from him, you sure as hell couldn't afford it, I'll tell you that. Sells a lot more than peaches."

"He certainly seems to have a profitable store," Fiona said. "Friendly guy full of advice, too. And his wife Mary was so sweet and helpful. I hated her on sight."

Jacque chuckled. "I'll bet. Mary Roundtree reminds me of old folktales, like Baba Yaga and her candy house. On the other hand, that old conjure woman down the lane helps his reputation for sure. She's a good one, Aunt Verna is, but she's dependent on his good will so you can't trust her one hundred percent, but she tries best she can and she's got some of the best remedies around, always has."

Henley leaned back in his chair. Fiona knew his back hurt and he was tired. She was too, but she wanted more. "Tell me the rumors."

"It's so crazy, you won't be believin' me, I tell you that," Jacque said, "why I didn't say anything earlier, along with it wasn't in the wind then. Now, though, I think you two have maybe walked into the wild side."

"Come on, Jacque," Fiona said. "You've known Julius forever, and you know we've walked on the wild side many times, so tell us."

Jacque finished his whiskey. "Zombies, that's what I'm hearin', girl."

Henley laughed. "Are you drunk?"

Jacque looked indignant, even his mustache bristling, hard to do after three whiskeys. "Nossir, I am not. You want to hear me out or not?"

Fiona shot Henley a look and patted Jacque's arm. "Apologies. Tell us more."

Mollified, Jacque went on. "Here's what I know, my friends. There's a few places out here that are thrivin' when it comes to profits, or so my bankers tell me. Some deservedly so, like mine, if I do say so, but others for no reason in hell. Spending money like water, fixing things up, crops growin' and harvested in big quantities with little labor that anyone sees. My men tell me stories and I know they ain't lyin'. There's something not right."

Fiona glanced at Henley. They'd heard that phrase too often today. "So they think it's zombies? They're just creatures in a scary children's story, not real. Old voodoo stuff."

Jacque shook his head and poured more whiskey. "Nope. Not anymore." He sat back in his chair. "I'm trusting y'all tellin' you this. I don't want people thinkin' old Jacque is going crazy in his old age. Cause I'm sure as hell not."

"So how does it work?" Fiona said.

"We figure maybe it goes like this. These zombies come from somewhere, maybe they bring them around at night. They work all day, or sometimes into the night. They don't need much food and all. Perfect. Just like the slaves of the old days, but even better, 'cause they're dead."

"That's impossible," Fiona said. "They can't be dead."

Jacque sighed. "Well, they are. If they weren't dead in the beginnin', they don't last all that long and then they're dead."

"How?" Henley was intrigued, but impatient. "Hypnosis of some kind?"

"Nope, don't think so. It's gotta be some sort of drug or poison. I've heard of this, from some frogs and fish. People take this stuff, sometimes too much, and they end up buried in the grave. Then somebody digs them up and they're walkin' around but not too much is going on the attic," Jacque pointed to his head, "you know? Hence, 'zombies'."

Henley, formerly a hard-headed New York police detective in his early years, shook his head. "That sounds impossible."

"Told you you wouldn't believe me, son," Jacque said with a heavy sigh. "But it's true. I've lived here all my life and I've known about this for years. Never encountered it before, but times haven't really changed about some things if you know what I mean."

"Christ Jesus, Jacque. I believe you," Fiona finished her whiskey. "Monstrous. I don't suppose these people live very long? Or do they?"

"Hell, I've got no idea, Fiona," Jacque shrugged and held up his hands. "I can't even say for sure if any of this is gospel truth, because I haven't seen it for myself, but I truly think it is. There's plenty of talk, though, always has been, but not like this. Nobody cares much for McDade, and he's not the only one. That place you two were sent to this afternoon? That wasn't Fox Run, or Marie's place. I don't think you were ever supposed to leave. Since you did, they'll be lookin' for you, be sure of that."

"Oh, I am certain you're right, no matter what's going on," Henley said. "You know what they say, though – be careful what you look for in case you find it, and never corner anybody meaner and smarter than you."

Jacque grinned. "Amen. Still, you two must be cautious. Think about how this came about: first, you ask about this Frenchwoman, which means somethin' to someone out here, but I can't quite figure her in yet; second, you stop at Oak Alley where you stumble onto another somethin' that you still don't know, then you meet Hiram Roundtree, who can't stop you from seein' Aunt Verna without raising suspicion, who he suspects may have told you another somethin' he doesn't want you to know, so then, just to be certain, he sends you into an ambush at the wrong farm, with a backup of an inn where you'd likely not live through the night. That about sum it up?"

Jacque didn't manage what was the most successful plantation in Louisiana without being extremely analytical and organized, and his suspicions and conclusions were well-founded.

"Yes," Fiona shook her head and glanced at Henley. "Unfortunately. We've been babes in the wood on this entire investigation. That's over."

Henley snorted. "Hell, that was over when you killed that guy."

"Don't be jealous, darling. You know I'm a better shot than you."

Jacque choked on his bourbon a little but it sounded suspiciously like a laugh to Fiona.

"Are you all right?" She patted him on the back.

Jacque coughed and reassured her. "Perfectly fine, my dear, but now we need to call it a night. Dawn comes early on this place. I will mention one more thing you should know. Marie Laveau does indeed have a place out here, her Le Petit Jardin. However, it's only about three miles down the road, and she's always been a delightful neighbor. From what I know, she's got nothing to do with any of this and I don't want to see her hurt. I'll give you directions over breakfast. You are safe here, I have four gentlemen that patrol at night. Sleep well, my friends."

The bed was soft, Henley's warm body was reassuring, and against expectations, they both slept well, strangers to such a thing as a guilty conscience. People who knew they did the right thing rarely had one.

21

"Here we are again at a crossroads." Henley pulled the bays to a halt at the end of Belle Fleur's drive. "Left or right, Fiona?"

Fiona brushed dust from her wrinkled dress. She sniffed heartily, but road worn as they both looked, they at least didn't smell too bad, but the day was young. "Going to Le Petit Jardin might be a waste of time, Henley, and I doubt if Marie is there." She squinted into the bright morning sun. "On the other hand, we're here and we might as well see for ourselves. I can't believe she'd be behind any of this zombie stuff, but someone there might have more information."

"I agree. Left it is."

Jacque's directions were perfect. Fifteen minutes later, they arrived at a well-kept farm, a sprawling one-story house with a wide porch and sparkling white paint coming into view down a neatly-scythed lane. The house was surrounded by large trees dripping with Spanish moss, a cozy and well maintained place, even without the antebellum grandeur of Belle Fleur or Oak Alley. Once again, there was a man on the porch to greet newcomers, but his hands were at his sides with no shotgun in evidence. Another difference was the welcoming grin on his face. Jim Washington waved in recognition as they stepped down from the carriage.

"Mornin, Miss Fiona, Mr. Henley. What brings you two out here?"

"What a lovely surprise, Jim," Fiona smiled. "Is Marie around, by any chance?"

"Not this day," Jim said, clearly curious. "I usually oversee things around here, she bein' who she is. If you want to get out of the sun and come on up here, maybe I can help you with whatever you lookin' for." He chuckled. "'Cause if I know you two, you ain't on a morning drive for nothin'."

"You are an astute gentleman, Mr. Washington," Henley said. "We will take you up on your kind offer."

Minutes later, they were settled on the shady porch sipping cool glasses of water, along with a lovely view of green gardens and Jim Washington's waiting stare in immediate cognizance. There was no point in dissembling. If they couldn't trust Marie Laveau and her people, they were in big trouble, not just here but in New Orleans as well.

Fiona started. "We've had quite a time the last day or so, meeting a few people, some helpful and others, well, not so much. As Marie may have mentioned, we came up in search of a woman, a botanist by trade and French by name, but it seems no one has heard of her. We stopped in here and there, met a man who runs the Vacherie general store, and then a conjure woman, Tante Verna. Somewhere along the line, we must've ruffled the wrong feathers, because late yesterday afternoon, some people tried to kill us."

Jim frowned but said nothing except "Go on."

Henley took up the narrative. "Clearly they didn't succeed. We took refuge last night with Jacque LaSalle," Jim nodded, "but before we go back to the city, he suggested we stop in and visit here. He mentioned there had been some rumors around in the last while and thought perhaps you had heard something disturbing about some of the plantation workers around here."

Jim sat back and peered closely at them both, weighing his response with care.

Finally, he stood up. "You talkin' zombies, I'm thinkin'," his voice low. He ran his hands through his hair and gave both Fiona and Henley a hard stare.

Fiona shot Henley a look and he nodded. *In for a penny, in for a pound*, she thought, crazy as it seemed.

"Yes," she said. "That would be the rumor."

"Come on into the house." He glanced around. "The trees a bit too close out here."

They sat in the large front room, the front door latched and the windows shuttered. A fan swirled lazily overhead, but even so, the air was warm and close, and only two lamps lit the dim space. Bookshelves lined the walls, an empty fireplace between them. The furniture was simple but comfortable. A girl brought another pitcher of water and one of sweet tea and left as silently as she'd come.

"Some things haven't been right around here for some time now," Jim said. That phrase again. "People tryin' hard to make their way and some doin' all right, and some even better, takin' care of folks, makin' a good livin', treating people fair.

"But there's some others that don't see things that way. They wantin' to make money at the expense of others, kinda like the way things was back in the day, you know? Some people just cain't seem to let go of their misguided notions."

"We do know." Henley poured some tea and handed Fiona a glass too. "How has this led to something like zombies? You have to forgive me and Fiona as well, because we'd never heard of anything like that before last night. Is this even possible?"

"'Course it's possible, but understandable you don't know,

most don't. It's been around. Some say from Haitian voodoo, but Louisiana kind of voodoo not the same," Jim said. "People always lookin' to accuse voodoo people and make up stories. It's all over the world, from what Marie has learned. Place doesn't matter and Louisiana ain't no different. People everywhere and in every time do terrible things to other people to get what they want."

No one knew that better than Fiona, Irish orphan as she was, and fighting against that way of thinking was what had brought her to America and eventually into Julius's world, since that was his mission as well.

"So how does it work?" Henley wanted details, as always the former New York policeman, before he met Julius and became part of his entourage. "Is it a drug, a poison? Where does it come from? What happens to the people that take it?"

"Slow down, Mr. Henley, you got a lot of questions. Some I got answers for, some I don't."

"I apologize," Henley said, somewhat abashed. "I do get carried away sometimes."

"It's quite understandable, Michael, it's a subject that tends to evoke emotions," said Marie Laveau, her white tignon and dress appearing out of the gloom like an ghostly apparition. "It certainly has done so for me." Fiona was not surprised to see her.

Henley shot to his feet. "Good morning, madame. We appreciate your hospitality and did not mean to show up on your doorstep with dark questions, but," he flung out his arm to encompass Fiona and Jim, "here we are. May we intrude a bit longer?"

She gave a throaty laugh. "You'd better. There are unanswered questions for all of us. Sit." It wasn't an invitation, but a command. Henley did so with alacrity, folding his long legs quickly to the side of the sofa.

"You two have had quite a time out here on the River Road, haven't you?"

Fiona looked at Marie's placid face. "No question about that, Madame. We found some very unfriendly folks up the road. Things didn't turn out well for them, but I don't know why."

"We have heard," Marie said. "It turns out to be quite fortuitous, however, especially so since you are both sitting here unharmed. Another two were not as fortunate, I hear."

Fiona shrugged. "I don't like being shot at."

"Justifiably so," Marie said. "That said, we now know the location of at least one place that could be part of this madness. Tante Verna has quite a network, the old dear, right under the not very clever noses of Hiram and Mary Roundtree, among others."

Henley snorted. "Those two."

"Yes, but they're not alone, I fear, likely only some of the conspirators. We know some of the end users, like McDade and his ilk, but we need to find the source. It could be the place you stumbled onto yesterday, but there could be others, and I think it's only a way station. Your talk of this Chambord woman has raised my alarm bells, so to speak. If she's out there, she's carefully disguised. I've not found anyone so far that could be part of this."

"What do they distribute, some drug or another?" Henley said.

"Yes, of a sort. Those of us that grow and use botanicals, herbs, spices, and other things, have often been suspect. I myself have lovely gardens of the more common plants that everyone is familiar with that I cultivate, even botanicals that could be accurately described as a "poison garden" after the old medieval European term. Those plants that fit that description are very useful in many remedies, especially for pain. There are some, such as wolfsbane or datura, that have been misused.

Datura can be used as an hallucinogen, wherein people are easily led or even put into a somnambulistic state. Its effects are fairly temporary, and that's far from what's happening here."

Jim poured Marie a glass of tea and she sat down on the chair beside him with a grateful smile, patting his hand. The affection between the two was clear, in this safe space with trusted friends.

"The reason I am so concerned, aside from the obvious humanitarian one, is that I have heard there are people spreading rumors about me and some of the old storied voodoo practices, to slide suspicion away from themselves and their own nefarious activities.

"What they are doing to people, from what I can determine, is entirely different from any effects that could be introduced with the plants I grow. They are using an old remedy, a poison derived from some types of fish or some frogs and snakes, called tetrodotoxin, which renders their victims mostly insensible. They become, yes, zombie-like, and completely under the control to the wishes of their handlers. They may sleep, occasionally eat or drink, but as long as the poison is in their system or continuing to be administered, they are slaves to the whims of their masters. They work past human exhaustion. Eventually, of course, they die. Nameless and forgotten, they are finally done away with, I assume, either buried or drowned in the river, when their physical usefulness is over. Then, more are recruited with advertisements that promote false promises of high wages and good living conditions. Expecting a better life, they are instead drugged and put to work. So the cycle continues."

Silence reigned when she finished speaking. There were few words to express the horror of what Marie's words invoked and it only seemed appropriate to spend a few minutes in mourning for the fate of those so victimized.

"Horrifying," Fiona finally said, her voice shaky. "I have

seen awful things, but I have never encountered anything like this."

"Few have." Jim rose and put his hands on Marie's shoulders. "It is up to those of us who know to stop it in any way we can. Even after a war, proclamations and laws, there are those who will always believe people with dark skin are less than human, and exist only to make their privileged ways more comfortable and profitable."

Marie glanced up at him and lowered her gaze to Fiona and Henley. "And now, my dear investigators, you are part of the few. You've already inadvertently played a part, so you know there are many that must be held accountable for the carnage that is being perpetuated here, and lives to be saved. As they say, 'once you know, you have a responsibility' and never has that been more true than now."

"We're in," Henley said, "have no doubt about that. Julius will undoubtedly throw in any resources we need as well."

There was an awkward silence at that proclamation. Henley looked at Fiona and she was as perplexed as he.

"That would normally make me happy, of course," Marie said. "However, there is something else at play here. Your search for this woman has been instigated by Julius's friend, the one whom we met at your Samhain ball. The Comte Saint Germain. It is his wish, I believe, that you search for this mysterious Frenchwoman, Annette Chambord. Is that not so?"

"True," Fiona said, "but honestly, what does that have to do with zombies?"

"Perhaps nothing, perhaps everything," Marie Laveau said. "But I caution you. Before you feel comfortable in divulging anything you have heard or experienced in the last two days, think hard. Who really is this man? How much does Julius trust him? How much do either of you?"

Fiona opened her mouth to speak, but Henley squeezed her hand, so hard she nearly winced. Apparently it could wait.

"One more thing for you to think about," Marie said, leaning forward. "The Cassinis are here, and they are not my friends, even though rest assured, we made peace long ago."

She smiled, and the regret was unmistakable. "You must be very careful, my friends. The Cassinis are not here for me. They are here for you."

22

Fiona left her dusty clothes lying on the floor and stepped into the steaming water of the tub, rose petals littering the surface, the steamy water bringing out their sweet scent, exactly the way she liked them. She sighed gratefully and rested her head on the small pillow on the lip of the tub. Christ, that was not a trip she wanted to make again soon, but she had a bad feeling that was a feeble hope. She'd never been a happy traveler if it involved discomfort, probably after-effects from crossing the Atlantic from Ireland on a crowded and disease-ridden ship. Floating down the Mississippi on a luxurious showboat like the Queen of Dreams was a world away from that, but she seldom felt the urge to suffer even minor inconveniences like a sore backside, dusty roads and getting shot at by some ruffian. Trains were fine, carriages were not, given choices. At the moment, choices were becoming limited.

"Here you go, Irish," Henley handed her a frosty glass of lemonade fortified with her favorite gin and sat down on a hassock beside the tub. He had his own glass of whiskey and sipped it with what looked like great enjoyment.

"We have certainly stumbled into a hornet's nest on this one," Fiona said. "I don't like it in the slightest, but as the King told Alice, 'Begin at the beginning, go on until you come to the end. Then stop.' All the way back, I kept thinking those very words. To get to the end, we have to go back to the beginning, as in Julius and the Comte Saint Germain."

Henley looked grim. He needed more than one whiskey in Fiona's estimation. "So right, as always. Not liking it is an understatement. What bothers me more than anything right this moment is that my mentor is no longer someone I completely trust. I think that's true of you as well." He glanced at her. "Julius has been like a father to both of us. It's possible he's not aware of the effects searching for this Chambord woman would have, but Saint Germain would have to be, don't you think?"

Fiona shrugged, the water rippling. "No way to tell, Hen. I do know Marie wouldn't make things up. No point in speculating, we simply need to have a discussion with them both as soon as possible. Hope they don't have plans for the evening as I'm in no mood to wait. I keep thinking some spooky Cassini fellow is going to float onto the balcony like some damned vampire."

Henley finished his whiskey and made even shorter work of his clothes. "I hate the cursed rose petals but I'm coming in anyway. No time to waste, we've got business to attend to."

He slid into the other end of the tub, sliding his long legs up beside Fiona's shoulders, his fingers trailing slowly down her legs. "Damn, that was an uncomfortable ride. This water feels good. Perhaps we can come up with an activity to ease our pain."

"Highly likely," Fiona said, reaching towards him. "We do tend to be quick thinkers and whatnot."

An hour or so later, they headed downstairs. Raphael was still at his desk, looking bored and munching on a beignet as usual. Mrs. Acante had been baking this afternoon, from the enticing aroma that wafted in from the kitchen. Fiona gave a passing thought to visiting the kitchen and grabbing a clove or two of garlic but figured her pistol was a better defense. Still... the old myths she'd heard as a child were silly but still frightening. Not, of course that the Cassinis were of that sort, but they were menacing somehow.

"Good afternoon, Raphael," Henley said, leaning on the desk. "You may as well lock up, looks pretty slow today. Have you seen Julius around?"

"I have," Raphael said, swallowing the last of his beignet. "He and the Comte left earlier. I don't know where they went but Julius had me make a reservation at Juliana's for seven."

Henley looked at his pocket watch. "Excellent. It's just six now." He took Fiona's hand and headed to the front door. "Go home, Raphael, we'll see you tomorrow."

Ensconced in a small alcove in the bar at Juliana's, they sipped a good Bordeaux and kept an eye on the entrance.

"Your plan?" Fiona sipped her wine. "Mmm. Quite good."

Henley eyed the door. "Greet them as they come through, join them for dinner. I already told the maitre'd we need a more secluded table for four."

"Hopefully it's just the two of them," Fiona said. "I don't think I can handle a dinner with the St. John sisters tonight. They're fun, but tonight I am definitely not."

Just as the words were out of her mouth, the door opened and Julius and Saint Germain made their entrance, ostentatiously as always. It wasn't as though they even tried, it was just their undeniable magic, even when they downplayed it, which was practically never.

"Showtime," Henley said, downing his wine.

"What a lovely coincidence," Julius said, as the four of them were seated in a back booth with curtains for privacy. "Just the people I wanted to see. How's the search going?"

Henley smiled benignly. "Actually, in odd directions, and there's been a wrinkle or two, Julius."

The sommelier appeared before he could elaborate, and they chose wines, then sat through the ritual before the welcome liquid splashed into their glasses. Before conversation could resume, the waiter appeared and regaled them with the evening's menu selections. That done, they watched him depart to the kitchens.

"So, back to the wrinkle?" Julius said finally, staring at Henley. "What could that be?"

Fiona shot Henley a sideways look. They'd agreed beforehand not to bring up anything about their troubles in the last two days, but instead to question Saint Germain, since that was where at least one of the problems had begun."

"To start," Henley said, "no one here has ever heard of Annette Chambord. Perhaps it is because the last time anyone by that name was ever heard of was in France around 1798, according to our research. Did she have a descendant by that name who may have come to New Orleans?"

"How peculiar," Saint Germain said. "I had no idea. Maybe she did and I've been looking for a great-great granddaughter." He seemed amused. "All this time. I've not kept up with history, it seems. Nevertheless, the book I'm searching for could be in her possession if that is true. From the information I've received, that is somewhat likely. But, that it is here is beyond question. I can sense it."

Julius was silent, so Fiona joined in. "Possibly so. However, here's an odd pleat to that wrinkle. Why is the Cassini Brotherhood interested in us, based upon the fact that we are looking for her?"

At her words, Saint Germain's face, always somewhat pale, went as white as the linen tablecloth and silence reigned over the table for a moment or two. Julius became still as a marble statue. Henley and Fiona exchanged knowing glances.

"What did you say?" Saint Germain managed, taking a small sip of his wine.

"The Cassini Brotherhood," Fiona repeated. "They're here, and not for Henley and me. We are not people to excite their interest." She stared at Saint Germain. "Unless we are asking questions about someone that interests them, say one Annette Chambord?"

Julius put his hand on the Comte's arm but he shrugged it off.

"Excuse me," said Saint Germain, "I must refresh myself." He slid his chair back and vanished into the nether regions of Juliana's.

Julius watched him go, and then turned his focus to Henley and Fiona. "You must be careful what you say, my dears. He is my oldest friend and I dislike seeing him upset. What is this Cassini nonsense? You mentioned this before but everyone knows they are a Catholic myth."

"They are not," Fiona said, "and no one knows Catholic fairy tales like I do. That was a story I heard as a child but a few days ago, Julius, we actually encountered one of them. Oddly enough, I don't think the Cassini Brotherhood is a myth anymore."

Now it was Julius's turn to grow paler. "If anyone but you two had come up with this nonsense, I would have walked away. How can you be so sure?"

Fiona sighed. It was becoming increasingly difficult to wade through all of the odd incidents of the last week without telling Julius everything they'd experienced but they had to manage to do so for now. How do you tell your benefactor and greatest friend that his old friend was not to be trusted, either by him, Marie Laveau or the Vatican? The short answer was you didn't, at least not until you had more information. Hopefully, either Julius or Saint Germain could supply the answers they needed to make sure that wasn't a viable option.

Saint Germain reappeared, looking somewhat better, just as the waiters arrived with their food, an excellent anecdote to the awkwardness of their earlier conversation. Plates were set, more wine was poured and forks and knives were utilized. Sometimes delectable cuisine took first place and supplanted other troubles. Fiona and Henley did their best, but occasionally the bites of carefully prepared seafood and sauces weren't quite as delicious as they'd been on other evenings. Appetite can be a variable thing.

Conversation was sparse during the meal, and Saint Germain himself pushed away his strawberry compote as the others were enjoying their desserts.

"It is time I was a bit more forthcoming with you," he said. "The Cassinis are here, as far I can determine from what you say, for me. It isn't the first time. They have tracked me around the world countless times in the past but I have eluded them. In a way, this is a good thing, because it means we are close to the item and the person we seek, I think. Or it could be that their goal is simply to find me. At any rate, here we all are."

"You've never told me this," Julius said, frowning. "Why would they look for you?"

Saint Germain stared at him. "Ah, my old friend. It's the book, and now, the elixir. Of that, there will be no more, unless I find Annette. They are determined, I am sure, to make certain both of those things never happen."

He leaned across the table and took Fiona's hand in his. "Please help me. My life and the lives of others depend on this. We must find her, and along with her, the book. Once that is accomplished, your work is done. Despite the Cassinis or any other obstacles in our paths, we must proceed."

"This is about much more than finding some woman," Fiona said, staring into Saint Germain's eyes. She took his hand in hers and squeezed it gently. "Tell me the truth, Comte. All of it."

He smiled, and regret was in his face. The chilly aristocratic façade faded before her eyes. "The truth, my fey little Irishwoman, is that I am 182 years old. That stolen book holds the secret to the last ingredient for the elixir to provide me with more life. Without it, I will die soon. That is the truth."

Julius and Henley sat in their chairs, gazing speechlessly at Saint Germain, but not the fey little Irishwoman.

"I know," Fiona said. "I've known for some time, since the first day you gave me a key to your laboratory and I had time to at least begin to absorb what you had in there. The Cassini Brotherhood consider you to be an abomination but they are deluded fools under the sway of historically even more bigoted deluded fools. I, on the other hand, do not believe in any of that nonsense, having been a victim of it early in my life.

"I believe you are not of their ilk, but instead a man whose life has been one of hedonism, of course, but with no malice in your pleasures. I also think you wanted to test me, as well as Henley, to discover that which has been hidden for so long and allow us to be privy to whatever arcane secrets you possess. It must have been very lonely for you, for all these long years, searching for those you can trust while on the trail of your treacherous mistress, long fled and clever enough to have evaded you for many years.

"More than that, your life has been one full of scientific discoveries and helping others whenever you can, very much unlike the Cassinis and the so-called benevolent Roman Catholic church. We will find your book, Claude-Louis, and we will find Annette Chambord, who I am beginning to suspect does not share your ideologies in any way."

Saint Germain leaned over the table and kissed Fiona's hand, his dark eyes full of gratitude and a genuine fondness.

"You know me like very few others ever have. You have all my gratitude as well as my trust, Fiona. It is not only for myself, but others as well that I have enlisted your help."

He turned to Julius and Henley. "You have both risked your lives and reputations to have aided me thus far and will have my gratitude, which is more than words can express, forever." He smiled, somewhat grimly and held up his wineglass. "Well, forever is a very long time, but as long as I am with you, which I hope is at its least, the latter."

23

An insistent knocking on the bedroom door woke Fiona with the grey light of pre-dawn the only illumination. She nudged Henley. "Go see who that is, would you, love? I'm not decent. If it's Raphael and he's confused, tell him croissants today, not beignets." She rolled over and snuggled into her pillow.

Henley blinked, rubbing his face and strode to the bedroom door. "Who the hell is this? Can a man have no peace?"

He jerked open the door. Daniel Fox looked uncomfortable, but worried. "Sean is waking Julius. There's trouble at the warehouse."

Henley was still half asleep. "What kind of trouble?"

"Some officials with a warrant and some strange people with them. They look like priests," Fox said. "Sean said bring Fiona, too. We'll meet you there."

Henley shook Fiona's shoulder. "Wake up, Irish. Looks like the Cassinis are making a move."

"I heard," she said. "Not a surprise. They're nasty, but clever bastards."

Early morning mist swirled in the breeze from the river as the carriage with Julius, Henley and Fiona pulled up at the warehouse. Saint Germain wisely stayed at Royal Street. Julius was furious. He jumped down from the carriage, his cape flying along with his silvery hair, looking like a veritable Zeus stepping down from Olympus.

"What in hell is going on here?" he demanded. Sean McKean and Daniel Fox, along with the two night guards, stood blocking further entrance to four New Orleans policemen, who didn't look much happier than Julius did. Two black-robed Cassini brothers, similar to the one Fiona had seen on Bourbon Street, stood silently to the side. One of the police officers stepped forward.

"Captain Murphy here, sir. We have a warrant to lock up this facility, pending a hearing with the City Council and Judge Dupree," he said, holding out a piece of paper in a shaking hand.

Julius snatched it up and read it quickly. "This is utter nonsense. 'Suspicion of illegal importation of religious items'? Of what religion might that be, may I ask? And who's suspicion would that be?"

Murphy's voice was as unsteady as his hand. "I don't know that, sir. I'm just following orders."

"This could be a very bad day for you, Captain Murphy, because I have no intention of allowing you and your men or," Julius glanced over at the two priests, "and whoever those ghouls are, locking up anything, especially my warehouse. Go away and take this with you." He shoved the paper back into the policeman's hand.

At this point, Sean and Daniel had stealthily drawn their pistols, as had Henley, all of them staring at Julius, awaiting his orders. Fiona touched Julius's arm. It was far too early for this shit and she was getting thoroughly irritated. Getting rid of six bodies before breakfast wasn't in her plans for the day. Men were always so quick to resort to the worst choices.

"Gentlemen. Surely there must be a way to resolve this without unnecessary bloodshed." She glanced over at the two priests, who hadn't moved but their eyes were gleaming with the anticipation of victory, foolish as that was. "What is it you wish to do, Captain Murphy? Surely your orders didn't involve dragging us out of our beds at this hour with this ridiculous order?"

Murphy flushed. "Apologies, ma'am. We were told by the City Council, working with the Archdiocese, that this was a crucial and dangerous mission and to waste no time."

Fiona smiled. "I understand, Captain. However, I believe you and your men have been misled. Perhaps we can resolve this mistake later this morning with more information and a visit to the City Council. What would satisfy you now?"

Murphy, clearly charmed, looking both chastened and relieved. "Yes, ma'am, perhaps that would be best."

Fiona reached over and took the paper from his hand. "Indeed. Why don't you and your entourage go back to your offices and we'll resolve this with our lawyers and the Council later today? That would seem to be a more fortuitous choice than to continue this confrontation. We are hardly violent criminals on the run, after all." She never took her hand from the pistol in her pocket.

"Yes, ma'am." Murphy turned to his men and the four of them marched quickly away. The two Cassini brothers didn't move a muscle. Julius turned to them.

"As for you two vultures and all the rest of your unholy cohorts," he said. "Don't ever interfere with me again. I've always loved shooting blackbirds out of trees, they make such good targets."

One of them glided forward, seeming to move soundlessly.

"You would do well to hold your temper, Julius DeMonte. This is just the beginning. You harbor an abomination and we will succeed in our mission. We always do, one way or another and we are no strangers to violence when it comes to God's work, because we are blessed. You are all damned."

Julius laughed. "Get out of my sight before I shoot you both and dump you into the river, if she'll be so kind as to have you. I suspect not even the alligators would relish a taste of your putrid flesh."

Daniel Fox shot at a bush close to the Cassini's foot and they both melted away into the pre-dawn mist.

Julius sighed. "Christ Jesus, these idiots. Back to business, my dears. I fear we haven't seen the last of those horrors. Feel free to shoot on sight when we do. They are much more dangerous than the police or any political nob that may interfere with us. I don't think God will mind in the least."

They climbed back into the carriage, while Sean and Daniel stayed at the warehouse. As the horses pulled away, Julius put his hands on Fiona's shoulders. "Thank you, my fierce one. You have such an affinity for knowing the right words to say. I have to take some credit for that, having tutored the best actress I've ever worked with." He kissed her gently on the cheek.

"I wasn't acting," Fiona said. "But I do give you credit for refining my stage presence. Next act, the courthouse, but that's all you and James Lebrun, Esquire. Hope your lawyer likes getting disturbed at breakfast. For me, I'm back to bed," she put her arm through Henley's and put her head on his shoulder, "or at least a bun and some coffee."

∽

FIONA WAS in her office going over old files when Julius and Henley returned mid-afternoon. Julius was clearly grumpy, slamming the door shut and throwing himself into one of the big leather chairs beside the desk. Henley eyed him and went to the small bar, returning with two whiskies, one of which he handed to Julius.

"Well?" Fiona said. "Are we sailing the glorious Queen upriver or did you work things out with the judge?"

"Quite the comedienne, aren't you?" Julius downed his whiskey and held the glass out to Henley. "The Cassinis got to that pompous little shit Montell, big friend of the church that he purports to be. I'll never know how much money changed hands, from Rome to the Archbishop to Montell, but it was obviously more than my contributions, which have now had to grow considerably larger and include a judge and likely some tawdry painted effigy of some nameless tortured saint for the Cathedral. Christ, these people."

He sighed. "Suffice it to say, all is well. For now. The case was dismissed for lack of evidence, because there isn't any. The message, however, was delivered. The Cassinis want Saint Germain, and probably the Chambord woman, wherever the hell she is, and we are in the way."

"Have you talked to Saint Germain about this, Julius?" Fiona said. "I can understand not wanting to incite more fervor in the Cassinis, but he should know."

"Of course I have, Fiona." He sipped his whiskey. "Because it's really all about him and that damned Chambord woman. No point in beating him about the head with it that I can see. Besides, one look at him and those two black-frocked idiots would have just made matters worse."

"Today we won," Henley said, handing Julius another whiskey. "They will try again, we can be certain of that."

"Definitely," Julius said. "I had Daniel send word to his people that we need men, and Sean went over to the Channel to recruit some old Irish friends of his. They want a battle, those black-frocked bastards, believe me, they'll get one."

"Another thing," Henley said, looking at Fiona who had sat

wordlessly through this. "Do not argue with me on this, Irish. You are amazing, a treasure to all of us, particularly me," he smiled but there was no mirth in his eyes, "but you are a woman, and more vulnerable to physical harm than we are."

Julius snorted into his whiskey and untied his cravat. "Christ Jesus, Henley. You are going about this entirely the wrong way. Fiona is a huntress, if you've somehow missed that. She's Boudicca, and she could take out both of us in a heartbeat." He finished his whiskey again. "You are not thinking with your brain, but your heart. Of course, we'll protect you, darling," he said to Fiona, "and make sure you're safe from," he glanced up at Henley, "was that 'physical harm'?"

Henley flushed, and finished his own whiskey. "Yes, and don't mock me, Julius. This isn't the day for it, is it?"

"Probably not," Julius said. "Apologies."

Fiona sat wordlessly through all of this. While she adored both of them, this conversation was annoying. She wasn't some doll with magical powers, she was a woman who had been forced to learn how to take care of herself in a society of wolves, mostly men, whether in Ireland, New York, on the river, or here in New Orleans, and she'd learned those lessons well.

The people she'd done away with, from New York to now, had only been self-defense or in retaliation to those who deserved it and she had no qualms or misgivings about protecting herself or those she cared about. That wasn't going to change now, especially with adversaries like the Church and its despicable minions, and whoever was enslaving and murdering black people upriver. She and Henley hadn't divulged any of that problem to Julius or Saint Germain yet although that it was connected somehow, she had little doubt. From today on, she knew only this: they were at war, she was a part of it, and they would win.

She stood up. "Stop quibbling, you two. I don't want to hear another damn word. Get Saint Germain, wherever he is. We are going down to the docks and having fresh shrimp and crawfish etouffee and all the gin and absinthe we can stomach, with Sean and Daniel guarding over us, if you're so worried. Tomorrow we strategize, but tonight we bond together, as we should've done from the start. Nothing can defeat us then."

24

Ruby Green lay back on her pallet, bone-tired but as often happened, reluctant to let sleep overtake her. It was only these few minutes of quiet before consciousness faded that allowed her to think logically about how to get her and Samuel out of this mess they'd stumbled into many months ago. She could still hear the sounds of the frogs croaking through the thin board walls that separated the old slave quarters from the laboratory, as the Frenchwoman called it. Hell would have been a better name for it.

They'd been looking for work, first in Mobile, then moving on, leaving the children in their grandmother's capable hands. They weren't alone. Many others, both black and white, were doing the same, but good-paying jobs were hard to come by in the South these days. Samuel's brother had left for Chicago, but they didn't want to go north. Not unless they'd exhausted every possibility in the South, the place they perversely loved and hated, even though it had never been kind to those with dark skin.

They first saw the advertisement in the Biloxi newspaper. Unlike many others, both Ruby and Samuel could read well,

Ruby having been taught by her mother, a privileged lady's maid, and she had in turn taught Samuel after they married. It had seemed a blessing, but had turned out to be the instrument of their doom. Roadworn as they both were, Ruby was aware they both looked as attractive as they always had, which also had its good and bad sides, some employers wanting more than just work from one or the either of them. The ad sounded too good to be true, as Samuel had said at first. High wages, housing and all in all a great opportunity with a growing business. Unfortunately, it was in Louisiana, a place neither of them had ever been. Still, Ruby saved the now much-thumbed paper in her pocket. Weeks later with still no jobs from Alabama to Mississippi, they decided to brave Louisiana and visit the farm that had left the advertisement, in hopes they were still hiring. They had grown desperate.

On the way, they took short term jobs – planting, harvesting, cooking, cleaning and painting, but nothing evolved into anything permanent and soon they were back on the road, heading west once more.

Following the directions in the old advertisement, they came to the meandering river road that followed the Mississippi. From there, the way seemed a little vague, the ad only said "turn west at the two black stone pillars" but they hadn't seen any. Just as they were ready to give up for the day and make camp, they spied two dark pillars nearly overgrown with vines, and turned into a lane shaded by trees that led forward through green fields.

"This is one pretty place," Ruby said, and Samuel agreed it certainly was. Still, it was after a mile or so they glimpsed a large house in the distance with a white sign that read "Fairhaven". Other buildings could be seen further on and somehow it seemed to beckon a welcome to those looking for just that – a fair haven.

Once they walked closer and the house came into view in

detail, it seemed the old mansion wasn't quite as well kept as the fields that surrounded it, but that was typical of many of the majestic old plantation houses. Many were no longer standing at all, while others were half burned. Since the war, that former architectural glory was difficult to maintain, for many reasons. Perhaps it was never meant to be, Ruby often thought, and now the people and places of such temporary grandeur were being reduced to the reality they had fought against for so long. Still, the place was hardly falling down, simply in need of a good coat of paint, at least on the outside.

Samuel knocked on the front door and within seconds, a pretty black woman answered the door, wiping her hands on her apron.

"Hello," she said. "How may I help you?"

"We don't mean to disturb you, ma'am," Samuel smiled. "We've come about the advertisement we saw where you lookin' for workers."

"Of course," she said, but the light in her eyes dimmed briefly. "Please come in and have a seat in the parlor. I'll alert the mistress."

Well. This sure was a friendly place and the first time they'd ever been invited into the big house, rather than directed to the back door, the kitchen or the barn. Ruby smiled at Samuel and he nudged her with his elbow, his brown eyes sparkling. "I'm thinkin' it was worth the trip, wife." Ruby couldn't disagree. Their luck was finally changing.

They were directed to a sofa and sank gratefully down on the soft cushions, glad to be off their feet. Ruby glanced around. The interior was markedly different than the shabby façade. A double staircase swept up to the upper floors, a crystal chandelier gleamed in the middle of the entry hall's high ceiling, and paintings in golden frames hung from the walls. A marble fireplace with a small fire warmed the elegant parlor and fresh flowers, their sweet scents perfuming the air, stood in vases everywhere in both of the rooms they'd seen. The house was large but they could hear the faint sounds of a piano, a violin and it sounded like someone singing. Ruby felt warmed by that for surely that was a sign of cultured and kind people. Music always did that for her.

Within minutes, a woman swept into the room, her blonde hair in an elaborate upswept hairdo, her satin gown embroidered with tiny blue flowers and delicate green vines, a smile on her pretty face as she held out her hands to both of them. "So happy to see you both but we don't often get a couple, especially such a good-looking one. We so need workers like you, and I'm very glad you're here." She had a faint accent but one Ruby had never heard before.

A younger blonde woman came in with a silver tray bearing a teapot, cups and saucers, even a tray of sugared pastries, and set it down on the table. She poured two cups of tea and handed them to Ruby and Samuel, the enticing aroma of hibiscus filling their senses. "Enjoy."

The next time Ruby opened her eyes, she was lying on the same pallet she was trying to fall asleep on now. The same blonde girl stood over her, but the smile was as non-existent as the tea tray.

"It's time for assessments. We always do these with the new ones. Some of you have hidden talents and Madame detests wasting resources. Get up."

RUBY HADN'T SEEN Samuel for some weeks, since she'd been kept busy in the kitchens and off warehouse duty. They hadn't had a moment alone since the night they arrived at Fairhaven, but for a while they'd caught glimpses of each other now and then, since she worked at the big house and he the laboratory, a far better fate than many of the others who had become prisoners at this place. Rumors abounded on those others, but no one knew what became of them. Those seconds of reassurance when she glimpsed her husband were the tiny threads she clung to, but she was becoming despondent.

Assessments had shown that she and Samuel were well educated in comparison to most of their peers, which delighted Madame. They could read, write, knew mathematics and even, in Samuel's case, knew some basic science, from his time working for a doctor who had his own pharmacy. Ruby was also an accomplished cook and Madame was thrilled when Ruby pored over the kitchen cookbooks and produced a dinner which she declared "fit for Marie Antoinette", whoever that was. From that day on, Ruby ran the kitchen, although she slept in the slave quarters, not the house. Even though she heard faint comings and goings, she was not allowed further access into the big house, only the kitchens and pantries.

Every once in a while, over the noise of the boiling pots or the water rushing into the sinks, she thought she heard the piano again. She yearned to hear more, but she'd learned the rules the hard way, and the hallways off the kitchen were not for her, only the door to the back. That was the least of her problems.

Samuel was less fortunate, which Ruby knew because she was sometimes delegated to bring food to the warehouse and the laboratory workers. The place was a nightmare, but she didn't mind the chore because it was her only opportunity to occasionally see Samuel. The old barn had been refitted into a workroom, factory, and Madame's laboratory. There was a warehouse as well, full of boxes and crates that she shipped all over the country, or so she said.

Madame called herself a botanist by training, also a scientist and an aristocrat, a refined woman of culture, great learning and curiosity. She grew many different varieties of herbs and plants in the big gardens and greenhouses of Fairhaven, and processed them all right in this barn, the long worktables full of strange equipment, crucibles, glass tubings and containers, all manner of minerals and chemicals, things Ruby could never have imagined she'd see. Some of the smells that came out of the place were gut-churning. But worse things than smells were happening in there.

There were animals - dogs, cats, foxes and stoats trapped in wire cages, snakes, lizards and frogs housed in large glass boxes, and the strange fish that lived in a huge aquarium at the north end of the barn. The second time Ruby had been sent there, Madame herself was seated at a worktable, the sharp smell of ether emanating from a small furry dog that lay unconscious before her. Blood spurted as she cut into the dog's brain, pooling on the table. Ruby gasped as she set down one of the trays and Madame looked up at her and frowned.

"Don't be coming in here unless you are quiet. This is delicate work. I cannot be distracted by some ignorant darky. Get out."

Ruby was only too glad to do so. She hated the place, but it was her only chance to catch a glimpse of her husband. After that, she steeled herself to look away from the atrocities she saw and remain blank-faced and silent as she witnessed more of the creatures being killed or tortured in a variety of different ways, dying from experiments with chemical concoctions or vile surgeries.

One day Ruby saw Samuel and two other men, all outfitted in strange leather gloves, catch some of the yellow frogs in another tank with a long barbed spear and put them in a roasting oven, and another time spear and grab some of the odd ugly fish from the aquarium. The fish would puff themselves up to twice their size to try and evade the spears but eventually they succumbed. Every time she left the place, she was dizzy with nausea at the things she saw, heard and smelled and she had to take a dozen deep breaths before she could make her way back to the house. Fairhaven was a haven only of horrors. While the barn was terrible, she and Samuel were both alive. It was the discovery of the rest of it that was the worst of all.

The slave quarters at Fairhaven were made up of two dozen clapboard cabins, with leaky roofs and plank floors. Ruby slept in the one closest to the house with four other women who worked in the house, and they had use of a washroom lean-to and laundry area. It was always quiet at night out there, only the sounds of the crickets and the whoosh of the bats on their hunting. The white overseer, and some of his trusted men, had quarters over by the stables, and were rarely seen. The women didn't talk much, as they feared someone was always listening, certainly during the day and even at night, whispering to themselves in their cabin, because Madame seemed to know everything. They were convinced she was a sorcerer or a witch of some kind, but were afraid to voice that more than once even in the quietest whisper.

In truth, Ruby was pretty sure it was the two young blonde women, that she suspected were Madame's daughters, who were always slithering around and spying on them. One was called Mistress Yvonne, and the other Monique and both were equally unpleasant. Punishments for the slightest infractions were severe, and swiftly delivered with the two small leather whips the girls carried at all times. They seemed to thoroughly enjoy enacting their punishments. Ruby had felt their sting more than once, as had they all.

Infringements of the rules were dealt with in beatings and slaps but the threats of what would happen to any of them if they tried to leave the place or even venture further into the house were appalling. Not only the threats of worse whippings, but having their Achilles' tendons cut, being raped repeatedly, and the most bone-chilling of all, being put into a wire cage in the barn, to be experimented upon like the other innocent animals housed there were warnings that terrified them all, trying not to scream when their nightmares woke them in the gloom of their small cabin. All the women had talked of escaping in fervent whispers at night in their cabin, but everyone was so terrified of the consequences should they fail, that none of them had ever tried.

The night Ruby woke to the sound of many feet shuffling past their door, she sat straight up on her thin mattress, straining for more. It sounded like a lot of people, and she'd never seen any others, besides the barn and house workers. Of course, she reasoned, there had to be some field workers for all of Madame's crops, but she'd never noticed any, likely an oversight on her part. She'd come to think there were no crops, just the gardens full of herbs. Still, frightened but curious, she inched open the door.

A large group of black men was passing by, guided by two other men carrying torches. It was eerily quiet - no whispers, coughs, sneezes or even heavy breathing that she could discern. There must have been at least fifty of them, barefoot and their clothes ragged on their bony frames. They faded into the night on their silent journey towards the end of the slave cabins and into the dark fields.

Ruby carefully shut the door, and just as she did, a voice she knew well spoke softly in what seemed only inches from her ear. She nearly jumped out of her skin but instead looked through a knothole in the board beside the door.

"Skeet, will we have to cull soon, you think?" It was Madame, not a voice Ruby would ever mistake.

Skeet Rawlins, the overseer, took a hefty pull on his cigar, the smoke nearly making Ruby cough as it wafted into the many holes in the walls of the cabin. They hadn't been built for comfort. "I been watchin' them boys close, and I think you're right, ma'am. I figger we got one more night on this crew and then it's sleepytime fer good."

"I thought so. Still, we have two more working, and one almost ready to go. Business is good, though, so it may be time to do some more advertising in the newspapers. Maybe go as far as Arkansas or Texas this time. There's people hungry for work all over.

"You'll get the usual bonus, Skeet, after the cull. You're so valuable to me. I don't know what I'd do without you."

"Thankee, ma'am. I never knew I'd be so lucky to find myself workin' for a countess, and a *caplata* at that. Whatever you need, I'm your man."

"Oh, I am quite sure of that, Skeet. You're quite a man indeed. One more thing. Have you heard any more about Jacque LaSalle and him and those others in his planters' association stirring up rumors about our boys?"

"That bastard," Skeet said, spitting out likely some loose tobacco. "The Colonel's got a big mouth on him. He even come around pestering Aunt Verna, but she knows what's good for her and she sent him on his way. Then there was those two that came into the other place we got, further up, one of them a damned woman. She shot poor Clyde in the shoulder right on the damn porch, and killed Gus Watson before he got off a shot. We had people lookin' for them two, but there's not been a word. My guess is LaSalle was harboring 'em. I got no idee where they come from, those two."

"Hmm. That bears more looking into, Skeet," Madame said. "Lately there's been too many people doing too much talking."

"I'll take care of it," Skeet said. "Don't I always take care of things for you?"

"Indeed you do," said Madame. "And so well, too."

The two moved off and Ruby finally took a deep breath. God on his throne, what in the world were these two devils doing to people? It more than likely had to be some poison Madame was cooking up in that cursed laboratory, and what in the world was a 'caplata'? Whatever it was, it didn't sound good.

Ruby knew she had to get herself and Samuel and the others out of here, and to stop it, scared to death or not. She crept back to her pallet, thoughts swirling in her head. It was time she followed her mama's instructions: "Ruby girl, remember this your whole life, no matter what God throws at you, always be brave."

She could almost see her mama's face and smell her comforting scent, one of vanilla, jasmine, and yes, the fried chicken she made better than anyone. She thought of her two girls, knowing they were being held close by their grandmother, and a tear trailed its way down her cheek. She brusquely brushed it away. No time for tears, Ruby Green. You got to think, you ever want to see your man, your mama and those girls again. Get busy.

25

"*Mon amis*! Come, we must celebrate." Jean-Claude St. Clair held up a bottle of champagne. He was standing in the doorway that connected their two business establishments. "I just sold another painting to that horrid Montell man. He thinks it's a Caravaggio, and for $10,000, I did little to dissuade him, of course. For that price he should've known better but I am in the business of art, not hand-holding."

Henley laughed. "I heard he had a windfall recently. Good work, Jean-Claude. That arrogant ass deserves it like no other. You're playing a dangerous game if he ever finds out, though."

Fiona smiled. "I wouldn't worry. The odds are with you on that one. The man's such a toad he'd never hire an art expert to find out and if he did, he'd never tell anyone."

"Exactly." Jean-Claude grinned, popping the cork. "I am an honest man, my friends, and I deal honestly with those who are honest themselves."

Raphael magically appeared with four flutes, the champagne was poured and they took no time in emptying the bottle, even if it was only two o'clock in the afternoon. Not a person in this building adhered to the rules of convention, even young Raphael, an adept learner to both fine wines and fine art.

Fiona and Henley had spent the morning with Julius and Saint Germain in his laboratory, planning their next moves. A dozen new men had been hired, split between Irishmen and Cherokees, and deployed at the moment between the warehouse, on the Queen and two here at their building. There would be no more surprises from the Cassinis or anyone else on those fronts. Henley methodically set out everything they'd learned from their journey up the River Road, and how they suspected Chambord or whatever she was calling herself, could be behind it.

Julius was horrified at the revelation of zombies but Saint Germain, while unhappy, was not shocked. "This has been a practice in other parts of the world many times before, my friends. I am sad it has come to be practiced here. Annette has never been a kind woman but for her to resort to being a part of something like this truly is appalling. She has become ruthless and evil, seeking the control she was privy to in France, by virtue of her birth and her beauty. It is even more reason to find her and stop her from damaging any more people."

It was decided the search for Annette should be their first priority, with a good sized troupe of men. Fiona was definitely not happy about another outing in the carriage, but there it was. This time perhaps she'd just ride a horse, which she preferred. Before Jean-Claude's champagne, she'd been planning to meet with Marie to coordinate and gather any further information on Annette's activities. She waved goodbye to Henley as she opened the door. Of the office.

"Hold on, Irish," he said. "You shouldn't go alone."

She looked at him and patted her thigh, where she had strapped her newly made leather sheath for her razor and held up her reticule for good measure, which held her pistol. "I'm not alone, Hen. Marie and I just need a woman-to-woman chat. You, Julius and Saint Germain all need to stop treating me like I'm a delicate teacup when you know full well I am not."

Henley sighed. "Fine. Just be careful." She knew perfectly well he was going to have someone shadow her, likely Daniel Fox, but she just smiled. There was little point in arguing. Marie had returned and had sent her an invitation this morning. There were lives at stake and they had little time to waste.

The short walk to the shop on Bourbon cleared Fiona's head and Evangeline waved her upstairs with a smile. Marie sat in a brocaded armchair and motioned Fiona to the matching one beside her. Books were stacked on the floor and one was open on Marie's lap.

"Find anything about our problem upriver?"

Marie glanced up at her, shutting the book. "Maybe. I also had a chat with Tante Verna yesterday before I left, which was revealing, more for what she didn't say than what she did. She's clearly frightened, and I've never seen her like that."

"I can tell you when I asked her if she'd ever heard the name Annette, she couldn't wait to get rid of me and Henley. Scared."

"I think I know why," Marie said. "Annette Chambord isn't just some botanist. I think she's a *caplata*. She's behind this whole business, I believe."

"That's a word I've never heard before," Fiona said. "What's a *caplata*?"

"Oh child, it's not a word you ever want to hear," Marie said, "but here we are. A *caplata* is a female Haitian vodou priestess, one who specializes in making zombies, using a poison called tetrodotoxin, which paralyzes its victims, and eventually kills them. I have come to think that's what we're dealing with. More common are *bokors*, male priests, but the feminine variety, from what I've heard, are less often active but even nastier. I am a Louisiana voodoo priestess, as you well know, but never of that evil sort, even though some of my enemies would like to slander me with that name and reputation."

"Christ Jesus," Fiona said softly. "Even though I didn't know what that was, I knew there was something truly nasty going on up there. How do you fight this sort of thing?"

Marie stared directly at her. "You don't fight. You kill her."

"Christ Jesus," Fiona said again, standing up and pacing around her chair, her worst suspicions confirmed. In a way, it was a relief, but in another, it was terrifying.

"Don't panic," Marie said, her voice steady. "We will work together. You will need extra help, because you aren't dealing with just a murderous and evil woman. There are other forces at work, and she is in league with them, be sure of that. So, we must combat this on both the physical and astral plane." She looked at Fiona's face and gave a faint smile. "I can tell you find this incredulous, and that this information is outside of your purview, Fiona Shanahan, but you must trust me. Otherwise, we will fail."

Fiona desperately wished she hadn't drunk that champagne earlier, because it was threatening to make an encore appearance. She sat down, swallowed heavily and took a few deep breaths.

"There is one other complication, and his name is the Comte Saint Germain, but I think you already know more about him than I do. I know there is something…off about the man," Marie said. "To give him some credit, I cannot believe that he is aware of what Annette Chambord has become, but I don't know. I also don't believe Julius would have sent you and Henley on her trail if he had any inkling of what you might find," Marie said.

"Nor do I," Fiona said. "But Julius knows about Saint Germain, at least now, as do Henley and I." It was way past time for secrets, as dangerous as they might be. Marie deserved to know the truth.

Fiona grasped both the upholstered arms of the chair, her fingers digging into the heavy fabric and leaned forward. "Claude-Louis Saint Germain is no ordinary man, as you have suspected. He is 182 years old, Marie. Annette Chambord is his former mistress and many years ago, stole a book from Saint Germain that he must have to continue to survive, as it contains the secret ingredients to an elixir that prolongs life, one that he discovered. It would seem that Annette has re-created it."

It was Marie's turn to be shocked, which wasn't an everyday event in the life of the New Orleans voodoo queen. She was genuinely speechless for a few seconds, gazing silently at Fiona.

Fiona took her hand. "He is not evil, Marie. He is a scientist who has let his secrets fall into the wrong hands. He wants nothing more than to repair the unwitting damage he has done by allowing her access to his work. Annette Chambord stole his ancient book and has been using it to gain power for many years. He has been in search of her for a very long time, knowing what she could become. He wants only to stop her in any way he can."

Marie closed her eyes. "Oh cher, we have work ahead of us. But now, I understand much more."

Fiona could not disagree. "Indeed we do. There has been another development." She related the Cassini Brotherhood's attempt to seize Julius's warehouse and how he thwarted it for now. Marie listened intently and shook her head.

"So, we are at war on two fronts, it seems, all stemming from Saint Germain and that infernal book, whether he meant to bring his needs here or not. It is the Chambord woman who is the cause of all of our troubles and Saint Germain is not responsible for what she has become.

"The Cassini zealots are annoying, but not dangerous at the moment. The poor souls that Chambord has claimed must be our first focus. Once she is found and dealt with, Saint Germain's problems will be over as well. I may have misjudged the man, but he is not as we are, Fiona. Do not forget that. Let's all meet as soon as possible, perhaps tonight. We must coordinate and waste little time in doing so. Can you do that?"

"Of course," Fiona said, rising from her chair. "I will send word."

Twilight was falling as she left the voodoo shop. Fiona hurried down Bourbon Street, anxious to talk to Henley and the others. Just as she turned the corner onto Royal, a street urchin crouched in her path, tears running down his bloodied face.

"Please, miss, you must help me," he cried. "Ruffians have taken my sister."

She could hardly go on her way and leave the child in his distress. She knelt beside him and took his hand. "Where did they go?"

He peered up at her, his smile malicious. "Somewhere nice, I bet. Unlike you."

Those were the last words Fiona remembered before a burlap sack was put over her head, that and the cloying smell of ether before everything went dark.

FIONA OPENED HER EYES, but could discern nothing in the darkness of the place where she lay on a cold stone floor. There was no longer a sack over her face, which was good because the champagne finally decided to make its sophomore debut. She sat up, wiping the drops of slime from her chin, her head still whirling. She quickly felt for her reticule, but of course it was gone. She did have other assets. She pulled up her skirts to unclasp the sheath on her leg, only to find it was as empty as her current prospects. *For one who thinks she's so clever and well prepared, Fiona Shanahan,* she thought, *you have been a very foolish woman.* Her eyes closed, and she fell back onto the floor, its coolness a welcome relief to her fevered face.

The next time she woke, it was the bells. The very walls and floor seemed to tremble with the cacophony of sound, and Fiona knew it was the Cathedral bells, since she only lived two blocks away and had learned to live with their constancy, but never this close. She was nearly afraid to move or open her eyes, but the nausea had passed, leaving behind a throbbing headache, so she sat up, prepared to meet the same blackness, but it was not so. A candle flickered on a wooden table, and two men in the long cassocks of the Cassini Brotherhood sat on each side of it, staring wordlessly at her. It was a small room, the walls looked to be earthen, roughly plastered, and a door with iron bars was set in one wall. A jug of water and a glass sat on the table. One of them pulled out a third chair, motioning her to it. She didn't give a damn for the chair, but she needed that water. She took her seat heavily, dizzier than she'd expected, poured the water and refilled it again. She set the glass down.

"So there are crypts underneath the Cathedral, then. I've always thought so. Your sort loves that clandestine kind of thing."

The two priests exchanged a glance, somewhat taken aback.

"Not up for a chat?" Fiona said, and poured another water. "That's unfortunate, you nasty vultures, because I want to know what in all that's holy you thought you were going to accomplish by putting me down here. You have just made a big fucking mistake."

This time they looked alarmed, especially the younger one, who flinched. The older one frowned at his fellow and turned to her, his eyes filled with hatred.

"Woman, you must learn when it is your turn to speak. Due to the filth that comes from your mouth, I know you for a witch. We know how to deal with witches."

Before she could react, he grabbed her hand and held it over the bright candle flame in an iron grip. There was little point in struggling. She knew he would release her when he'd made his point. She waited it out with no reaction because she knew he wanted one and that was never going to happen, but it hurt, a lot. This was a man who truly hated women, and perhaps everyone else. After about a minute, he threw her hand back in her lap, the skin blistered and sizzling. He stared at her, a faint smile on his lips.

"What's next, drowning?" Fiona said. "Good thing the River Styx isn't down here on this hallowed ground." She spit in his face. "You imbeciles in your ball gowns would sink and I'd float."

What was next was a backhand and she fell out of the chair. She never did know when to keep her mouth shut. Well.

The younger one helped her up, clearly not pleased with his superior. "Father Martine, these actions are uncalled for."

Father Martine didn't agree. "I am in charge here, Gregor, and I will deal with this as I see fit." He coughed. "I did lose myself for a second there but God will understand."

"I doubt that, and I can assure you that I won't," Fiona said. "Once again, what do you want with me?"

Father Martine gave her a scathing glance. "It isn't you we want, witch. It's Saint Germain, of course. You are nothing but a means to an end." He stood up, taking the candle with him. "Come, Gregor. We have work to do."

They walked to the barred doorway, opened it, and locked it again from the other side, leaving her in inky darkness as their footsteps died away. Fiona felt carefully for the water pitcher and poured some of the cool water onto her hand, wincing. She was simmering with anger and pain, but there was little she could do about either of those things at the moment, except prepare for their next visit. Hopefully the bastards weren't going to leave her down here to rot. Damn, her hand hurt.

Her fingers slipped into the neckline of the dress she'd chosen for the day, untying the silk ribbons of the corset she'd decided to wear, just in case. She pulled out her slim pearl-handled straight razor from its carefully concealed resting place inside the center boning of the corset. It rested in her hand, an old familiar friend, before she slipped it into the pocket of her skirt.

She was eager for another chat with the Cassinis and her old sharp friend was keen with anticipation as well.

26

Saint Germain stood up and began pacing throughout the office, around the desk and the leather chairs that held Julius and Henley, and turning at the bookcase, resumed his steps. His face, as usual, was composed and emotionless but his actions belied that façade. He smoothed his waistcoat, impeccable as always, glancing at the darkness beyond the window. They'd been continuing to hatch plans for their foray upriver all afternoon. It had been tedious, but necessary.

"She should've been back long before now. Something's amiss," Saint Germain said, stopping before the desk and facing the other two. "I'm sure Laveau is a knowledgeable woman but not quite this entertaining."

Henley bristled a bit. "I sent Daniel Fox to follow her so I've not been concerned. That said, he's a clever fellow, but to be honest, I should've gone myself. I was afraid Fiona would make me before she'd gone two blocks. That woman has a sixth sense, and we all know that."

"That doesn't mean she's impervious to danger," Julius said, rising from his chair. "I have to agree with Claude-Louis, and no blame to you or any of us, Henley. It is late. We should've been more conscious of the passing time."

The heavy door to the office was thrown open, banging off the wood-paneled wall. Nico, Fiona's pet street urchin, stood before them in all his slight raggedy glory, eyes blazing. "They took her, you idiots."

Henley moved as swiftly as he was known to do and grabbed Nico by his scruffy collar. "What the hell do you know, brat?"

Nico angrily shook him off. "More than you. The man you had following her is out cold in the alley on St. Charles but I don't know who did him in, it happened so fast. What I do know is this: I was down the block when I saw her stop to help this little ruffian I know of who will do anything for a few dollars, pretending to be in distress in front of her on the sidewalk. She crouched down, kind soul that she is, and before I could run to warn her, the next thing I knew, she was grabbed and spirited away by someone in a fast carriage."

Julius took Nico's arm and sat him down in a deskside chair. "Don't run, my man. We appreciate you and it was brave of you to come here, and a good thing you did." He glanced up at Henley and shook his head almost imperceptibly. "A brandy, perhaps?"

Nico looked at Julius as though he was gazing at a god and settled into the soft chair. "That'd be lovely, gov."

Henley refrained from rolling his eyes because he'd been susceptible to Julius's ways himself, or he wouldn't be here in New Orleans at this moment himself, but back in some New York police precinct unhappily taking bribes from city councilmen. He'd been lucky enough to make the right choice. Maybe the brat would too.

Nico accepted the brandy snifter from Julius, wide-eyed. He took a sip and coughed. The little imp had likely never had such a drink, Henley surmised. Julius sat down beside him.

"Sometimes things happen so quickly that we can hardly take it in at the time," Julius said. "However, when we think back, calm ourselves and even close our eyes, we remember things we may not have noticed during the event. Do you know what I mean?"

Nico nodded and sipped a bit more brandy. "Think I do, gov."

"Good. Let's try that very thing, shall we? Lean back, close your eyes and play the whole incident before your eyes, like you were watching one of my stage plays. I'll walk you through it as best I can. Breathe easily. You are safe here."

Julius's voice was soft and soothing, and Nico did as was suggested. "So, you were down the street, having discovered our man unconscious in the alley when...."

Nico took up the narrative, his diction slow. "I looked up and saw Miss Fiona down the block, bending over to help that nasty Jemison...a carriage pulled up beside them....yes, I remember more now. A man in a dress put a bag over her head and picked her up. He put her into the carriage and then jumped in himself and off they went. There was another man at the reins."

Nico opened his eyes. "He had a funny-lookin' hat on, he did, and I couldn't get a good look at his face, 'cause o' that, you see."

Julius smiled. "Excellent, Nico. Tell me more about his 'dress', as you call it. Was it black?"

"Yessir, it was. What sort of man walks around in a dress? Me old mum would've throttled me goin' out on the street like that."

Julius laughed, Henley smiled and even Saint Germain's lips twitched. It was the first hint of humor they'd had all day and it was relieving.

"Never spent much time in church, have you, lad?" Henley said. "Which is just as well, you ask me."

"Nah, they have some peculiar ways." He polished off the brandy. "Me mates have told me stories about them creepy bastards." He looked at the three men before him. "Did I help?"

"Very much so," Henley said. "I'll tell Raphael to be sure to get extra beignets from now on. You've earned them."

Nico grinned. "Thankee, sir. I usually steal one anyway. Raphael's a bit slow, but that'll save us both some time."

"Off you go." Julius chuckled, standing up and holding out his hand. "We are going to find Miss Fiona, Nico. You've been quite an asset. I have a feeling you might make a good investigator, and I'm always interested in raw talent. Take care."

Nico wobbled just a trifle as he made for the door. "Tell Miss Fiona I love her and I'll see her soon." Realizing what he'd said, he blushed, clearly visible under the grime, he scurried out the door, nearly colliding with a surprised Raphael, who was still there, obviously waiting for Fiona to return. He carried an envelope in his hand.

"What are you doing here?" Raphael said, but Nico was gone before he uttered the last word.

"He's fine, Raphael," Henley said. "Let him be from now on. What's that?"

"Some little ruffian just delivered it." He handed the envelope over. Henley ripped it open and read the enclosed note aloud.

"If you ever want to see your witch again, we will trade her for the abomination known as Comte de Saint Germain. Be at your warehouse at ten tonight or she will be with God."

There was no signature, but they already knew who it was from, thanks to Nico.

Saint Germain sighed and held up an elegant finger. "Abomination here. There is no point in waiting until their ten o'clock deadline, because I know where Fiona is, along with our Cassinis. If you're willing, gentlemen, let us retrieve her now."

Henley eyed him suspiciously. "How could you possibly know where she is?"

"Because I know how these cowardly bastards think and who they work for." Saint Germain said. "This is far from the first time we've had our run-ins. You must remember there is only one place where they will be met with appreciation, welcomed, and housed. Here, it is your St. Louis Cathedral, likely the archbishop's guest quarters, and if they are hiding someone, it will be in the crypts under the basilica floor."

Henley wasn't ready to give up yet. "There are no crypts under the cathedral floor. This is New Orleans, we place our dead above ground."

"You are mistaken." The Comte's eyes flashed. "Do not doubt me, Michael. I have had the advantage of time to find out more things than you. There is a passageway under the altar."

Julius held up his hands. "Gentlemen. Let us not quibble. Saint Germain is correct. It is not public information, but it is true. Now, let's collect poor Fox and get our rescue party together. The longer we delay, the greater the possibility of more harm coming to Fiona."

Julius pulled a Colt .45 from the cleverly concealed leather holster under his coat, checked that it was loaded, and returned it to its snug resting place. Henley took his own revolver from the desk drawer. Saint Germain merely smiled. There are other weapons than those that shoot.

HER HAND HURT. There was no more water, either to drink or bathe her blistered palm. Fiona was becoming impatient. Whatever these fools wanted, she'd wished they'd get on with it because she needed some of Marie's burn concoctions, and some food wouldn't go amiss either. They'd been gone a long while, although she couldn't be sure. In complete darkness, the mind plays its tricks with time.

A flickering light appeared, outlining the iron bars on the door. The younger Cassini, keys clanking, unlocked the door and came toward her where she sat at the table.

"I brought you more water." He sat the candleholder down, along with a pitcher. His voice was nearly a whisper. "I am sorry for what my brother did to you." He poured her a glassful. "This will all be over soon."

"What were you thinking, to do this?" Fiona gulped down some water. "I've done nothing to you."

He didn't meet her eyes. "That is true, but you consort with the devil's own. Taking you is a means to flush him out. It is God's plan."

Fiona had nothing to say to that. Trying to reason with fanatics was something she'd learned was a futile endeavor a long time ago. She fingered the razor in her pocket just as the barred door opened again and Father Martine strode in, clearly a man on a mission. "Get up, devil's whore. We go to meet your master." He jerked her to her feet.

Fiona had had enough. Wincing, with her burned hand, she swung the stoneware pitcher into Gregor's face. With the other, she grabbed her old friend and slashed upwards at Martine's throat. The light was dim, but they were very close. Martine loomed over her for a few precious seconds, eyes incredulous and hands scrabbling at his throat before falling to the mercies of the unforgiving earthen floor. She stood over him and after a minute, the gurgling stopped while the liquid on the floor pooled outward, black in the candlelight. Gregor lay on the other side of the table, sodden and groaning.

Fiona sank down on the chair, the razor still in her hand. She took a few deep breaths, glancing over at the younger Cassini. Perhaps he'd learn. Perhaps not. Let their God sort it out. She wiped the razor clean on Martine's hassock, pocketed it once again and headed towards the doorway.

She started down the tunnel-like hallway. Stealthy footsteps and another light ahead drove her into an alcove where she huddled in the shadows, scarcely daring to breathe, her hand going to her pocket. As the three men passed, she smelled Henley's familiar cedar soap and stepped out behind them.

"My white knights have arrived, I see."

Henley, Julius and Saint Germain whirled around. Following closely behind them, holding torches, were Sean McKean and Daniel Fox, a bandage on his head. The five of them gaped at her for a second or two until Henley grabbed her up in his arms and held her close.

"Oh god, Fiona."

"He had nothing to do with it," she said. "But I am a little dizzy. It's been a decidedly tiresome day."

"Christ Jesus," Julius said. "Where's the bodies?"

"Oh please," Fiona said. "There's only one. The other will be fine, I'm sure. Death by water pitcher is rare. However, we may have uses for him. He's in the cell back there, rather wet but perhaps worth keeping. Or, you could just lock him in." She held up the iron keys. "I never make hasty decisions."

27

Fiona winced as Henley carefully applied ointment to her burned palm, rewrapping it in gauze as the doctor had shown him the night before. The ointment was from Marie, and it had a clean sharp scent, perhaps of tea tree and other herbs, along with the sweet tang of honey. It was soothing and Marie had assured her the burn would heal without damage if she was diligent about its use. Her face was another matter. The entire right side was a colorful mix of purple, green and yellow but that would likely heal faster than her hand, although it looked worse at the moment.

At Julius and Henley's insistence, she'd spent the day in bed, which truthfully she didn't mind. The floor in her little prison had been cold and hard, and her head still ached a bit from the ether. She had dreams she hadn't had in years, since leaving Ireland and her foul husband behind, as well as memories of St. Hilda's which had resurfaced. The beatings, the hours on her knees on a stone floor and the condemnation of the priests, all reminiscent, stemming from the treatment she'd endured at the hands of the Cassinis. As darkness fell, however, she was becoming restless. The need for justice, not just for herself, but those who had fallen prey to Annette and her schemes, woke her from both dreams and nightmares.

She woke to Henley's concerned gaze, his hand brushing her hair from her face. She tried to smile but her face hurt too much.

"I assume you've all been hatching plans while I slept," she said, sitting back on the feather pillows stacked behind her. "What about our driven religious friends?"

"Not to worry, darling. One is fish food, of course, I enjoyed taking care of that. The Mississippi is a welcome mistress. The other is enjoying the hospitality of one of the warehouse storerooms for now. No questions have been asked about their whereabouts and I doubt there will be. Rome may sanction them, but I don't think the Archbishop here knew or would have approved of their activities under his church. If he did, there's not been of whisper of interest from the diocese or any other authority, since the scandal would not benefit them. Julius and the Comte would like to squelch any more Cassini Brotherhood interference, so we're keeping our younger crusader on ice, so to speak, until they decide how to deal with that situation. A little time for silent reflection and penitence may benefit him. Clearly, he's a misguided young man searching in the wrong places for the holy glorification of his soul."

Fiona doubted that but approved of the incarceration. She would've preferred to let him rot in the crypts but this was more humane. Possibly. His fate was yet to be determined, as far as she was concerned. He could've helped her, but he had chosen not to do so. Forgiveness was not high on her list of personality traits.

Henley settled himself on the bed and handed her a crystal flute of champagne, raspberries floating in the bubbles. "We're not celebrating, of course, but I know how you love raspberries, and they don't go as well with gin."

She laughed and it felt good. "Such an epicure you are, love."

"I aim to please." He sipped his own glass of whiskey and gave her a sideways glance. "You're a woman a man needs to keep happy. Sometimes you even scare me. Just a little."

The raspberries were delicious and she rolled one around on her tongue. She swallowed the tidbit and stared at him. "You've known that since the beginning."

"Indeed I have," Henley said. "And I hope it never ends, Irish." He put down his glass and gathered her into his arms.

TWO DAYS HAD PASSED PEACEFULLY, with no news or untoward events but everyone was constantly thinking how to proceed. This evening, their tenuous alliance had gathered in the S&H office, in chairs around the leather-covered conference table: Marie Laveau, Jim Washington, Julius DeMonte, Saint Germain, Henley, and Fiona. Distrust hovered in the air, an unwelcome guest.

Sean McKean and Daniel Fox were keeping watch in the outer reception area with Raphael, who viewed his new colleagues with some trepidation, but kept them supplied with copious amounts of coffee and pastries. Young Raphael longed to be as adept as these men, but he knew it would take time and training to become so. In the meantime, he was intimidated but fascinated by his new companions. Already, he was learning to look at people on the street, in restaurants and anyone who came through the door with different eyes. Naivete was quickly fading, but other than suspicion, he wasn't yet certain what would replace it. Fiona watched him and never ventured a word. This was not a path for everyone.

In the back room, the conversation kept circling around the big question: where exactly was Annette Chambord and how did they find her? They were all agreed she was the engineer of the zombie situation, but she'd kept herself well hidden. Despite the open windows into the courtyard, the air was thick with doubt and frustration.

"For one thing," Saint Germain said, "she's clearly not using her real name. Time has passed, yes," he duly noted Marie Laveau's sideways glance at him, "so I was foolish to send Fiona and Henley on what has proven to be a fool's errand in that regard." He nodded at them both. "My apologies, dear friends. I had no inclination she had sunk to the vile depths she has."

Marie waved her hand with impatience. "As you should be, but let us put that mistake behind us. What is important now is to put a stop to her activities and rescue any that are still worth saving, even under her control."

Julius spread maps of the country north and west along the River Road. "Since this is at least one of the areas in which she has been employing her drugged workers, this is where we need to concentrate."

"We didn't stop at many places on our foray before," Henley said. "Of the two that we are certain of, Hiram's store and the fake farm he directed us to where we were attacked, they only remain as way stations for her activities. I don't believe either of those to be her main establishment. Worth our attention, but the true place where this woman has gone to ground lies elsewhere, although not far, I think, and perhaps disguised as something else."

They all pored over the maps for a few minutes. Fiona was silent, her brain whirling with thoughts, but none of them coalesced into anything useful. She wasn't alone, she knew. After a few minutes, everyone sat back in their chairs.

"This is a needle in a haystack," Julius said. "We need more to go on. I suppose we could go torture your pal Hiram into yielding some information, but that's all the ideas I've got so far. The other option is to take a troupe of men out there and go door to door. We'd need a base and supplies. Perhaps LaSalle would let us invade his privacy, or set up some tents. Unless you could provide accommodations at Le Petit Jardin, Madame." He glanced at Marie.

The voodoo queen looked at him, her eyes filled with disdain. "It is a small effort, my Le Petit Jardin, and a small house. Not many know it even exists, Julius. I cannot have careless white men and their horses trampling my gardens. As much as I respect you, that will not do. Perhaps you should load them all on that big boat you have out there and steam it upriver, eh?"

Christ Jesus. Fiona shoved back her chair and stood up. This extremely tenuous alliance was deteriorating fast.

"Stop this," she said. "Everyone take a moment, please. Perhaps just Henley and I should go upriver again alone and talk to more planters. Jacque LaSalle indicated there are others who are concerned and suspicious. We know more now and won't be stumbling into traps. Maybe take Sean and Daniel with us for added protection." She looked around at each of them. "It is indeed a needle in a haystack, but it gleams with its own malevolence. She is not invisible, just clever. We can find her.

"This time we know what we are looking for, whereas before we were stumbling blindly into dangerous territory, territory we didn't even know existed. Now we understand more, and know what she's doing. She's not magical, simply well-concealed. Rather like the crypts, she's hidden out there, but like them, visible once you know how to look."

Everyone nodded, looking around at the others gathered around the table.

"You are right," Julius said, "as always, Fiona. What a treasure you are, darling. My only objection is putting you in the line of fire again. You are precious to me and all of us and you've already paid a price none of us have yet to endure."

Saint Germain rose and took her hand in his. "If you go, I go with you, Fiona, providing Henley agrees." He bowed in his usual formal style towards him. "I owe you a debt and it's one I must repay."

Before another word could be said, there was a pounding at the door. Sean McKean opened it, another man close behind him. Jacque LaSalle, looking a bit road-weary, shoved him aside and burst into the room.

"Thank god you're all here in one place," he said, "so I don't have to explain more than once. I've brought a woman out there you need to meet. We could both use a whiskey, too."

28

Ruby Green rode bareback, as she'd learned to do as a child, the horse responsive under her hands on the bridle she'd hastily managed to put on him. There hadn't been time for a saddle but she was fine with that, her bare heels urging the stallion into the darkness. She remembered the lane to Fairhaven was a good two miles from the main road but the moon was high, illuminating the track. That was both a blessing and a curse because she could sense the dogs and men behind her, following her scent and silhouette. She urged the stallion on and he responded, his strong legs carrying them forward, likely as glad as she was to leave this foul place.

She'd been planning for days, even stealing a kitchen knife and some matches, but she hadn't come to any conclusions, except for one: that she had to leave and find help if she and Samuel were going to survive. It was only a matter of time before Madame decided otherwise, she made a misstep that was unforgivable in their eyes, or the whole thing blew up, and the former was likelier than the latter. Every night before she fell into a restless sleep, she thought of ways to leave and discarded plan after plan. This night had been different.

Skeet Rawlins and some of his men were talking close to her cabin, their voices rousing her from her troubled dozing.

"Giselle told me earlier this evenin' she ain't feelin' well." Ruby could smell Skeet's usual foul cigar. "So I'm off duty, boys, if you get my meanin'."

Coarse laughter followed. "We surely do, stud. You are one hard-workin' man, Skeet, but a lucky one, come to that," another said. "'Course I'd stand in for you anytime if you needed. She is one sweet piece, she is. Smells like a flower all over, I bet."

"Shut yer fucking mouth, Dupree. I don't like talk like that about my lady, comin' from a no-account like you." There was a sound like a slap.

"I didn't mean nothin', Skeet, swear to god. Just ramblin'."

"All right then. So's I was thinkin' about ridin' over to Baton Rouge, get some entertainment. We're been sitting around too long tonight until we're near out of whiskey and we could stand to resupply."

"Well, hell, Skeet we got quite a bit here, even though we been at it since sundown. Still, better more than less." There was more muffled conversation she couldn't make out. "Saddle up that buckskin mare, Dupree. I'll be back before noon tomorrow. She needs anything before then, tell her I went to check on the boys."

They moved off. Ruby could smell the whiskey from inside the cabin. So Skeet was leaving, and he was the worst threat. Horrid as he was, the rest of them were just as bad, as just as stupid, and now she knew they were drunk. After Skeet left, nobody should be guarding the stables. He was the one that scared her most.

She heard him ride off and waited another half hour, best as she could judge. The men had decamped to their bunkhouse on the other end of the lane. She crept out of the cabin and over to the stables, her bare feet scarcely making a whisper. There were a half dozen or more horses there, but the big bay stallion responded to the slices of apple she'd hidden in her pocket as she usually did. They made a tasty snack if no opportunity presented itself, but tonight was different. He was a beautiful horse, the best choice for speed and strength, both of which she needed. She stroked his nose and ran her hands soothingly onto his flank. She loved horses, always had, and they responded to her in turn. Her father had been the head groom on the plantation where she'd grown up.

"Beauty, you ready for an adventure?"

He whiffed softly and she set the bridle on him, only then unlatching the door and leading him out. She tied the reins to the board on the stall door and went to take the saddle from the rack behind her. Just as her hands lifted the heavy saddle, a man appeared in the doorway.

"What the hell?" He strode in. "What you think you doin', gal?"

She dropped the saddle like it was on fire and whirled around to grab the pitchfork leaning beside the stall. She couldn't back out now. Before he could say another word, she lunged forward and stabbed the tines into him, pinning him into the straw-covered stable floor, the handle wobbling as she jumped back, shocked at what she'd done.

Blood dribbled from his mouth and the wounds in his chest. "You dumb bitch. You'll die for this."

Ruby stood there for a second. She'd never hurt anybody in her life and she didn't like it one bit. But things were not the same.

"I don't think so. Not tonight anyway." She thought about stabbing him again but didn't want to murder the man. He didn't look too good anyway.

She untied the reins and jumped on the stallion's back. She

edged him out of the stable doors and galloped down the lane. Samuel would have to wait. If they had any chance at all, it was solely up to her.

Frightened as she'd ever been in her life, she clung to the stallion, her knees tight, her hands clenched on his mane. She leaned forward over his strong neck and whispered in his ear. "Run, my friend, like you've never run before. Like the devils in hell are chasing us. Because they are."

She still heard them coming closer as she reached the River Road, the one she and Samuel had walked to get to this godforsaken place. She slowed the stallion as they made the turn east, hoping her pursuers would take some time to decide which way she went but even if they split up and there was only one or two, she would be in dire straits if they caught her. She urged the horse forward, even faster now that they were on more solid ground. He responded like a dream, his gait as smooth as the road they ran on, the moon lighting the way. Her heart soared and her blood pounded in rhythm with the creature beneath her, both their freedom denied for too long. For a time, the sounds of pursuit died away and Ruby began to hope.

She had no idea where she was headed, only that New Orleans was east and south and Baton Rouge north. Surely there would be somewhere to go to ground, or some people that would listen to her story and help. She knew it wasn't much of a plan, but it was all she had.

Miles flew by, and Ruby knew the stallion couldn't keep up this pace much longer. She'd have to slow or find a place to hide. There wasn't much cover between the road and the river, and she hadn't seen much habitation, so her options were limited. Unfortunately, she could faintly hear hoofbeats behind her.

The hoofbeats grew louder. She tried to stay calm, but fear threatened to overtake her. If they caught up, they'd likely kill her, especially after the stable incident. Even if they didn't, the punishments that had been described for trying to run were nearly as bad, maybe worse. God, how she hated these monsters.

Foam flecked from the stallion's coat into the wind, and his breathing grew labored. She couldn't let her valiant friend die with her. The road curved closer to the edge of the river and she slowed the horse and turned carefully into the brush and trees toward the water. It wasn't far, only a few hundred yards but screened by trees.

Moonlight gleamed on the ripples, and the stallion was eager for a drink. They reached the bank, and she led him to a shallow spot and slid from his back, holding the reins in her hand as he drank. The sand and gritty pebbles felt good on her feet for a moment but the water was bitter cold.

Refreshed, the stallion raised his head and eyed her, flanks heaving. She could almost read his thoughts. You want to keep going, woman? I've got a little more, he seemed to say. She stroked his neck.

"Not tonight, my friend. You've done me proud and I hope to meet you again. I'm going to leave you here for a bit and go on best I can." She tied the reins loosely to a bush beside the bank. "I'm going a different way for now."

She heard riders pass out on the road but the stallion didn't make a sound, seeming to know he should be hidden for a time, rather than communicate with others of his tribe. Ruby waded into the water, the current as strong as she figured the Mississippi would be. She pushed the log she'd found on the bank in front of her and wrapped her arms around it, legs pushing and feet paddling as she made her way downstream. The water took her, the current strong even close to the bank, and she didn't want to go further out. This river was so wide she couldn't make out the other bank. It was also much colder than she'd anticipated, and before much time had passed, she could no longer feel her legs and feet but she kept moving them anyway.

As the dawn broke, the river rippled and glittered like it was sprinkled with gold in the rising sun. That, and the water she swallowed, woke her, arms still clinging to the log she'd found. She choked, spluttered and looked around. Her side of the riverbank was some distance away, although not so far she couldn't swim to it if the current wasn't too strong. Lord, her arms hurt. In truth, everything hurt, but that was a good thing because it meant she wasn't dead yet. She couldn't see any men or horses on the riverbank so she turned the log towards it and pushed with the last of her strength. She reached the bank and staggered into the brush and weeds, the muscles in her arms and legs feeling like they were melting wax from a burning candle as she slogged through the cloying mud. Finally, she could go no further and collapsed on the thick growing vines. She closed her eyes, just for a second, but that second was all it took.

"Good god, Mary, go get Mr. Jacque and some help. This woman's in bad shape, looks like she's been half drowned. We ain't doin' any fishin' today." Strong arms lifted her and turned her over. "Honey, what happened to you?"

Ruby opened her eyes and looked into the man's kind eyes, his coffee-colored face creased with concern. She gave a sigh of relief. She tried to talk, but all that came out was a croak, and she closed her eyes again. It would have to wait, just for a time.

29

"Good god, man, bring her in, my friend," Julius said, pushing back his chair and clasping Jacque's hand. "You seem disturbed. Does she need medical attention? Do you?"

A very pretty black woman stood behind him, her hair coiled in braids atop her head, but attractive as she was, the fear in her eyes and the apprehension on her face overshadowed it. Jacque took her arm and led her to a chair which Fiona quickly pulled up beside her own. She limped slightly in the leather moccasins she wore and her arms were deeply etched with red scratches and mosquito bites.

"This is Ruby Green. We found her this morning on the riverbank, DeMonte. The tale she told me and what we are about to tell you is astounding and, I believe answers many of the questions we've had for months." He leaned over and whispered in the woman's ear and she nodded, peering tentatively at the people gathered around the table. Julius seated Jacque and briefly introduced everyone else, and her eyes widened, lingering on Fiona, Saint Germain and Marie Laveau in particular.

Fiona took Ruby's hand in hers. "You are safe here, Ruby Green, among friends even though we are new to you. You have been through something terrible; I know that because I have been in that place even though it may not seem so now. Please," Fiona held out a glass of whiskey and Julius poured another for Jacque, who tossed it back quickly and got a refill. "Although it may be difficult, know that you can trust every person in this room to help you."

Ruby took the glass from her hand. Her eyes watered at the first sip but the second and third went down easier. Her shoulders eased and she gave Fiona a faint smile that disappeared quickly.

"Thank you, ma'am," she said, her voice soft and pleasant to the ear, the deep southern cadence evident even with three words. She gave a tiny cough and looked at Jacque, who nodded reassuringly. "Tell them, Ruby."

"Yessir, I surely will." She took a breath and launched into a tale that was so horrifying every person at the table sank into silence. Everyone had questions, but once Ruby began to speak in her low modulated voice, no one wanted to interrupt her, understanding how traumatic her experiences had been and the effort it took her to relate the story. From the time she and Samuel had seen the ad, to coming to the farm where they were enslaved, to the horrors that were concocted in the workshops and barn, and seeing the men turned into zombies, the words fell from her mouth as the group listened with increasing dread. If she was telling the truth, everything they had suspected was true.

She stopped for a moment and Henley silently gave her a glass of sweet tea, and she drank it, thanking him and continued her story once more from stealing the horse, stabbing the man in the stables, the ride through the night, to her journey down the river that ended on the riverbank early this morning.

"Mr. Jacque has been so kind to me, and he and his people saved my life. Now, I must do all I can to save Samuel's life and everyone else who's stuck at that place." Her eyes flashed for the first time with anger. "But not those who run it. I want to burn it all to the ground with them on top of the fire."

"In that event, Ruby," Fiona said, "you've come to the right place."

No one demurred. They sat in silence for a few moments, digesting everything Ruby had said. Henley went to the desk and set a notebook on the table atop the maps, uncapping the pen in his hand. Always the detail man.

"Ruby, if you're up to it, we need to have you try to give us more information. Names, overheard conversations, details of what goes on in the barn, where people go – anything that may help us find Fairhaven. Can you do that?"

Ruby glanced at Fiona, who still held her hand. Fiona felt the tremors of exhaustion that coursed through Ruby's slim frame.

"Not tonight she can't. Pressing as the matter is, Ruby needs rest," Fiona said. She squeezed Ruby's hand and gently placed it back in the woman's lap. "You too, Jacque. We have guest rooms in the east wing, and armed guards. You are safe here and we can reconvene in the morning."

"I'm sure we all agree," Julius said, standing up. The theater impresario's commanding presence brooked no argument. "Nine o'clock? Breakfast, of course." He turned to Ruby Green. "Rest well, my dear, if you can. I assure you, justice will be served."

Everyone filed out and said their good nights. Julius and Saint Germain conferred with Sean and Daniel, while Fiona and Henley escorted Ruby and Jacque upstairs to their rooms. Ruby sank into the lace-trimmed down comforter on the four-poster bed, kicking off her moccasins, while Fiona produced a soft cotton nightgown from the armoire, and laid out towels on the dresser.

"This is heaven, Miss Fiona. You been so kind I can't think how to thank you, all of you. Jacque said you would help but I didn't expect this."

"It's just Fiona, Ruby," Fiona said. "It's not heaven, I assure you, but the Cathedral bells will likely wake you. Try to ignore them." She smiled. "If you need anything, Henley and I are just a turn down the hall, at the double doors. See you in the morning." She glanced back as her hand touched the doorknob to see Ruby's eyes already closing.

"Christ Jesus, Henley, I cannot fathom the evil in this world sometimes," Fiona said. They were sitting out on their balcony, watching the dimming lights of the city. "As was often said, we knew 'things weren't right' but this is worse than I imagined by far."

"Ah, Irish, we'll fix it, I promise. I had a hard time not wanting to press her further, but you did what was needed." He sighed. "I want to get on a horse and go find those people tonight, but of course I won't. It's a fool's errand and doubly so since we need to narrow our search with more information. Ruby will be better able to remember more details tomorrow and I have to curb my impatience."

"It seems surreal, but it's definitely not," Fiona said. "Believe me, you're not the only one eager to mete out justice, and it's not only me. Did you see Saint Germain's face? He feels responsible for this, and in a strange way, he's not wrong. If Annette didn't have the resources and education he provided her so long ago, none of this could have happened."

"Perhaps, but as the bard said, 'there are more things in heaven and earth', and fate finds an avenue to people's worst nature in a variety of pathways if they seek them, as we well know. I don't believe Saint Germain to be any of the things the Cassinis or even historians might think he could be – an 'abomination', evil, or the most ridiculous, a vampire. He is a learned man but still a mortal one and has contributed more good and scientific learning than any harm he has done."

"We are in complete agreement on that, darling. In fact, despite his formality and distrust, I have become quite fond of him and I think he enjoys my company as well."

"Take me to bed, love. I need to be with you and put terrible things away for a few hours," Fiona ran her hand softly down his cheek.

"As you command, princess," Henley said. He scooped her up from her chair and carried her inside, depositing her gently on their bed. "An arduous task you've set for me but I am up for the challenge."

"So I see," Fiona said, untying the ribbons on her neckline while Henley busied himself with her skirts. "We may not even hear those damn bells tonight."

"What bells?"

30

Morning dawned, bright and sunny, a perfect New Orleans autumn day, a counterpart to the dark plans that had to be made. Fiona thought a sky full of threatening thunderclouds, wind and rain would be more appropriate, but the storms held off this year and blue skies made her feel hopeful that all this would soon be behind them.

"Morning, my darlings," Julius greeted her and Henley as they entered the office. Sunlight streamed in through the louvered shutters and a breakfast buffet had been set up – silver trays full of croissants stuffed with ham and cheese, sugary beignets, strawberries and melons, and carafes of coffee and juice. Ruby Green was already ensconced in a chair beside Julius, a full plate in front of her. She smiled at them both, scarcely looking like the frightened and hunted woman from the night before, her eyes bright and face more serene.

"Thank you all again for your kindness and hospitality," she said in her musical low voice. "Best night's sleep I've had in a long time."

Julius waved his hand. "Of course, my dear. First of many to come, I hope." He looked up as Saint Germain and Jacque entered, Jacque making a beeline for the buffet. Saint Germain was attired in his usual impeccable black suit, cheeks glistening from a close shave, perfectly composed but his dark eyes took in every detail of the room and the people in it, a faint smile on his lips.

"Good morning. I see you are feeling better, Mrs. Green, and I am happy to see that. We have but one goal and that is to make certain you continue to do so, and that your husband and others do so as well." He turned as Raphael entered with another heavily laden tray. "Julius, I've taken the liberty to include champagne and orange juice to our repast, which you always overlook, old friend. I must take credit for inventing this concoction and I do hope it catches on."

Julius laughed. "I knew you would do so, Claude-Louis. I wished to allow you to include your own touch, as you're so excellent at details."

As Saint Germain instructed Raphael in mixing his contribution, Marie Laveau and Jim Washington arrived, Jim carrying a large basket and Marie attired in another colorful tignon in green and gold that matched her flowing dress. Fiona sincerely hoped there wasn't a snake in there, recalling some of the previous baskets she'd seen in Marie's company. He set the basket on the floor beside the conference table and it didn't move. Fiona hadn't expected it would but she had a morbid fear of snakes and she'd always had a vivid imagination so she kept a surreptitious eye on it.

Raphael left, everyone settled with food and drink, they turned their attention to the maps still spread on the table and Henley once more took up his notebook and pen.

"Now we three or more meet again to plan the hurly-burly," Julius rather dramatically paraphrased MacBeth and Fiona grinned. God, the man just couldn't resist. Once a showman, always a showman. That said, he wasn't wrong. A hurly-burly was exactly what was to come.

"Before we begin, curiosity is killing me, Marie. What's in the basket?" Henley said.

"Things we will need, Michael Henley, but it's not for now." She turned to Ruby Green. "I see you look better. We will help you to remember details of your incarceration and where we might find this woman and her cohorts. Let us start with the basics and then we will delve deeper if we need to. Are you ready?"

"I am," Ruby nodded, clearly enchanted by the voodoo queen, which in Fiona's estimation, was perfectly natural. She had been too, the first time she'd met her, and still was.

Ruby began. "In the advertisement we saw, it said to turn when we came to two black pillars, and that is how we would know the road we sought. We finally spotted them, hard to tell if they were black as they were overgrown with thick growing vines, but pillars they were and we hadn't seen any others except some white gates and fences. So, we took a chance. The lane just kept going after a long time and we thought about turning back until we finally saw buildings ahead and a sign that read 'Fairhaven'. There was some other smaller lettering on it but we didn't take the time to read it, tired as we were. We knocked on the front door and were welcomed inside. It was so pretty in there, much more so than what we expected from the exterior which could've used some repair."

She sipped her coffee. "The girl was so nice and kind. We were actually seated in the parlor, even though we were dirty from the road. Then this woman arrived, one we were introduced to as 'Madame'. She was lovely. Blonde, tall and elegantly dressed, a faint accent but one I couldn't place. She offered us tea and cookies, which we eagerly took. Now I know the tea was drugged because the next time I woke it was on a straw pallet in the old slave cabins and that was the beginning."

Henley made notes and looked up. "The night you ran, how far do you estimate you traveled on the road and then the river, Ruby?"

"I wish I could be more accurate, but I was so frightened and it was dark. Once we got out on the road, I ran that horse hard. I could tell that stallion was nearly blown I ran him so hard and I was worried for him, so it couldn't have been no more than three or four miles on the main road." She stopped and glanced at Jacque. "Did you find him? How is he?"

"He's fine, Ruby. We found him yesterday, wandering near the riverbank. Hard to tell how far he'd come, but he's in my stables and safe." He smiled. "He's your horse and he's waiting for you."

Ruby smiled. "Thank you." She looked back at Henley. "As for the river, I've no idea, but I would say much further. Even after I fell asleep on that log, the current was carrying me some and I was swimming behind it fast as I could before that for a long time. Seemed like a lifetime but I would guess anywhere between ten to twelve miles. That's the best I can reckon."

"River's runnin' about mile and half an hour right now," Jacque said, swallowing the last of a croissant. "She pushin, maybe get up to three or more but no way to tell how long that lasted. My guess would be around the same as Ruby's."

"So, the place was maybe ten miles upriver from Belle Fleur," Henley made some notes. "Called 'Fairhaven'," he rolled his eyes, "a bit off the road, black gateposts. We're making headway." He looked around. "Anybody ever heard of a plantation called Fairhaven?"

"Nope." Jacque started in on another croissant. "Never." Heads shook around the table.

"What else, Ruby?" Fiona encouraged. "Anything that would give us more to go on?"

"I'm sorry," Ruby said, "I wish I could, but I never got off the place until now and most of the time I was in the kitchens and never got further than the barn and the cabins."

Saint Germain leaned forward. "Let's try something else, if that's all right with you, Ruby. I want you to close your eyes and block out everything in this room, this time and these people. I will guide you and together we will go back into your memories. Can you do that?"

He whispered to Julius, who rose and closed the louvers, dimming the light in the room.

They all watched in fascination as Saint Germain's mesmerizing voice took Ruby back to the very day she'd arrived at Fairhaven. Everyone breathed quietly, not even wanting a bite or a sip to disturb the scene.

"You went inside the house, and it was lovely, wasn't it?"

"Yes," Ruby said, her voice low but clear. "It was. Paintings. Flowers. The chandelier, so beautiful."

"What did you hear?"

She smiled. "Piano music, quite beautiful. And a violin, I think, or maybe a harp."

"Very good, Ruby," Saint Germain said. "Did you ever hear music in that house again?"

"Yes, every now and then, but it was faint because I was never allowed out of the kitchens after that, but every once in a while Marita or Daphne opened the door and I heard the piano again. Once someone singing."

"Tell me about Yvonne and Monique, Ruby. What did they look like?"

She frowned. "Like Madame. Maybe her daughters? They were pretty but cruel."

"What was Madame's name, Ruby? Did you ever hear any other names?"

"The foreman's name was Skeet Rawlins, I told you that. Never knew the others. Although one night I heard him call Madame 'Giselle'. I'd never heard a name like that before."

Saint Germain was quiet for a time. "How much food did you and the other women cook in a day, Ruby?"

"Quite a lot, not that we got much of it. I always wondered. Especially the teas sometimes in the afternoons, 'cause it wasn't for Skeet and the men. It was scones and pastries, delicate stuff, sometimes for much more than the three people I saw."

Saint Germain was silent for a time. "Is there anything else unusual you remember, a smell, a sound, something odd?"

"Men walking by. Wagons," Ruby said. "At night sometimes. Wagons. Don't know where they went."

"Ah," Saint Germain said. He snapped his fingers and nodded at Julius who opened the louvers. Ruby opened her eyes and light streamed back into the room. Fiona, along with everyone else, blinked and felt as though they too, had been under a spell. Marie Laveau smiled in approval.

"Very good, Comte," she said. "Couldn't have done better myself." Saint Germain gave her a nod and a slight smile.

Henley finished scribbling in his notebook and looked up. "We now have a lot to go on. Let's plot the map and see where to begin."

Julius stood up and shoved in his chair. "Carry on. I'll be back in an hour." Before anyone could speak, he left, shutting the door firmly behind him. Fiona looked at Henley, who shrugged. Julius had his ways and detested being questioned. They'd find out soon enough.

Jacque knew the area better than anyone, even Marie, so he took charge of the mapping. Considering the somewhat snake-like curves of the Mississippi as she wound her way down to the Gulf, along with the fact that they couldn't determine with any accuracy how far Ruby had floated with her log, there was no way to pinpoint the location.

Jacque pored over the maps for a while, marking points here and there. Finally he sat down, some satisfaction on his face. "Best I can determine, it's somewhere in the stretch between Belle Fleur and Vacherie."

Henley groaned. "That's a lot of territory, Jacque."

"Hell, boy, I know that. Thing is, we got us variables here. The river runs both fast and slow through them curves, but sometimes real damn fast. Ruby is one strong woman, she was scared and swimmin' for her life. Hate to miss something that's just a few miles further up, is why I say what I do."

"The odds are it's closer than Vacherie but there's a chance it's even further," Marie mused, and Jim nodded. "My place isn't far from Belle Fleur and I've never seen anything like those pillars Ruby described. I do go to Vacherie once in a great while, to see Tante Verna, but I usually take the back roads, which is likely why I've never noticed any pillars along the way."

"They're not easy to spot unless you're walkin'," Ruby said. "And, lookin' hard."

"So, we should concentrate most of our search at least eight miles up from Belle Fleur," Henley said, closing his pen. "That's a little better."

All seven breathed a sigh of relief and began to relax in their chairs. Jim Washington got up and brought a plate of croissants back to Marie, along with more coffee. Saint Germain delicately ate a few strawberries. All Fiona could think of was that place where she'd shot the two men. Was that Fairhaven? From Ruby's description, it didn't seem to be, but it was worth returning to make sure.

The door slammed behind Julius at his return. His cape flowed behind him and he stopped beside the conference table, smiling like a cat that had indulged in a saucer of cream.

"I think I may have discovered our villainess and her lair, my darlings. It is much different than we thought. Fairhaven is not known as a plantation nor even a farm of any kind, nor is she known as a botanist.

"I have just been to the Opera House and talked with Monsieur Thibodeaux, the director, as well as some of the young women in the chorus. They tell me Fairhaven is known as a Conservatoire, a musical school for select young ladies, who travel there for a three-day tutorial twice a month. True, it is expensive, secluded and difficult to travel to but that only adds to its alluring reputation, and it's considered to be the best in all of the South. Its proprietor and much vaunted teacher is one Giselle Grateau, who bills herself as the former leading lady and star of the Paris Opera Company. Voila!

"I even have directions, courtesy of a lovely young lady who will be singing Aida next month. We must be sure to attend. I do hope there's going to be an elephant."

"My dear Julius," Saint Germain rose from his chair, "you never fail to astound me in all the years I've known you." He clapped his hands and everyone followed suit. If there was some relief before, now it was elation. "I should've picked up on the clues myself, *mon ami*."

"Excellent deductions, Julius," Marie Laveau said, nodding at Jim Washington, who placed the mysterious basket on the table. "However, we must be extremely cautious in our approach. Finding her is one thing. Defeating her is quite another. This is not just a clever and evil woman. She has long ago become a caplata, a voodoo priestess. This is how she controls the men she enslaves and we underestimate her abilities at the peril of our lives."

Jim opened the basket and handed an amulet to each person in the room. They were small, easy to fit into a pocket or on a chain or string around the neck, consisting of a smooth rock, golden in color, wrapped with reeds and herbs.

"These are known as gris-gris," Marie said. "These amulets look simple, but they will counteract the evil our caplata emanates and keep you safe. Wear one next to your skin as you go to confront her."

Henley looked dubious, and Marie noticed. "Believe what I say, Michael Henley. You will come to find I am right."

As each one found its way into the hands of their recipients, a warm vibration pulsed through them and just as swiftly ended, having seemingly to have made its mark.

Saint Germain bowed to Marie. "*Merci,* Madame. It is beyond fortunate we have you with us, else I fear we would be ill-prepared. Now we have an opportunity we would have never had without your skills and knowledge."

They agreed to reconvene for dinner at a new Creole restaurant on Chartres, Le Baronne, run by a friend of Jim Washington's, all except for Jacque LaSalle.

"I have to get back to Belle Fleur, my friends." He shoved a few more croissants into a napkin. It was a long ride.

"I've a harvest to attend to, and there's not a crystal of sugar I don't try to oversee. My home is open to you and whoever you bring along on our coming venture." He turned to Ruby Green and hugged her. "You take care, Ruby. All will be well. We'll make sure of it. You'll be seein' your man in no time. Thanks for the hospitality, y'all."

Within minutes, Marie and Jim left as well, along with Ruby Green, who was still clearly exhausted and recovering from her ordeal and in some need of a nap. Julius, Saint Germain, Henley and Fiona remained, although no one seemed eager for more conversation. That could come later tonight.

"Well." Fiona broke the silence. "We've got a bit of a war on our hands. As Julius said earlier, the hurly-burly is upon us. Sooner started, soonest over, don't you agree, gentlemen?"

31

Still dark, the moon high in the trees, shadows played against the old bricks caressed by the pre-dawn breeze, while most residents of the Vieux Carre were still fast asleep.

"You're staying here," Henley said, shoving two shirts into his saddlebag. "Don't even think about arguing with me, Fiona Shanahan. You're strategy, not cannon fodder."

"Oh please, I'm more than strategy as you know quite well, and smart enough to stay out of the way of a bullet, let alone a cannonball, which I doubt these people have access to anyway. Let's not get fanciful."

Fiona finished lacing up her boots and pulled the trousers she'd borrowed from Raphael down over the tops of the stiff leather. She'd topped off her ensemble with a linen shirt and a leather vest and she twirled around on the toes of the boots. "See? Armored up and all. Don't make me say, 'I'm all dressed up and have nowhere to go,' Henley."

Heaving what Fiona thought was a rather theatrical sigh, he sat down on the bed. "Seriously, Fiona. This entire raid or whatever it is we're doing, to a place we aren't even sure is where Julius was told it was, or even if it's the right place, will be physically taxing and very dangerous. I don't want you anywhere closer to this mess than right here on Royal Street."

She sat down beside him and put her arm over his shoulders. "I know all this, love. I'm not a fool and this is not a lark. I've a few ideas of my own." She kissed his cheek. "Besides, you know perfectly well if you don't let me come with you, I'll come behind you."

This time Henley actually groaned. "That is true, God save us."

"Absolutely, and now that you bring Him up," Fiona said, "God will be with us, too."

"What?" Henley nearly jumped off the bed. He'd become quite high-strung through all this.

She smiled. "I sent Sean to ready my dear friend Father Gregor. Saint Germain and I think it's time the Cassini Brotherhood knew who their true enemy is. Clearly, our misguided priest has been much too sheltered by life in the Vatican and has trouble with that old Catholic bugaboo: lack of discernment. He needs an education in that arena and he's about to receive it. What could be more illuminating than an encounter with the devil herself?"

"The hell." Henley shot out the door. "Julius and Marie will never go along with this."

He bolted down the hallway. Fiona watched him go but he didn't hear her whispered reply.

"They already have. I do love you so, silly Henley. Needs must when the devil drives."

She stood there in silence for a few minutes, thinking through everything that had led to this point, a place she'd never imagined any of them could be, when the whole affair had begun with searching for a wayward French botanist. It had gone so wrong so fast, threatening people she cared about and some she'd only just met.

She shook her head and began to move, coming to life like Giselle, the ballet they'd seen just a few weeks ago at the Opera House. She touched the replacement leather sheath on her thigh, and buckled the holster with her new pistol onto her shoulder, shrugging on a light leather jacket to cover it. She put Marie's gris-gris amulet around her neck, along with Henley's. She'd tied them both onto silver chains and shoved them into her shirt. She grabbed Henley's saddlebag and her own, both their hats, and of course his gun and holster. She'd meet him downstairs after he spoke with Julius. That he'd be angry, she had little doubt, but that wouldn't last. It never did.

She took one last look at the room she adored, the place of so much love and delight, and turned down the lamp. They'd be back. She couldn't think of it any other way.

JULIUS GREETED HER WITH A HUG. "Morning, darling. We're off on a grand adventure, what?" He grinned and released her.

Fiona eyed him suspiciously. "Any reservations, Julius?"

"Of course not," he said. His eyes were guileless, as usual. Henley glowered by the doorway to Royal Street and wouldn't meet her eyes. That was ridiculous but there was little to be done for now. He wordlessly held open the door for her, and she swept through without a glance his way.

The big carriage with four horses was waiting at the curb, while a slew of riders gathered behind it. As requested, the palomino mare she usually rode was tethered to the carriage, her rifle in its scabbard on the empty saddle. Sean McKean and perhaps twenty of his men milled on Royal Street, the horses' breaths steaming in the dawn chill. What a procession they made.

"I wasn't sure whether you'd prefer to ride the mare or be more comfortable in the rig," Julius said, coming up behind her. "Ruby Green is in the carriage, we'll leave her at Belle Fleur. Our misguided priest is also inside, but as you know, there's plenty of room for at least three more if you're so inclined. Saint Germain will be trading off, as he gets bored without travel options."

"Indeed I do," said that worthy gentleman, joining them at the curb. "For now, the carriage looks comfortable. 'Tis early for exertion." He climbed up the steps and disappeared into the depths of the carriage, smiling at Ruby Green and taking a seat beside her.

"I'm sure Father Gregor will be aghast at the company he will be keeping," Julius said, "but he likely won't die of anything but fear by the time we arrive. Who knows, he may even learn something." He smiled mischievously.

Fiona couldn't resist. This could prove to be amusing and there was little chance of outside confrontation in the beginning leg of this journey into hell. She climbed into the rig and seated herself between Ruby and a smiling Saint Germain. The Cassini brother sat across from them, hands securely tied, eyes closed rather than gaze at his infernal companions.

"Delighted to have your company, Fiona," Saint Germain said. "It isn't a terribly long journey, but we have an opportunity to chat with our friend here. I doubt he will be willing to renounce his vows on this short trip, and frankly, I don't give a damn. However, truth is a shining beacon, is it not? One the Church has fought to extinguish with thoughtless damnation for anything they don't understand or revere for two thousand years or so." He smiled benignly.

Oh, this was going to be an interesting ride, Fiona thought. *An ancient learned nobleman against a jejune indoctrinated priest.* She'd had worse treks in her life with far less interesting people. She settled back as the carriage pulled away and smiled at Saint Germain with malicious satisfaction, and he returned it with a grin, the first time she'd seen that. The man was in his element. He wasn't alone. She nudged Father Gregor's knee as the carriage picked up speed. "Wakey, wakey. You're not fooling anyone, and it's quite rude. Let's discuss theology, what do you say, love?"

The priest's eyes flew open. "Untie me and let me out now, witch."

Fiona rolled her eyes. "Well, that's not going to happen so you need to mind your manners. The Comte and I have some questions and I'm sure you have some of your own, so quit acting like a wounded dove, wake the fuck up and talk to us."

Saint Germain made a slight choking sound but quickly recovered, a smile lingering on his lips. "Heed the lady, Gregor. It would be best. We may have need of your admittedly limited services, because of course, we keep an open mind and even you and your devotions, scant as they are, may come to be of help. Now, let's discuss your oh-so-dedicated beliefs." He brushed unseen dust from his spotless shirtcuffs and leaned forward. "Enlighten us."

As the sun rose higher and the miles sped by, Father Gregor failed dismally in his task of enlightenment, not to mention persuasion. His positions were met with argument, disdain, short lectures, justified ridicule and eventually silence. Saint Germain threw up his hands and turned to Fiona. "The greatest mistake one can make when seeking reason is to debate a fool, my dear. I fear that is what we have done."

"I cannot disagree," Fiona sighed. "Though it has been interesting to see the blindness of what is called faith, which simply means that your position is indefensible when confronted with science, facts, instinct or sense."

She smiled at Father Gregor, whose eyes burned with undiminished fervor. "Don't worry, Father. Soon you will meet true evil, and perhaps confronting it with fallacy and a cross may bring you absolution of a sort. In the real world, we refer to it as death."

The carriage slowed, turned and finally halted. Fiona pulled back the curtains. They had arrived at Belle Fleur and the sun was still high above them. She could hardly wait to leave the stuffy carriage with its atmosphere of strife and the body odor of Father Gregor's holy sweat. She knew Saint Germain, from the many retreats to his perfumed handkerchief, agreed wholeheartedly.

Jacque greeted them from the pillared verandah. "Heigh-ho, Julius. Looks like you got quite an army there, and likely a good thing."

The men dismounted to give the horses a rest and milled about in the yard, smoking and talking, using the conveniences and getting water themselves from the pitchers on the tables. Sean got Father Gregor out of the carriage while she, Julius, Henley, Ruby Green and St. Germain followed Jacque into the house.

Seated in the kitchen, Julius turned to Jacque. "So I was thinking we may want to stop in Convent at the St. James Parish Sheriff's office and let him know what's going on. Perhaps enlist his help and cooperation."

Jacque shook his head emphatically. "Not a good idea. Some of the other planters and I tried to talk with him about this situation, but our good Sheriff James Beaufort wants no part of it. I can't say if he's just a coward or if he's in on the whole scheme. Either way, it's not a sound idea, as he's only got one deputy anyway, and if he's in on it, he'll alert his pals."

Henley agreed. "These local sheriffs pander to their constituents, and I'd bet our charming Frenchwoman has long ago bribed him to look the other way. I agree it's a waste of time."

Fiona left to use the privy and as she was returning, Henley caught her in the hallway.

"Irish, hold on." He took her arm. "I'm sorry for my reactions earlier this morning, but I can't help but be concerned about you being in the thick of this mess. I don't want to be distracted by keeping you out of harm's way once the shooting starts."

Fiona put her arms around his neck. "Henley." She stood on the tips of her boots and kissed him, mainly to stop him from talking and also because he was so dear. "You don't need to worry. I'm not going to go charging into a shooting war. I'm looking for that woman and once we have her, there may not be any shooting anyway."

"Still, I'd feel better if you stayed here at Belle Fleur."

"I know you would, but I would not." She took his hand and led him back to the kitchen. "And don't go thinking to enlist Jacque to keep me here because I won't have it and I'll find a way to follow, which will only make things more precarious for you."

"Jesus God, woman, you'll be the death of me."

"No, I won't if you just listen." She squeezed his hand so hard he winced.

Julius grinned as they came back. "All is forgiven?"

"More or less," Fiona said. "What's the plan?"

"Well, according to what I was told," Julius said, "the place isn't that far west from here, and as we plotted on the map, perhaps less than twelve miles or so. I think we keep it straightforward and not do a night raid or any of that nonsense. Ride in, find her, shut down the operation, take some prisoners probably, and free those she's got captive."

Henley nodded. "We may give up the element of surprise once we get close, but we gain the advantage of not stumbling around in the dark in a place we don't know. That could be a disaster."

"I'd like to go with you," Ruby said. The woman had been silent as a mouse all morning.

"Absolutely not," Julius said. "You are staying here with Jacque, my dear. I know you are eager to be reunited with your husband, but it's just too dangerous. We'll bring him back to you by nightfall, I promise."

"But I can help," Ruby protested. "I know the layout of the place. You'll need me, and it'll save time and I'll make certain you've identified the right people. The good from the bad. There's a lot of bad, and some of them don't look it. Besides, Fiona's going."

"Fiona's a special case," Julius said. "She looks like an angel but she's the most dangerous of the entire crew, even if it doesn't seem so. She's mean as a cobra and can shoot out the eye of a squirrel at a hundred yards."

Ruby looked at him dubiously. "Well, if you say so."

"Let's not get carried away. I do have virtues," Fiona said. "Just not a lot of patience."

Henley patted Ruby's shoulder and chuckled. "See? He's not lying."

"I understand," Saint Germain broke in. "But be assured I can identify Annette and her companions as well. Trust me."

"Let's compromise," Henley said. "We should've thought of this before. Ruby, can you draw us a map of the house and outbuildings, the barn, old slave quarters and all? That would be extremely helpful and keep you out of the melee."

"Of course," Ruby said. Jacque produced pen and paper and within minutes, Ruby skillfully drew a map of Fairhaven and the placement of the structures and roads, pointing out there was a back road that led through the fields.

"Perfect," Henley said, passing the paper around. They all perused it and Henley got up and took it outside to show it to Sean and Daniel, who would be with him at the head of the riders.

"We'll be back before you know it," Fiona said to Ruby. "Stay here with Jacque, go visit with your horse and we'll return with Samuel. Can you do that?"

"Yes," Ruby said, "I can do that, Fiona. God bless you all and take care."

"Good," Fiona said. "And now, gentlemen, I've a mind to go take some piano lessons or hone my vocal skills. Let's get on with this."

"Christ Jesus, Fiona, stick with acting. You sing like a croaking frog and there's no honing that," Julius said. "Thanks for the hospitality, Jacque. We'll be imposing again soon."

Outside, they debated about taking the carriage or using one of Jacque's wagons, and decided on both, as a wagon might be sorely needed. Horses were harnessed, and they set off, Fiona now on her mare, waving back at Ruby and Jacque standing on the verandah. She hoped Ruby would stay put but she didn't fully trust her to do so. Saint Germain rode beside her, bored of toying with his errant priest like a cat with a mouse. The priest rode in the carriage again, with one of Sean's unlucky men to keep an eye on him and his holy stench.

Fairhaven might not be far away in miles, but it was a world away from justice and mercy, both of which they were bringing to its inhabitants, captors and captives alike.

32

Fiona was happy to be on horseback again and not stuck in the stuffy carriage. Saint Germain clearly agreed, throwing her a brief smile as he spurred his horse to the front of the troupe. It was a beautiful autumn day, the bright green of the fields fading as the year dwindled, but still pretty in their golden dress. After they'd left New Orleans, before and after Belle Fleur, they passed small hamlets, an occasional enterprise of one sort or another – a blacksmith, small general stores that reminded her of Vacherie, then plantations, some thriving, some not so much, houses, barns and corrals but not many travelers. The miles passed but there was still no sign of the pillars Ruby had described, black or otherwise and Fiona was becoming slightly anxious. She rode up the column until she was beside Henley.

"Think we missed it?"

He shook his head. "No. There's been nothing and we've all been hawk-eyed for those damn pillars. Maybe they took them down." He laughed. "Heard we were coming."

"Not likely. I like it better up here with you," she said. "Not as noisy and all."

"So stay. No one said you had to ride back there."

"I know, I just thought I'd give you some peace of mind, you know, not being the first one to get shot at and all."

"Sweet Jesus, Fiona, let it go. Besides, I like having you beside me and you know it."

Fiona smiled sweetly. "That's good, because I'm never leaving."

More miles sped by. Just after a big curve in the river, so near she got a close look at a large paddle wheeler churning past, Henley let out a shout.

"Here." He held up a hand and stopped, as did everyone else. There they were, two black marble pillars about five feet tall, covered with vines but clearly discernible underneath the leaves, one on each side of a dirt road that looked somewhat traveled.

Julius leaned over in the saddle. "This is it, has to be. Unless there's a big demand in black pillars, which I haven't seen before. We'll know soon enough." He turned his horse onto the road, and they all followed.

Fiona, Henley and Julius rode at the head of the column. She turned to Henley and then Julius. "How do you want to handle this?"

Julius shrugged. For a theater director, he wasn't as prepared for this as he was for The Taming of the Shrew, which is what worried her. "Knock on the door and see what happens. We've got a small army at our backs, Fiona."

"I've got a better idea," she said. "At least worth a try, because I think our Frenchwoman has a small army, too."

She explained as they rode and by the time the white sign with elegantly scripted black lettering came into view, they had both agreed. 'Fairhaven' it read in big letters and in slightly smaller ones, 'A Conservatoire'.

Fiona snorted. "Conservatoire, my sweet Gaelic ass."

Saint Germain rode up at Julius's signal and after a brief

word, entered the carriage, tying his reins to carriage rack. The curtains were tied back, leaving a clear view.

It was as Ruby had described. Once pristine, the big house could use a coat of paint, and the statue of the small black jockey hitching post was covered with moss. Leaves littered the porch and crunched under her boots as she approached the imposing front door, dropping the iron knocker soundly twice.

The door was opened swiftly, as though someone was right behind it, as well as they should be with a troupe of riders close on their lawn. A pretty young blonde woman stood there.

"How may I help you, ma'am?" She smiled, not showing much alarm, but the smile didn't meet her eyes, eyeing the riders with skepticism.

"Good afternoon. My name is Fiona Shanahan. Please forgive my entourage for causing any disturbance, it is the fault of my father who insists on them accompanying me whenever I venture from the city to what he considers the wilds of America. So silly, really."

The young woman's shoulders relaxed slightly but her eyes remained suspicious despite the smile. "I understand how protective parents can be."

"The thing is," Fiona continued, "Marie Dechamps at the Opera House told me of the amazing teachings you have here, and as long as we were passing on our way to Baton Rouge, I thought it may save time to simply stop in, rather than waste time with messages back and forth. Go to the source, as my father always says. I am in need of a vocal coach and training and I have heard Madame Giselle Grateau is the best."

"She certainly is."

"I wanted to just introduce myself and set up some times for lessons in January if that fits her schedule. Is she available?"

"I shall have to see. Would you like to come in?"

"Actually, time is pressing. We should have been in Baton

Rouge by now but we had a late start. I'm fine to wait here as the weather is pleasant and I know this is an inconvenience."

Fiona had no desire to get trapped in a house of horrors. The blonde woman nodded. "I'll be right back." Fiona glanced back and shrugged. Henley and Julius had heard most of this, and she saw Saint Germain's face at the carriage window.

Minutes passed. Fiona couldn't help but think this might have been a bad idea, certainly not the first time she'd had one, when the door was opened once more by the young woman. Behind her stood another figure who stepped onto the threshold. She looked remarkably like the younger woman, but with a heightened elegance and presence that could only come from a good stage actress or the aristocracy. She was beautiful, with only slight lines on her face and neck betraying her age from jejune to mature. Her hair was piled in a towering updo threaded with strands of pearls and her black silk gown flowed around her as she stared at Fiona.

She smiled but her blue eyes were cold with disdain. "What have we here? A new hopeful? I see so many, you must forgive me. And so unexpected, which I don't care for, Miss," she turned to the other woman, "what was it again, Yvonne, 'Shana' something?" She had a French accent, not pronounced, but there.

"*Desole, Madame,*" Fiona said. "I see how rude I have been, but I was so eager to find you." She glanced back at the carriage where Saint Germain was nodding and opening the door. "Unexcusable, as so many things are, wouldn't you say?"

Before the woman could respond, in a few rapid steps Saint Germain stood beside Fiona on the verandah, his face expressionless, eyes dark.

"At last, Annette. How delightful to see you again. We have such a great deal to share, do we not?"

The two women moved so fast it was slightly uncanny, the

massive door slamming shut in Fiona and the Comte's faces, the sound of bolts being drawn resoundingly evident.

Saint Germain turned to Fiona. "So much for the easy way. I should have been quicker. Now we must be very fast, Fiona. This woman is the devil herself."

They ran back to their horses, their alarm enveloping the column like a cloak, the horses milling nervously awaiting commands from their eager riders.

"Around the back, Sean," Henley shouted. "I want three men on the back door, three more on the front. Anybody that comes out, stop them. The rest of you, the barn and stables. To me."

Dirt clods flew as they turned their horses swiftly toward the outbuildings, Henley in the lead. Saint Germain and Fiona held back when Julius held up his hand.

"It's definitely her?" Julius said to Saint Germain. "Hate to roust a woman like that by mistake, old friend. Lovely thing."

Saint Germain frowned, looking impatient for the first time in Fiona's experience of the man. "Do not be of any doubt, Julius, and do not be fooled by her beauty as it masks the rot inside. It is Annette, and the other? Her creature, *certainement*. And equally evil, I assure you." He mounted his horse and called to the three men left to guard the large house. "Let no one leave that building, gentlemen."

He spurred his horse towards the barn, and Julius and Fiona followed close behind. From Ruby's description, who knew what horrors they would discover? Fiona was filled with as much trepidation as excitement, but the latter won out as it usually did, and she was equally eager for a further confrontation with Annette.

Their arrival had obviously not been without notice, probably from the first step onto the property, and Annette's forces were ready for them, shooting first with no warning. The boom of a shotgun followed by shouts greeted them as they entered the barnyard area, now a melee of men on horses, others on foot and taking cover behind a wagon and haybales, while more gunfire erupted from the barn. Return fire poured into the open doors of the large barn but it was difficult to tell how many bullets hit their marks in the gunsmoke-clouded air. Henley was smack in the middle of the morass, shooting from horseback while yelling commands at his men. For a few seconds, Fiona was paralyzed, not knowing what to do, and Julius grabbed at the reins of her horse.

"For god's sake, get off that horse before you get shot," he said. "You're a perfect target." He wasn't wrong. She grabbed the rifle from its scabbard and smacked the mare on the rump to get her out of the line of fire. He and Saint Germain did the same, and the three of them ran around to the side of the barn.

"Now what?" Fiona said.

Julius shrugged."Hell, I don't know. Maybe the back? Shoot the rats as they leave the ship?"

"Excellent idea," Saint Germain said and took off at a run. They followed. Rounding the back corner of the building, they saw four men pour out of the back doors, all holding pistols.

Saint Germain aimed his rifle. "Halt or be killed," he shouted in a gentlemanly fashion. It didn't seem to be his first battle, but that didn't surprise her.

It did seem to surprise the four men who stopped only to turn and aim at them. Saint Germain shot the first one in the eye, Julius the second, and Fiona hit the third in the stomach. She frowned, because she was rattled and her aim wasn't quite as good as usual. The fourth man took off running, throwing down his pistol, but Saint Germain shot him anyway. He walked over to the man Fiona had shot, who was moaning in agony and fired again.

"Vermin," he pronounced and went through the back door.

"There will be no mercy here," Fiona said.

Julius glanced at her and reloaded. "Nor should there be,

Fiona. You coming?" There was still plenty of shooting around the front. She hoped Henley was all right.

"You know I am, Julius." She sure wasn't staying out there.

They walked into hell. It was dim in the cavernous building except for small fires that had broken out here and there on the big worktables, likely from alcohol ignited by bullets. The surreal scene reminded Fiona of a stage set for Dante's Inferno. It took a minute before her eyes adjusted from the sunlight outside to the shaded barn.

Men, all of them black, were cowering in corners or under the tables, some in chains. Others, these white, were shooting at the men from New Orleans who were now converging in the entrance. Henley rode into the barn, an impervious avenging angel, pistols in both his hands, the reins hanging loose as he fired again and again at the few defenders left. Fiona waved toward him as she and her companions entered from the rear, not wanting to get caught in the crossfire, but she doubted he'd seen her. A man near her focused his weapon on Henley but before he could fire, she shot him in the back and scuttled towards the safety of the wall, as did Julius and Saint Germain, trying to keep their heads down.

A few more shots rang out, but it was eerily quiet within seconds, the gunsmoke hanging in the air like Spanish moss, dissipating into the barn rafters. Only the still bodies on the dirt floor gave evidence of the fierce battle that had ensued, ended almost as quickly as it had begun. It was less than half an hour since they'd arrived at Fairhaven and it seemed to Fiona that the world had paused while justice was served, but she knew it was far from over.

"Henley," Julius called out. "We're over here." The three walked cautiously towards Henley and the rest of their men.

"What a mess," Julius said. "I was hoping it wasn't going to go quite this badly."

Henley shrugged. "They didn't give us much of a choice,

Julius. We're damn lucky we only lost two people that I know of." He swung off his horse.

"They knew we were coming," Saint Germain said. "She likely sent someone to warn them while we were at the front of the house. At that point, they had choices: parlay, surrender, or shoot it out." He brushed some dust from his coat. "They made a poor choice. Based on what we're seeing, just in here, I don't have any sympathy for any of them. Annette has a way of corrupting everyone around her. I am sorry for the men you lost."

"So am I," Henley said. "Two of the Irishmen Sean hired last week, unfortunately. The first one got the shotgun blast that started the whole thing. I'll have him check on their families and make sure they're taken care of. Sean's handling things outside and getting the wagon."

Henley and Fiona went to the first big worktable. He leaned down and gently touched one of the men underneath on the shoulder. "You can come out, it's all right. We're not here to hurt you, but to get you all out of here."

One by one, they crawled out of their shelters under the tables, eight of them, dressed in ragged shirts and pants, most barefoot. Two wore leg chains, and Henley found keys in a drawer, unlocking the cuffs. They were very frightened, staring at the people they'd just watched kill their jailers, not sure what was going to happen next.

"Samuel Green?" Fiona said. "Are you here?"

"I am Samuel Green," said a tall man, one of the two who'd been in chains. "What's going to happen to us now?"

Fiona gave what she hoped was a reassuring smile. "We've got a wagon and horses. We thought you might want to leave. We're going back to New Orleans and we'll help you get settled there, if you like. Ruby is at a friend's house, not far down the road, waiting to see you."

"Oh Lawd," Samuel grabbed her hands, tears running down his face. "Thank you, thank you. Is she hurt?"

"No, Samuel, she's fine, just worried about you." She patted him on the shoulder. "She's the reason we found all of you. She's an amazing woman, but you already know that."

"So, can you men show us what goes on in here?" Henley said. "Doesn't look like anything good."

"No suh, it surely is not," one of the other men said. "Look here." He led them to a row of cages filled with all sorts of animals – among them foxes, dogs, cats, rabbits, even a pig, and field mice. Some looked normal, if skinny, but others had stitches and bandages, one of the foxes blind. "The devil queen herself come in here and do awful things to these poor creatures, seemin' to like they's sufferin'."

Fiona's stomach churned. She opened one of the cage doors and took out a small furry puppy, stitching across the top of its head. The puppy mewed and nestled into her hand, trembling. That foul bitch was going to pay for this.

Saint Germain was rummaging through the drawers and cabinets, pulling them out, searching each nook and cranny with growing impatience, throwing vials and bags this way and that, clearly not finding what he was searching for.

In the back corner of the barn, Julius and two of the former prisoners pulled a big muslin covering from what looked like a huge crate. It wasn't a crate, but a huge glass aquarium.

"God save us," Julius said. "What in hell are those things?"

The ugliest fish Fiona had ever seen were surging about in the murky water, huge things with big mouths and bulging eyes, some up to three feet long and half again as wide.

"Them's the poison fish, suh," Samuel said. "John and Roman here, she makes them catch those things and kill them. She makes her zombie poison from them. She makes me help."

Holy shit, Marie was right about everything. Fiona clutched the tiny puppy closer. This really was hell.

Saint Germain came up beside her, cradling a shotgun he'd picked up from beside one of the dead slavers. "This cannot stand. When we're ready to leave this abattoir, I'll take care of this."

It didn't take long; they had other business to attend to. They released the wild animals, and took the few dogs and cats that remained out to the wagon. The freed men climbed into the wagon bed, along with the two wrapped casualties of the gunfight. The bodies of the slavers were left in the barn, along with the three they'd shot outside behind the barn, ten of them altogether.

Before they set fire to the chamber of horrors, Saint Germain pointed the shotgun back at the aquarium. The blast was ear-numbing in the confines of the barn, shattering the glass. Water and fish poured out, the fish flopping in the quickly dissipating inches of water that lay in pools on the thirsty dirt floor. Henley poured alcohol over some hay bales and set them afire. The old wood caught quickly, flames licking hungrily as Sean drove the wagon back to the front of the big house.

Fiona gently settled the puppy into her saddlebag, swung into the saddle and stood beside Henley for a few seconds, watching the foul place burn. "Time for a meeting with the 'devil queen'."

Henley's face was grim. "I've got a few things to say to her myself, Irish. Along with some other ideas that are far from vocal."

33

1794 FRANCE

Once Annette had made the decision to leave, she couldn't pack fast enough. She'd arranged for passage on a fishing boat at St. Malo, and a friend in the village to take her there.

"Damn you, Claude-Louis," she muttered, folding clothes into her trunk. "It's been two months and I warned you not to return to Paris, but would you listen? Had you ever?"

They'd been at war with each other for over two years and she'd planned on leaving him and France both for some time, but especially when the queen met the guillotine, the entire country had plunged into anarchy. So far they'd been lucky here at Chambord, out of the way of the mobs, but there had been increasing incidents. Even with Saint Germain gone, she was still a target by virtue of her own aristocratic birth. They would come, she knew it, so better she, as a magnet for their hatred, be gone when they did. Chambord, Saint Germain's estate and her adopted name, was too beautiful to be destroyed by mindless violence. At least that's what she told herself, trying for some righteous and altruistic reasons, when in truth she didn't really care about anything of Saint Germain's *anymore*, except for his discoveries, which she'd had a hand in as well.

She folded the last of the dresses she could stuff in the trunk, and sat down on the bed to catch her breath, thinking of him and wondering how he was faring. Likely as dead as the queen and king, along with so many others. They had not parted on good terms but for some years, life had been a delight with that magical gentleman and she had learned a great deal. He could've had such power, but chose not to use it. In her opinion, he was a compassionate dreamer. She, on the other hand, knew in her dark heart, that power over others was the stuff not of dreams, but reality, and the only path to ascendency in a world fraught with danger and malice. If Saint Germain had not chosen to use it, being the kind fool he was, she would not make the same mistake.

Aristocrats like her should be in charge of so much in this world of turmoil, where life would be serene and returned to the orderly way things should be. In the small bag beside the trunk, she had stolen and stowed Saint Germain's ancient book, packets of seeds for the black lily, as they'd named the precious herb, and all the remaining vials of the elixir Saint Germain had concocted with both the knowledge of the book and the plant that had been deemed extinct and gone from the earth forever. Only a few knew it was not, and she was one of them. The possessors of arcane knowledge such as that contained in the book could keep them in power forever. All she had to do was escape France, this abattoir of misguided allegiances and murderous fervor to elevate street scum to the heights only those who could appreciate and guide a person, a country or a world to the correct place all should be. She would show them the correct way.

Annette Chambord heard the wheels of the cart outside on the paving stones. She leaned out the window and there was Rene, as promised, outlined in the moonlight. He looked up at her and she motioned him in to carry her heavy trunk. She'd left the latch open on the kitchen door and the servants were long asleep, she hoped.

She threw on her cloak, picked up the precious small bag that held her future, and her fingers on her lips warned him to be quiet as he came through the bedroom door. He nodded and balanced the trunk on his sturdy shoulders without so much as a heavy breath. Within minutes, she turned on the wooden seat of the cart and looked back at the towers of Chambord. It was lovely and she hoped it didn't burn with half the rest of France. She was off to a new future where only she would rule and she had the tools to ascertain that would be true.

FOR MANY YEARS SINCE, Annette had succeeded in ways small and occasionally much larger, to mold her place in a fractious world, both the old and the new. Once or twice, Saint Germain had nearly caught her, but she'd been a step or two ahead of him. One morning in Shanghai and again a very near miss in Prague, he'd been so close she could smell his distinctive scent and something in her psyche had wanted to taste him once more but she'd remained in her hiding place until he'd passed on, and he never knew just how close he'd been. Since then, she'd traveled to America with its new opportunities.

New York had been amusing, but overcrowded with people just as greedy and power-hungry as she was. Then, Virginia, which bored her, to Savannah, where she'd spent some years as it was a charming place filled with people that shared her views. After the silly war the Americans fought with each other over nonsense, she had arrived in New Orleans. She fell in love with the old French influences in this city that seemed to honor the old culture of her beloved homeland. Still, even here, despite its many graces, the aristocracy, such as it was, had been decimated and punished for simply doing what was required to maintain the lifestyle that should have been theirs by right.

She'd searched upriver, sensing that others of a like mind

might be not that far away, and had come upon Fairhaven. It was perfect, the house's old elegant charm, the green fields, set away from the dusty bustle of the road and the river, an oasis. She'd deliberately kept the exterior of the Georgian mansion looking somewhat ill-maintained, while lavishly decorating and rehabilitating the spacious interior, all three floors of it, in the style of Chambord that she'd so loved. Here, in this safe place with its easy lifestyle, she researched and adopted the ways of the previous owners of this lovely plantation. It was the old slave quarters that sparked an idea she quite agreed with. Coupled with learning all she could from Tante Verna, an old woman who carried no malice, but knew the ways of the voodoo practitioners in the area, Annette came across one who educated her in the darker ways of the practice, including how to enslave people with concoctions and was happy to teach her, especially when he was provided with hefty rewards. She was a quick learner, and from that *bokor,* as the male priests were called, she became a *caplata,* a female priestess of the strange and hidden side of Haitian voodou.

Now Annette had found her element. She could grow her herbs in the fertile Louisiana soil, and provide herself with the unseen privacy to experiment with animals and even people, if she chose, brewing and distilling the elixirs, potions and even performing surgery in her workshop in the barn. It not only provided her with the power she craved and enjoyed inflicting upon others, especially those she considered worthless, but she had branched out to establishing a very profitable business from her efforts.

She created what was termed 'zombies' with her poison and rented them out to plantation owners who needed workers and shared her own beliefs, that the slaves should have never been freed in the first place. They were not capable, in Annette's view, of establishing lives for themselves as they were mentally inferior to those with lighter skin, among other qualities, so she felt no remorse or guilt, not that she was capable of either. Sadly, it was true they didn't survive long in their already close to death state but she had found there was a near constant supply of people looking for work if only they knew where to go to find it. The phenomenon of advertising for workers was continuing to bring them right to her door. Once one group of zombies had succumbed to complete death and could not function, a new group was ready for work, and so it continued, to the satisfaction of her contractors and her.

To mask the business of the workers, she'd devised the idea of establishing a conservatoire for young ladies from New Orleans and Baton Rouge under the name Giselle Gateau, an impoverished but noble Frenchwoman. The school was highly exclusive and ridiculously expensive, which only added to its allure for those who could afford it. She taught voice, piano, violin and harp, all of which she'd become extremely proficient at over the years. Life was good and for some time Annette had been at peace, or as much as she could ever be.

When the riders had arrived at Fairhaven, and with them Saint Germain, her nemesis for all these years, she was enraged. How dare he invade her little empire, destroying all she'd built in this place she considered her Eden?

For a few weeks, her overseer, Skeet Rawlins, had warned her there had been some talk but she'd ignored his warnings for the most part. While he was good at satisfying her physical cravings, he was a mongrel lout and never the sort she could have true feelings for. Never in her wildest dreams had she thought Saint Germain himself could have discovered her. It was good she had an escape plan, never dreaming she'd have to use it.

Today, she would. Saint Germain and his men would be occupied and with any luck, killed in their ill-advised assault on her property. If not, she was ready. Annette Chambord gathered up that which was of paramount importance, namely the book, seeds and bottles of the elixir itself, carefully packaged. She had some ready cash for instant use, but her accounts were well established at banks in New Orleans, New York and Paris. This could be a blessing in disguise. She was growing bored with languid Southern culture. Time for some excitement, which Saint Germain had always provided, and today, in his own peculiar way, he'd done it again and may have done her a favor. She'd heard interesting stories about San Francisco. The so-called gold rush might be over, but the money pouring into the cities in the West was just the beginning of boundless prosperity, especially for someone with a great deal of ambition and absolutely no scruples.

34

"Open the door," Julius demanded after pounding on the sturdy front door. "If you do not, we will break it in and be quite annoyed. Save all of us a great deal of useless trouble, please."

Henley and Fiona arrived just in time to hear his demand, dismounting and joining Julius and Saint Germain on the pillared porch. Surprisingly, bolts were drawn and the door was opened by a black woman, clearly frightened to death, trembling where she stood.

"Please, suh, we had nothin' to do with this," she said. "The house is yours." She opened the door wide, and they stepped inside, followed by Sean and five of his men. The place was astounding in its opulence. The entry hall was huge, dominated by the biggest crystal chandelier Fiona had ever seen, and the black and white marble-tiled floor gleamed in its reflection. Gold-framed paintings hung on the walls, and a gigantic vase of flowers sat on a Louis XIV table that had likely last been seen at Versailles. Twin curving staircases swept majestically towards the upper floors.

"Damn me, this is magnificent," Saint Germain said.

"Although knowing Annette, it is not a surprise to me. She is a whore to luxury." He turned to the woman. "Where is your mistress?"

"I don't know, suh, I truly don't."

In Fiona's opinion and everyone else's, that was unlikely, so they searched the mansion, spreading out around the first floor and its receiving rooms, and then up to the second and third floors and the bedrooms. The entire house was just as elegantly appointed, even the music rooms furnished with an ornate grand piano, harpsichord and two beautiful harps. It was also, elegantly appointed or not, completely empty of human habitation.

They all returned to the first floor and gathered in the kitchens. There, three more women were standing as though waiting execution, their eyes wide.

"Where is she?" Saint Germain demanded. "The doors have not been opened, and we checked the attic."

The same woman who had opened the door stepped forward. "She say she kill us if we tell. She see everything, even when she not have eyes on you. She is *caplata*."

Fiona's voice was soothing. "What's your name?"

"Isobel." The other women were crying now, wringing their hands in their aprons and shaking their heads.

"Isobel, she is a liar." Fiona held up the amulet Marie had given her and all the women's eyes widened. "We bring gris-gris. She can't hurt you ever again. Go outside. We have a wagon out there with the others. You are safe now. But first, you must tell me how to find her. I know there is a cellar here, an escape hatch for her and perhaps her daughters. It's hidden, but you must show us where it can be found."

"Come with me," Isobel said. She straightened her spine and looked Fiona in the eye. "You have power in you and you see things better than Madame. I will show you where she went. It was open one day when I went to clean the silver and she didn't know I saw it." Her eyes flashed. "Find her. And kill her."

Isobel pushed open a swinging door that opened into a cavernous dining hall. Floor-to-ceiling glass-fronted cabinets that took up two walls held an amazing array of china, silver and crystal, the other two walls and ceiling painted with trompe d'oeil murals. It was breathtakingly beautiful, but no one in their party had time for any adulation of the French countryside. They'd been through here once already and seen nothing out of place. Isobel stopped before one of the cabinets, opened the door and pressed a hidden lever. A three-foot wide section of the crystal-filled cabinet swung open to reveal a staircase leading downward into darkness, the path they had to follow.

Julius shuddered. "Christ, I hate dark narrow places. Why did the bitch have to flee through here?"

Saint Germain gave a dry chuckle. "It is her nature, *mon ami.* You know that. She has become a creature of the dark. Into the abyss we must follow, *desole.*"

And so they did. Sean took charge of the enslaved women, depositing them in the wagon and sending them off to Belle Fleur with the others, while instructing the remaining men to remain vigilant under the leadership of Daniel Fox, and wait for further signals, some of which that might come from much further from the house than expected but there was no way to tell. He returned with lamps and makeshift torches.

"Sean, I need you out there," Julius said. "Daniel is good, but I sense more trouble coming and you are the man I want to confront it when it comes." Sean took one last look at the dark tunnel. He didn't seem terribly disappointed.

"I'm always your man, Julius," Sean said. Fiona silently agreed with Julius; Sean had been stalwart and the man that'd been at Julius's and her own back many times before. There was no one she trusted more. They lit the lamps and torches and descended into the depths of Annette's lair.

Henley led the way, Fiona close behind him, then Saint Germain, and Julius bringing up the rear. At the bottom of the long staircase, they emerged into a tunnel, dank and dirt-packed. It smelled of damp earth, worms and death. Fiona hated it more than anything she'd ever encountered in her life, even the horrid cottage she'd been forced to occupy in Ireland. She, like Julius, had a dislike of dark and narrow places and it took every ounce of determination she possessed to keep walking. Only the thought of confronting and defeating this terrible woman they sought kept her moving forward. Occasionally, she clung to Henley's arm. He smiled at her in the dim light of the lamps.

"You can do this, Irish. You've been through worse."

She wasn't sure of that. Not at all. For all they knew, this was a false trail and Annette had found some other way past the guards. It wasn't until the faint smell of a cloying perfume drifted into her nose that she was certain they were on the right trail. Unfortunately, then there was a split in the tunnel, one going north and the other south.

They stopped, unsure which way to go. Fiona held up her hand. "It's the perfume she wears." The men looked at her quizzically. Apparently, they hadn't noticed it. "Let me go ahead into both tunnels and see if I pick up a scent. Give me a torch."

She didn't smell anything in the south tunnel. If it was there, it had dissipated into the swampy air. She hurried back to the main tunnel and walked as quickly as she dared into the other one. Within seconds, she smelled the musky scent and returned to the others. "This way. She's not that far ahead, either."

Henley stared at her and then shook his head. "Jesus, Fiona. You're like a bloodhound on a trail."

"Indeed," Saint Germain said, "and a damn good one. Lead the way, darling."

So she did, until the tunnel ended less than 500 yards further. An iron ladder with rungs led upwards. Henley took the lead, testing each step as he went. Now they were in total darkness, needing both arms to climb. Fiona followed, Saint Germain below her and Julius last. Fiona's arms were tiring when Henley stopped. He pounded on the heavy wooden door, but it didn't open more than three inches, showering dirt down upon them.

"Goddamnit," Henley said. "Fiona, hold onto my belt. It's going to take all I've got to push this thing open."

His second try lifted the door a couple of inches more, but it fell back down with a thud. The third didn't go much better. Saint Germain sidled past Fiona and joined Henley on his narrow rung, hooking his belt onto it.

"Perhaps we two can manage it," he said. They repositioned, and together, the door lifted high enough to swing open and crash on the other side, along with the two heavy bales of hay someone had placed on it. They clambered out onto the straw-littered floor of the empty stables, the barn they'd set afire not more than 300 yards away, the heat intense.

Fiona brushed dirt from her clothes and hair, and took a few deep breaths. Even the smoke-filled air above ground was preferable to the vile air in the tunnels. Henley strode to the open door, staring outside, pulling his hat brim lower on the glare of the setting sun.

"Shit. There she goes with her minions, whoever they are."

In the distance, they could make out three riders galloping quickly through the fields.

Wordlessly, all four of them ran towards the big house and their own horses. This time, Annette Chambord could never ride fast enough to escape her fate.

35

Sean McKean and the remaining fifteen men were sitting on the porch, along with Father Gregor, released from his isolation in the carriage, all of them enjoying food, water and lemonade from Fairhaven's kitchens, a needed respite and Fiona glanced at them enviously as they ran towards them.

"She's out, and she's running," Julius said to Sean, who was chewing on a sandwich that he guiltily swallowed, standing to attention. "We're going after her. You stay here for now. I'm not convinced there isn't more to come, so keep your guns close, as make sure everyone's got one of the gris-gris things Fiona handed out. This woman is as devious and strange as I've ever known."

"You got it, boss," Sean said. "You need any help?"

"No. We can handle her, we just need to catch up," Julius said, mounting his horse. Fiona Henley and Saint Germain were already heading out. "We'll be back."

They raced down the faint track in the direction Henley had seen Annette take, not a well-trodden path, but visible. Annette had turned onto the main road and was headed upriver towards Vacherie. They pressed the horses to their maximum limits, all experienced riders. Within three miles, they turned into the Vacherie store, the place Fiona knew held friends of Annette's. Though the dust was still settling, there was no sign of Annette and her two companions as they pulled up to the store, the place dark and shuttered and seemingly vacant, only a glimmer of light between the louvers, but no sign of Hiram or Mary Roundtree, Annette's allies.

"They're here somewhere," Fiona said. "I can practically smell them, and I can certainly smell treachery."

The words had hardly left her mouth when the first shot rang out, perilously close to her right ear, coming from the shuttered store. She swung off her horse, as did her three companions, taking cover among the now empty fruit stands and boxes. She hadn't figured Annette for a marksman, but that may have been a miscalculation, considering how long the woman had been around to learn just about anything.

Saint Germain crab-walked up beside her where she huddled behind an overturned table. Henley and Julius were a few feet away, doing the same. She could smell the peaches that had been stacked there ripening in the sun not long ago. The Comte was holding the same shotgun he'd picked up from the barn. "You know these people?"

"Yes, they're hers. Henley and I met them the first time we came up here. I think they're a distraction," Fiona said. "There's an old voodoo herb woman down the lane, and that's where I think she went." She checked her rifle. "Can't be sure, though."

"Let's make sure," Saint Germain said. "Shoot at them. More than once. To the left side."

As directed, Fiona fired towards the store. Seemingly immune to return fire, Saint Germain walked up to the flimsy door and blasted it to pieces with the shotgun. Hiram Roundtree fell out onto the dirt yard, his rifle tumbling from his hand. His wife followed, screaming and falling onto his lifeless body. Saint Germain jerked her up, impervious to her cries.

"Where did they go?"

One look at his face stifled her sobs. "Tante Verna's. Just down the lane."

He dropped her to the ground like a pile of rags and turned to Fiona. "You know her?"

"Yes," Fiona said and snatched up Hiram's Winchester, leaving Mary Roundtree to mourn her husband. She didn't need a gun for that. "It's not far."

Henley and Julius were silent as they mounted their horses, Henley taking the lead towards Tante Verna's cottage. It was becoming clear Saint Germain had an agenda that eclipsed anything they had previously expected. Only Fiona realized that Annette Chambord was an evil he'd been seeking to nullify for a long time and tonight he fully intended to do so, closer to his prey than he'd been for many years. Fiona did not disagree with his desire or his intent.

Mary Roundtree was right. It wasn't far. However, it was getting dark, so they approached cautiously, the horses' hooves moving delicately down the mossy lane. A single light burned in the window of the little cottage and it was deceptively quiet.

Only Saint Germain dismounted, waving a hand at the rest of them. He approached the cottage, still holding the shotgun in his left hand.

"Come out, Annette. There is no more hiding. Not this time."

A minute passed, perhaps two, and the door slowly opened. Annette Chambord stepped out, holding a trembling Tante Verna as a shield, a knife at the throat of the old woman.

"Ah, Claude-Louis. At last we meet again. It has been some time, darling."

"So it has, Annette. Don't be a coward, release the old woman. She has no part to play."

"Does she not? I will kill her, you know."

He shrugged. "What is she to me? You kill her and your pitiful bluff is done."

She seemed to consider his words, but Fiona knew an actress when she saw one. She glanced at Saint Germain, so certain. Annette released the old woman and smiled, holding out the knife, hilt-first. Tante Verna shrank back into her cottage and collapsed onto a chair.

"You have me. At last. What do you intend to do now?"

"There is a gentleman who is eager to meet you and bring you to his masters. I am sure you are familiar with the Cassini Brotherhood?"

Annette laughed. "Not so much as you, my love."

Saint Germain smiled. "That is true, but they will lose interest in me once they have you, Annette. That I am sure of, especially given my testimony and your history, which I've documented quite thoroughly. Hand over the bag."

Her smile faltered, just a little but she was mostly unperturbed. She held out the bag and he snatched it up along with the knife. "Would you like to meet your daughter?"

"Oh please. That is a joke. God knows how many lovers you've enjoyed. I cannot have children, in case you didn't know."

Two lovely blonde women stepped out of the cottage to stand by their supposed mother. Annette gestured at the closest one. "This is Yvonne, your daughter, and her sister Monique. Say hello to Papa, Yvonne."

The girl bowed and gave an impish grin. "*Bonne soiree,* Papa. Delighted."

Saint Germain sighed. "Nonsense. I don't have any idea who these mongrels are, but they are most definitely not of my blood. Shall we go?"

Henley spurred his horse forward and dismounted, coiling ropes in his hands. "I have had enough of this nonsense. Come to me. It's late and I've had a very trying day, thanks to you three damnable hags. My choice would be to shoot you all right now and bury you in the next cane field. Which could still be an option."

Fiona loved watching the results when Henley lost his temper because it was always interesting, as long as it didn't involve her. Within minutes, the three women's hands were tied and tethered to the pommel of the saddles on their horses that Julius retrieved from the woods. He and Saint Germain held the reins.

"Where now?" Annette said, as though they were going on a picnic. "Nice evening for a ride but I always prefer to know my destination."

"How unfortunate," Henley said. "Also, shut the fuck up."

The journey back to Fairhaven was mercifully silent. It wasn't far, but it was far enough that Fiona had time to ponder the entire situation, and she didn't care for her thoughts. Given what she knew of Annette Chambord's history, it seemed remarkable that the woman had no further plan of escape, and her suspicions grew as the miles passed. This had been too easy, this supposed capture, much too easy for a murderous conniving woman like Annette. She drew her horse close to Henley's as the burning torches at the big house came into view across the fields.

"I don't like it, Hen," she said. "Something's not right."

He glanced over at her. "I'm aware, Irish. She's too devious to get caught so easily. Be on your guard. I don't like any of this either."

36

"Success, I see, boss. Not that I had any doubt." Sean McKean strode towards them as they dismounted, taking the reins of Julius's horse, a big grin on his face. His red hair looked even ruddier in the light from the torches. They'd made quite a few more torches from the hay bales outside the stables, staking them into the ground in front of the house, and brought some lanterns outside to the porch.

Julius snorted. "I had a few, but here we are." He surveyed the area. "Damn place is lit up like a Mardi Gras parade, Sean. Scared of the dark?"

"Well, not exactly. Have to say, though," Sean looked around, "place is a little unnerving. Keep thinking we're hearing things, but can't find anything."

The hair on the back of Fiona's rose. Sean was not one for fancy. She looked over her shoulder and then back at the house and as far as she could see, into the dark paths beyond that led to the old slave quarters. They hadn't searched any of the old buildings, assuming them to be empty, especially after they'd discovered the barn. That may have been an oversight. Even so, all seemed quiet, only the night birds and insects making their usual music.

Fiona turned to Julius. "We still need to find the workers that she's turned into zombies, the ones Marie and Jacque have talked about. We know she's done it but we don't know where they are. Apparently, she rents them out so they could be at any plantation that does business with her."

Julius was tired, she could tell, and impatient. "Another day, Fiona. Let's return to Belle Fleur and make plans with Jacque and the other planters. We won't be going back to New Orleans tonight anyway. I prefer to deal with the undead in the light rather than the dark."

Fiona couldn't disagree with that, especially as uneasy as she was. Daylight sometimes made all the difference and childish fears of the dark weren't helping her make good decisions.

Annette and her daughters still sat silently on their horses. Henley spoke with Sean, and three of the men stepped forward, untying the ropes that bound them to the saddles, and lifting them off the horses. They took the women's arms and led them to the porch steps so they could sit down before being transferred to the carriage.

"Thank you kindly, gentlemen," Annette said, sitting gingerly on the stone steps. Her daughters mimicked her words and gestures like trained puppets. Father Gregor stood up from his chair on the porch and approached, staring at them. Sean had untied his hands long ago when they'd taken him from the carriage, little threat that he was among armed men. There was, after all, no place he could go.

Fiona turned to Julius and Saint Germain. "It would seem our work here is done," Fiona said. "Do you want to burn the house? Rather seems a shame, since there's some priceless artwork and antiques inside. Perhaps we should have Jean-Claude come out and take some things back to the gallery? Let's decide and get away from this awful place. Besides, I'm hungry."

"So practical, Fiona," Julius chuckled. "I am hungry as well. However, that's not a bad plan. Your thoughts, Claude-Louis?"

"Tainted," said the Comte. "Knowing Annette, those are likely fakes, anyway. The whole house should be razed to the ground, and everything in it." He looked over his shoulder as Fiona had done earlier. "Something isn't right. We need to leave this foul place."

Henley grabbed Fiona's arm. "How many damn times do we need to hear that to heed it? Julius, we need to get out of here now." He was as nervous as she was, which didn't make her feel better.

"Sean, get the women and Father Gregor into the carriage. We can return tomorrow and take care of the house." Henley said. "Tonight, we're leaving."

Before Sean could take a step towards the women on the steps, Father Gregor flung out his arms, his slight form in its black cassock backlit by the flames of the torches. "Father, help me now in my hour of need." He made the sign of the cross and pointing towards the three women in front of him, screamed, "Abominations."

Annette Chambord moved as swiftly as a striking snake, lunging at the young priest with her bound arms. The force of the blow felled him instantly and his head struck the stone floor with a sharp crack, blood pooling beneath his skull. She pulled a silver whistle from the necklace she wore and blew it three times, the piercing sound nearly deafening to those close by. She turned towards Saint Germain out in the yard, a triumphant smile on her lips.

"You've left it a little long, my dear, as you've always been wont to do. I always had better instincts." She waved her still-bound arms, and blew the whistle three more times. "Skeet, I am here."

From out of the darkness behind the house came a white man waving a pistol over his head, guiding a surging tide of black men, at least twenty strong, all of them brandishing sugar cane cutting blades that gleamed in the torchlight as they charged towards them. Annette laughed. "Hello, my darlings." She made some gestures with her fingers and for a second. "Chop them down, as Mama commands. You have been taught your work. These men are nothing but crops to be harvested."

Two of the men from New Orleans fell instantly under the deadly knives while the rest began shooting at the invaders as they scrambled off the porch to find shelter from the blades and fire back.

"Make your amulets seen," screamed Fiona. "They will know." Most of the men listened to her, flinging the gris-gris outside their shirts and jackets. It slowed the zombies, for there was no question that is what they were, and even in some cases, stopped them, leaving them open to a bullet that ended them, finally falling forever. Others looked confused, but kept coming, eerily silent as they ran, forging mindlessly ahead and swinging their machetes as though they were chopping crops rather than people.

Their troupe of men were panicked, but as they saw the creatures were not super-human and could be killed, regained their confidence and began shooting as fast as they could into the invaders. A few of the black men fell, twitching, as though they were imbued with some supernatural force and would rise again, but they did not, much to the relief of those who stood against them. Still, many more pushed forward toward the group in the yard and there was little shelter to be had. There were so many. At first, Fiona was terrified but her fear quickly transformed into action, followed by anger at the horror Annette Chambord had created. These poor men were already dead, even if still dangerous, their existence only ended by a true death which she and these men beside her would have to deliver to these unfortunate souls, and still hope to survive themselves.

The nightmare battle continued, the torches illuminating what looked like a scene from hell, men shooting and reloading their guns time and again, bullets their only defense against the slashing knives. The air was thick with gunsmoke, and bodies began to litter the ground. Their leader continued to urge on the few remaining zombies until Henley put the man down with a shot to the head. As he did, the last of the zombies slashed at him as he stopped to reload and Henley fell to the ground before Saint Germain stepped in and shot the creature between the eyes.

For the moment, all was quiet. Fiona ran to Henley. He staggered up, bleeding profusely from deep cuts on his leg and chest. She pulled her leather jacket off and wrapped it tightly around his wounds. In the yard around her, Sean began to assemble his men, three of them lying dead on the ground, while the survivors milled about in stunned disbelief.

"Get him into the carriage," Fiona screamed at two of the men, and they carried him into the vehicle. She pulled the tiny puppy from her saddlebag and tucked him in beside Henley. Before she could climb in beside him, Annette's whistle blew again. Fiona turned towards the house. She could hardly believe her eyes. No wonder Sean had heard strange noises. That damned tunnel apparently had another turn and they'd been massing inside all this time. A second group of zombies, machetes raised, emerged from the front door of the house and ran outside, wielding their weapons towards the weary group in the yard. Annette made the same hand gestures, laughing as they ran towards the stunned fighters outside.

Saint Germain took charge. His words rose above the carnage and they all heard him, even the most terrified of the men. Firm and clear, he gave orders like a Roman general.

"Listen to me. Reload and form two rows," he ordered. "At

my order, first row, fire, then kneel. Second row, fire. Reload and repeat until they're dead. No mercy and no pause."

His voice was compelling, firm and determined, and the men responded to it as though clinging to a lifeline, lining up as he directed.

Julius, breathing heavily, stared at Fiona as she reloaded her rifle, standing beside him as he quickly did the same. "Classic technique, should've thought of it myself. Steady on, Fiona."

He kissed her cheek and sighted his rifle. "First row, Irish."

She knelt beside him. "On one." The damn things were only twenty feet away. The gunfire was deafening and after the first round, between the darkness as the torches began to smolder and the gunsmoke that blinded them all, they kept shooting regardless.

It took three barrages before no one with a blade was still standing. They stopped coming because they were all dead. Finally dead.

They walked through the scattered bodies towards the big house. Fiona knew no one felt pride or triumph in their accomplishment, only relief they themselves were still alive and sadness at the fate of the poor men who had endured Annette's poison that had led to their eventual end. It was a mercy killing, really. Fiona looked at the carnage around her, the bodies of those proud men who had been deluded and poisoned by this terrible woman. Now they were at peace at last, but she had no way of knowing who they were or how to contact their loved ones, just more victims of the horror that Annette had perpetrated on those she could dominate. Since stepping into the grounds of Fairhaven, looking for honest work to support them and their families, they had been doomed, falling prey to Annette's cruelty and rapaciousness.

Sadness turned to white hot anger when she saw three more of their men lying in pools of blood. She could only think of Henley near death in the carriage, and Saint Germain in danger from a slash on his leg. Sean and Julius began barking orders, wrapping makeshift bandages around the other wounded men and carrying them all to the carriage for the ride to Belle Fleur.

BEFORE JULIUS COULD STOP HER, she ran up to the porch where Annette and her cursed daughters were still sitting, the corpse of poor Father Gregor beside them. So much for him taking Annette to the Vatican. The Church's accuser and escort was dead as last Friday's flounder.

Annette sneered up at her. "My little surprise didn't turn out as well as I'd hoped, but perhaps your handsome lover and dear Saint Germain will soon join the rest of these scum." She held out her hands. "Take me to justice, you incompetent little whore. I won't be held long."

"Ah, madame, you need not have a concern. There will be no delay. Your justice is here." Fiona raised the bloody machete she'd snatched from the ground and with one vicious swipe, Annette Chambord's head rolled onto the porch, her death accompanied by the funeral screeches of her daughters. They were quite annoying, and had contributed to a very trying day. Fiona raised the machete again.

"Fiona, no!" Julius shouted, but Saint Germain reached out and grabbed his shoulder, shaking his head. "We do reap what we sow, old friend. Be assured they are no blood of mine."

Before his words were finished, two more blonde heads lay on the porch floor. Fiona threw the bloody machete down as though it was contaminated, strode to the carriage, and climbed up onto the seat beside the driver. Her heart was hammering but not from what she'd done. It was concern for the men inside, two of whom were precious to her very existence. She leaned down to Julius. "Don't burn it yet, maestro. It might need a further search, now that we're unimpeded. The last act is yet to come." She turned to the man at the reins. "Drive, as fast as you can."

Julius waved and slapped one of the bays on the rump. "See you at Belle Fleur, my darling. Intermission. Act IV will come soon enough."

37

"Honey, y'all need some time in that bed yourself, right beside that man. He goin' to be fine."

Fiona's eyes flicked open. She'd dozed off again. Marie Laveau was gently shaking her shoulder, tsk-tsking as only she could. Even in the cold pre-dawn light, her ensemble of tignon and flowing dress of purple and green was dazzling as usual.

"How is he?" She leaned over to check Henley's breathing, which was slow and even.

"I told you already, woman. That spooky man over there be fine, too. My healer be back later to check on them."

Fiona looked over at Saint Germain, who seemed to be sleeping as soundly as Henley. "Thank you for everything," she said, grasping Marie's hand. "So much – not only your medicines and the healer, but the advice, the gris-gris...for just being there for all of us."

Marie stared at her. "Don't be goin' stupid on me now, Fiona Shanahan. You know I care for all my people and I do what it takes to be sure they safe." That familiar tsk came again and she pointed to Henley's bed. "Do like I say, Irish girl. Love and comfort are the best healers of all." With a swish of her dress, she left the room, only her usual scent of lavender lingering behind.

Fiona stood up from the chair she'd been sitting on all the long night, swayed a bit but rounded the bed and lay down gently beside Henley, the skin on their bare arms touching. She sighed at that meager comfort as her eyes closed.

The creak of the door roused her from a dreamless sleep and she opened her eyes to the dimming rays of the setting sun and Tante Verna's smile. The old conjure woman was the very accomplished healer that had tended the men's wounds the night before and now stood beside her.

"You feelin' some better, Miss Fiona?" She set her basket down beside the bed. "Let me tend to these gentlemen. You may want to go refresh yourself while I get started. It might not be pretty."

Fiona slid off the bed. "Don't worry about me, Tante Verna. I'm far from squeamish. Besides, I want to learn."

Both men came awake, groaning, at the commotion but Fiona could see neither one of them were entirely conscious, their eyelids barely open, which was likely just as well. A servant girl came in, carrying a large bowl of steaming water and white cloths, and Tante Verna set to her work, first holding up both the men's heads and making them swallow some concoction. She then peeled off the old bandages to reveal the neat stitches underneath on both Henley's chest and leg. Fiona took a breath, as there were so many. Christ Jesus, he had come so close to death.

Then Verna did the same procedure for Saint Germain before she and the girl re-cleaned the wounds and applied a sharp-scented salve. Fiona watched carefully as Tante Verna rewrapped the bandages with clean white gauze. Both men fell back asleep and the old woman nodded in satisfaction. She cleaned her hands again in the second basin and Fiona recognized the welcome acrid scent of carbolic acid as Tante Verna dried her hands.

"You want them back in New Orleans but that won't be until tomorrow at least before they can travel without openin' up them stitches. Even then, don't take them out for ten days and watch for redness or infection. That'll do them in faster than anythin' else. You watch what I do here?"

Fiona nodded. "Yes, ma'am."

"Good, cause that's what you'll be doin' for some time. Get you some carbolic and bandages back in the city. I'll leave you the other things." She set down a jar of salve, and a bottle of the sedative, whatever it was. It didn't smell like laudanum, which was good, and Fiona trusted it was even better.

She patted Fiona's hand. "I'll be back in the mornin' one more time." She eyed Fiona as she packed up her bag. "You're a smart woman and I thank you for deliverin' me and all those afflicted from that fiendish woman and her friends. Y'all did a kind thing. You got friends upriver any time you need."

Fiona hugged her even though she knew Tante Verna wasn't used to that, but after a second, the old woman hugged her back. "You have friends downriver too." Fiona stepped back. "Any time you have a need."

Fiona sat and observed her patients for a few minutes but they were both sound asleep again, sleep being the other best healer, according to Marie and Tante Verna. She reached down into the small bundle at her feet and checked on the puppy she'd taken from the barn. She was sleeping soundly, her tummy full from the saucer of milk she'd lapped up, and Fiona rubbed a bit of the salve on the line of stitches Her stomach rumbled and for the first time, she realized she was ravenously hungry, with nothing to eat since yesterday's quick breakfast. Downstairs, she could hear voices, the clink of china and the enticing aroma of frying chicken.

Dinner was over but they still sat around the table,

reviewing the events of the past few days. While Fiona had been occupied with her patients, Julius and Jacque had organized a sweep of the places they suspected could harbor more zombies, but found only a mass grave near Oak Alley. As Ruby had testified, Annette did what she termed a cull and then revived a new group or two periodically when the others were no longer of use to her. It looked as though that had only been a short time ago, and the two hordes they'd dispatched had been the last of them she'd made with her foul poisons. Sean opened another bottle of bourbon, the third one, Fiona noted, as drinks were topped off, including her own. It seemed these men had a trying and possibly interesting day.

"We had an especially lively chat with Andrew McDade at Oak Alley," Julius said. "He's eager to return to New Hampshire and go back to raising hogs or whatever he does up there." He turned to Jacque. "In fact, I believe he's on his way as we speak. Wouldn't you say?"

Jacque grinned. "Unless he's even dumber than he looks and the train's delayed."

Sean McKean laughed out loud. "Oily little bastard."

"What should we do about Fairhaven?" Fiona said. "We can't just leave things as they were when we left last night. We've a lot of cleanup to do."

Silence followed her words and the fifteen men around the table exchanged uneasy glances.

"Ah, even so," she said. "You made it into a funeral pyre, didn't you?"

"Yes, my darling," Julius said. "We did. We took a work crew over there this morning to dig graves but once we saw it again in the light of day, we had a change of heart, or one could call it a frenzy of vengeance if poetically inclined. Five good men of mine lost their lives there, along with that poor priest we dragged along, and a host of others that were likely good men when they were once alive before being poisoned by that witch.

"Saint Germain was right: the entire place was tainted and vile and had to be destroyed. We did say a few words for whatever comfort that may bring to their souls. I was hopeful you would agree."

Fiona stared at him for a few seconds and then downed her bourbon, setting the glass down with a resounding thunk on the table. Everyone tensed further.

"Goddamnit, Julius. I should have been more clear. I was rather hoping to learn to play that fucking harp." She shrugged in her best Saint Germain impression. "*C'est la vie*. Gentlemen, do we have more bourbon?"

New Orleans saved most of its decorating for Mardi Gras, but during the Christmas season, it had become increasingly popular to adorn itself with more northern décor. Raphael had taken it upon himself to install a pine tree in the office of S&H Investigations, replete with glittery garlands and holly sprigs. Fiona vetoed candles on the tree, her history with flames of any sort painful rather than celebratory. Jean-Claude had even outfitted the gallery with garlands and featured gruesome religious paintings of Christ tempered by manger scenes for the more sensitive. For the group on Royal Street, their festivities this year were more sedate and private than in years before. Recovery, both emotional and physical had been in the forefront of their minds, and Saint Germain had been closeted in his laboratory as soon as he could walk there.

Fiona had installed a tent in the courtyard as a cover against possible rain, and on Christmas Eve, they gathered there, with a buffet of delectable food warmed by charcoal burners, a well-stocked bar, and chairs and tables set up under the lush foliage, lit by small torches and warmed by larger charcoal heaters. The guest list was small, populated only by those they truly cared for, missing some who were too far away or with their own families, like Raphael, Jean-Claude and Abel Hamilton.

Fiona watched them all take their places. Saint Germain walked with a still noticeable limp, but forsook his cane. Henley, not quite as fortunate, still needed his, an ebony one with a wolf's head, a gift from Julius, but he was improving every day. The St. John sisters and Ramon were lively as always. Sean McKean and Daniel Fox, always on guard until they'd had a few drinks, sat stiffly at first. Samuel and Ruby Green arrived with a Chantilly cake, three layers of delectability. They had opened a bakery and boulangerie over on Chartres Street, where Ruby's mother was spending Christmas Eve with their children in the spacious rooms above the shop. Marie Laveau and Jim Washington came for cocktails, and left for their own festivities after a taste or two of etouffee.

Altogether, Fiona knew a success when she saw one. It was a lively gathering of delightful people, delicious food and strong drink on a night for celebration. Julius, always the impresario, regaled everyone with stories. It seemed the man had an endless stockpile of entertaining anecdotes.

As one by one, people departed with Merry Christmases and Joyeux Noels, each with a small gift, only those who the horror had impacted upriver were left, and the tone became a bit more somber. Fiona, Henley, Saint Germain, Julius, Sean and Daniel were left sitting together in the garden.

"Joyeux Noel, my dear friends," Saint Germain said, raising his glass, "to all of you that I unwittingly led down a path of hell itself. I could never have dreamed that was where my search would lead us all, but more importantly, what you all had to endure on my behalf and to the redemption of so many. I will be forever humbled and grateful to all of you."

Mirth faded, but the true feelings of warmth and hope did not. Sean and Daniel left shortly thereafter but the four of them remained in the garden in a comfortable silence, broken only by the soft whimpering of the puppy who wanted to be on Fiona's lap. She'd named her Athena and she was healing nicely, an amazingly clever little dog, a sort of miracle after all she'd suffered.

Saint Germain produced a small crystal vial from his vest. He looked at Julius for a long moment, and then Julius nodded. Saint Germain tipped the vial and two drops fell into Julius's wineglass, which he drained and set back on the table. Saint Germain stared at Fiona and Henley, his dark eyes intense.

"I cannot offer you immortality but now I can give you longevity, my dear friends, as I have done for only one other, the man at this table. It is your choice."

She'd always suspected, from that first day in his laboratory. Before she could voice a response, she looked up. Snowflakes floated around them, so magical and so rare in these southern climes. Fiona held out her hand and watched as each perfect snowflake landed on her palm, quickly melting away, their beauty so exquisite and sadly, so fleeting. She caressed Henley's cheek as he turned to her, this extraordinary man she would love forever.

"The world is a strange and wonderful place, my love. Do you not agree?"

ABOUT THE AUTHOR

Award-winning author Kathleen Morris is a graduate of Prescott College in Arizona and lives and writes in the desert Southwest. She loves immersing herself in the lives of her characters, bringing to life charismatic women and men, both real and imaginary. Meticulous research and dedication to detail are the hallmarks of her work. Kathleen is a member of both Western Writers of America and Western Fictioneers, and judges entries for WWA's prestigious Spur Award and Western Fictioneers' renowned Peacemaker Award. Her own novels have twice been Spur Award finalists and she has won the Peacemaker three times. She has also ventured into contemporary territory, with two thrillers, Risk and Never Touch Down, both set in the American West. Visit her website for more at www.KathleenMorrisauthor.com

www.ingramcontent.com/pod-product-compliance
Lightning Source LLC
LaVergne TN
LVHW010157070526
838199LV00062B/4398